TAPESTRY

A DEADLY CURIOSITIES NOVEL

GAIL Z. MARTIN

SOL

eBook ISBN: 978-1-64795-081-1
Paperback ISBN: 978-1-64795-082-8

This book is dedicated to all the wonderful readers who love Cassidy and the gang, to my amazing editor, Jean Rabe, and to my awesome husband, Larry N. Martin, who makes sure all the essential behind the scenes stuff happens right. Thank you, all!

TAPESTRY

DEADLY CURIOSITIES BOOK 6

By Gail Z. Martin

CHAPTER ONE

"If I had a secret room, I'd think of better things to do with it." Teag Logan looked around the dusty space with wariness and disappointment.

"Oh really? Like what?" I asked.

Teag stood with his hands on his hips and slowly turned to take in the whole room. It was bigger than the average modern powder room or walk-in closet and smaller than most bedrooms.

"It would be perfect for a reading getaway." He sounded a little wistful. "A daybed, plenty of squishy pillows and soft throw blankets, a little table for drinks and snacks, and good Wi-Fi. Add a nice rug and some pictures on the walls for a little punch of color, and it would be the perfect retreat." He sighed. "I would have loved a space like this when I was a kid."

I nodded. "Yeah, I can see that. I'd do the same thing. But I don't think that's what the previous owner had in mind."

From the room's contents, whoever last used it had been a practicing witch. An altar with occult symbols and pillar candles stood on a small mahogany table. A tarnished silver bowl held a mixture of dried leaves and flowers. Next to the bowl sat divination tools—yellowed Tarot cards, a crystal ball, and flat, rectangular ivory tiles marked with runes. Several old leather-bound books were on a nearby shelf with glass bottles that had questionable contents.

The circular rug made from a coiled cloth braid marked an arcane workspace. Materials used in spell work hung from hooks on the wall or dangled from the rafters—animal bones, carved stone amulets, and small leather poppets, along with other items I didn't want to examine too closely.

Other than the altar and bookshelf, the room held more shelves with dusty boxes and glass jars, a wooden chair, and a pallet and pillow for sleeping. The only decoration in the room hung above the altar, a tapestry of a forest glen. The wall hanging was three feet square and, despite the neglect of being locked away, appeared to be in good condition.

"What do you make of the tapestry?" I asked Teag. Woven items are his specialty.

He kept his distance and looked at the wall hanging as if it might bite. "I don't like its energy. There's something wrong. Don't get close to it, and for God's sake, don't touch it."

"Haunted?"

He shook his head. "I don't think so. Dark magic. Not exactly cursed, but it's definitely bespelled—and since we don't know what the spell does, that makes it a loaded weapon with a hair trigger."

Unfortunately, this kind of thing wasn't unusual for us at all.

I'm Cassidy Kincaide, and I own Trifles and Folly, an antique and curio store in historic, haunted Charleston, South Carolina. The store's been in my family for 350 years, and it's more than it appears. I'm a psychometric, which means I can read the magic and history of objects by touching them. Teag's a Weaver witch, so he can weave spells into cloth, and he's also one hell of a hacker. My business partner, Sorren, is a nearly 600-year-old vampire who founded the store with my ancestor back in the 1600s. We're part of the Alliance, a coalition of mortals and immortals who keep dangerous supernatural objects out of the wrong hands and protect the world from supernatural threats.

We don't advertise that part of our work for obvious reasons, but a few key people are in the know. The store has been around long enough that we have a reputation for being "good" with spooky stuff, so people contact us when they run into something that might be cursed or haunted.

Which is how we got the call to come look at the hidden room.

The new homeowner had discovered the hidden space when he needed to replace wiring in the historic house and contacted Trifles and Folly to see if anything locked away in the forgotten room might be valuable.

I wasn't convinced anything here would bring a windfall at auction, but there were definitely occult items that should be handled with extreme care—including the tapestry.

"Any guesses on the tapestry's history?"

Teag's eyes narrowed as he stared at the panel, deep in thought. "It looks old. Older than the house. From the subject and art style, I'd say northern European, Flemish maybe? And in spite of being locked up for a long time, it's still got a lot of magical juice. That makes me wonder if there aren't spells blind stitched into it to reinforce its magic and add focus."

He's been studying weaving since before he realized his talent was partly magic. Teag takes his craft seriously and looks into the lore and history.

I thought I saw something move in the tapestry, deep in the shadows under the trees.

It probably wasn't my imagination. I'd seen Nephilim step out of cursed paintings and ghosts move through mirrors, so I had no reason to trust a wall hanging that could turn out to be a doorway to somewhere I didn't want to go.

"We should get Rowan in on this." Teag named a mutual friend who is a powerful witch. "She can help contain it until we figure out more. Right now, we don't know whether the tapestry was meant to store power, like a magical battery, or focus power for another reason."

"Freaky, isn't it?"

The homeowner's voice behind us made both Teag and me jump. Ron Zimmerman was a corporate accountant with a passion for restoring old houses. With his collared polo shirt and chinos, he looked like he would be right at home on a golf course or at a barbecue. I didn't figure him to be the type carrying out clandestine occult rituals, but I've been wrong about people before.

"What do you know about the people who owned the house before you?" I asked.

"This house was built in 1822 and stayed in the same family until last year," Zimmerman said. "Passed down through the generations until the line basically died out. I had been watching it for a while and snapped it up when it came on the market. It's a real gem. I just didn't count on finding something like…this."

"Are there any stories about the house?" Teag asked. "Ghosts, scandals, strange things that happened?"

Zimmerman laughed nervously, and I figured he knew something that made him uncomfortable. "You know how it is in Charleston—every house is haunted, depending on who you talk to."

"Good stories add to the provenance." I kept my tone light as if I didn't believe such things could be real to put him at ease.

"I heard a few things, while I was arranging financing," Zimmerman admitted. "Apparently there were rumors about the family back in the day, which might have contributed to why the house never passed to other owners."

"What kind of rumors?" Teag pressed.

"I'm not saying I believe any of them," Zimmerman disavowed. "I thought the real estate agent might have been embellishing things to justify the price. Some people will pay extra if they think a place is haunted."

"I promise you won't shock me. My family's been in Charleston—running Trifles and Folly—since the city was founded. I think by now we've heard it all."

"One of the stories said a man disappeared from the room next to this. Went inside, never came out. No one ever found him." While Zimmerman tried to pass it off as gossip, I could tell he was nervous. "There's also a story about a gray man who shows up before a tragedy."

"Like the Pawley Island Gray Man?" Teag asked. Everyone around here knew the legend of the protective ghost who showed up to warn about disasters.

Zimmerman gave a bitter chuckle. "Not exactly. People believe he *causes* the tragedy instead of warning people."

That certainly didn't sound good.

"The house has a reputation with housekeeping staff for being haunted," Zimmerman went on. "Some flat-out won't work here. Others come, but they won't stay. The reasons are everything from saying they feel watched to saying that the house gives them the creeps."

I trusted the housekeepers' opinions. They had nothing to gain by making up stories.

"Anything else?" I asked.

"The man who built the house, Lee Harris Grantham, was the owner of a shipping company with an uncanny ability to turn a profit," Zimmerman said. "His luck was so good that his enemies wondered if he had unholy help."

Contrary to what people see on television, making a deal doesn't need to involve the devil. A talented witch, root worker, or Voudon mambo can work spells to make a wish come true—for a price. Everything in magic comes with a cost, especially if gain to one person causes harm to another. "What goes around comes around" isn't an idle threat.

"Did his luck ever turn on him?" Teag asked. "Him, personally, or the family as a whole?"

Zimmerman looked like he was weighing how to answer. "You know this is all hearsay—"

"We won't repeat it." I knew he was probably protective of the home's resale value. People think ghosts are fun, but curses? Not so much.

"Grantham died wealthy. But after the house was built, while he was still in his fifties—relatively young even in those years—he caught a 'wasting disease.'"

"Yellow Fever? Malaria?" Teag pressed. Both were scourges in the past before modern treatments, and Charleston's sultry summers were the perfect incubators.

"The documents are cagy, but they don't name either of those as the cause, which wouldn't have been shameful at the time," Zimmerman said. "There are a lot of things that might cause 'wasting,' from tuberculosis to other diseases that weren't understood at the time, but the decline was quick. People started to talk then about what price Grantham paid for his wealth."

"How did the family fare after that?" I asked.

"They hung onto their money and their interest in the shipping company, but the firm never hit the peaks it did under the old man. On a personal level, wealth certainly didn't buy happiness," Zimmerman observed. "The family history reads like a soap opera. Questionable deaths, feuds, and just plain bad luck."

Teag and I exchanged a glance, and I stole a look over my shoulder at the tapestry like it might be listening.

"Which is how the house ended up coming on the market because all that misfortune left the last remaining Grantham without an heir," Zimmerman concluded.

"And the story didn't scare you off?" I was genuinely curious. I know most people don't believe in "woo-woo," and some go to great lengths to avoid seeing what's right in front of them.

"I'm not superstitious." Zimmerman's sharp laugh sounded nervous. "Not usually, anyhow. When the workmen opened up the hidden room, and I saw inside, I'll admit it freaked me out."

Glad to know his hindbrain warning system is still working.

"Is the house haunted?" Teag questioned. In Charleston, it's almost a demerit if a house isn't.

Zimmerman fidgeted. "I haven't experienced anything malicious, but strange things happen. Cold spots, small items go missing and turn up in odd places, that sort of thing. It's common to hear footsteps when there's no one else in the house, or catch a glimpse of movement out of the corner of your eye, but you're alone."

"Have you seen the gray man yourself?"

His eyes widened. "No! And I really hope I don't."

So the house had active ghosts, and Zimmerman—despite being a professed non-believer—wasn't denying it. Interesting.

"What kind of help do you want? We know people who can bless the house, help the ghosts find peace and move on, remove questionable objects, and cleanse the hidden room of its negative energy. It all depends on what you have in mind."

I've found that when I'm talking to most people, they respond better to the idea of getting rid of "negative energy" than if I come straight out and tell them we need to break a curse and untangle dangerous spells. Even folks who aren't comfortable with religious or paranormal phrases seem to be okay with "New Age-speak."

"I bought the house intending to renovate it and then decide whether to sell it or keep it," Zimmerman said. "Right now, I can't do either."

"Fair enough," I answered. "Let me make a few calls and gather people I know who have special skills to help. But in the meantime, please stay out of the room and don't touch anything. We don't know what materials the person used on their altar and in their potions, and even some natural ingredients can be toxic to the touch."

Zimmerman nodded, and his eyes went wide. "I definitely won't bother anything."

"I'll let you know when I've talked to my contacts. Then we can give you a better idea of how fast something can be done. Do you have somewhere else to stay for a few days?"

"I don't mind a hotel as long as the situation doesn't drag on." He agreed quickly enough that I figured he had been planning his escape before we talked. I couldn't blame him. I wouldn't want to spend time alone in the house, either.

"Does anyone else have access to the house?" Teag asked. "You'll want to pass along the warning to them as well. Personally, I'd suggest everyone stay out until we can handle the problem."

"I can reschedule the construction people. That shouldn't be a problem."

"I think that's everything for now," I told him. "Let's walk out together."

Spells and ghosts have a way of knowing when someone's planning to reduce their power, and often they take action to keep the status quo. Zimmerman didn't argue, and I felt certain that the house scared him even more than he wanted to let on.

Once we saw Zimmerman lock up and drive away, Teag and I got in my car and headed back to the shop.

"More than you bargained for?" Teag asked as I drove.

"Yes—and no. I was expecting a spook-a-palooza, but not the wicked witch's workshop. The gray man legends worry me. And I think we need to take care of the problem before the Grantham family's bad luck transfers to the new owner."

"Yeah, I thought about that," Teag admitted. "And I think Zimmerman was seriously spooked, even though he tried to play it off that he didn't believe."

"I agree. That's an advantage since he's more likely to accept our help."

I was already thinking through our friend list and whose abilities would be most useful. *A priest, a witch, a medium, and a necromancer if things get dicey. I sure hope that covers what we need because if not, we're up shit creek.*

"What do you think about the tapestry?" I asked Teag. "Other than it being creepy."

"I don't recognize the image, which means it's not one of the famous pieces that have gone 'missing' over the years. Or the records could have been lost since it's clearly old. Maybe Sorren would know. I don't know if it can be neutralized or destroyed. We might end up passing it off to the Briggs Society for safekeeping."

Sorren looks like he's the same age as Teag and me, late twenties, even though he's close to six hundred. We make quite a trio. Sorren has blond hair, high cheekbones, and gray eyes; Teag's tall and slender with crow black hair cut in an edgy, asymmetrical style, and then there's me with strawberry-blond hair and skin that freckles in the Carolina sun.

I was counting on Sorren. He's got a long memory, and he's been part of the Alliance for five hundred of those years, so he's come across a lot of cursed and haunted pieces.

The Briggs Society is a haven for adventurers who got misplaced in time and objects too dangerous to keep and too lethal to destroy. It exists outside regular space and time—don't ask me how—and can appear and disappear in different locations.

"I'll make the calls when I get to the store," I said. "Once I know everyone's schedule, we can get back to Zimmerman with a time."

"I take it you're not interested in handling any of the items?" Teag asked.

I shivered. "I'd rather not if I don't have to. It's pretty easy to tell from the vibes that the Grantham family witches were on the dark side of magic. Unless we need details about a crime, I'm fine with not getting up close and personal."

While my touch magic can come in handy to answer questions about the past if the resonance has imprinted on an object, like every other magical ability, it has a price. Teag has seen me get knocked on my ass more than once from the strength of the connection. I can feel the emotions of an item's owner and see what the object "witnessed," which takes a toll on me. Sometimes it's just a bad headache, but in severe cases, it will put me in bed to recover.

"I'm glad—because I was going to have to have a sit down with you about taking crazy risks otherwise," Teag replied.

"Same goes for you with the tapestry. Just because you probably *can* read its energy doesn't mean you *should*."

He gave a solemn nod. "Oh, believe me, you don't have to twist my arm. I wonder if whoever closed over the room did it because of the piece."

"Bricking up the space because they didn't know how else to get rid of it?" I hadn't considered that possibility, but now that Teag mentioned it, that made sense.

"Maybe it's the kind of artifact that gets more powerful from magic done around it," he speculated. "It could have gotten strong enough to frighten the witch if he or she couldn't control it."

"For all their generations of magic, the family didn't prosper from it," I said. "Not in a lasting way." That's usually the way it goes when people use supernatural elements to cheat.

"Plenty of witches and witch dynasties have figured out how to use their magic to benefit without having it boomerang that badly on them," Teag pointed out.

"I guess people who overreach get burned." It seems like a simple lesson, but Charleston's history is littered with the casualties of people who didn't learn it until too late.

I parked and we walked into the store. Trifles and Folly has the look and feel of a shop with a centuries-old history. The gold lettering on the big plate glass windows is vintage, as are the massive carriage lights on either side of the door. Inside, the glass cases and display shelves are as antique as the goods they showcase. The property is heavily warded for protection, and we screen all the items we buy to weed out those with dangerous vibes or bad magic.

It feels like home to me. I can sense the protections wrap around me when I walk in the door, and I love the feeling.

"How'd it go?" Maggie asked from behind the counter. She retired from teaching and got a job helping at Trifles and Folly because she was bored. Maggie jokes that she got way more excitement than she bargained for. She doesn't have magic of her own, but she knows all about what we really do behind the scenes and is always quick to help. Her free-spirited, boho fashion sense hides business school savvy, and she has no patience for fools.

Today, her short hair was cotton candy pink, and she rocked the look.

"Haunted historic house with a tragic story and a witch's workshop someone bricked over and tried to forget about." I realized that wasn't nearly the weirdest way I had ever described my day.

"So…pretty typical," Maggie replied. "You didn't miss anything here. Got some window shoppers and a few browsers. I think a lady is going to come back for one of the silver tea sets for her sister's birthday. No bus tours today."

"I'll come up front so you can take a break," Teag said. He's not just my best friend and sometimes bodyguard; he's also the assistant store manager. "Cassidy needs to make some phone calls."

Maggie doesn't miss anything, and she gave me a look. "Calling in the troops?"

"Yep. There's some pretty dark stuff in there, and we need to get it handled ASAP."

Maggie poured a cup of coffee and relaxed in the break room while I went into my office. The shop is on the main floor. Upstairs is an apartment we use as a safe house when needed because of the strength of the wardings. Sorren has a day crypt in the basement so he can go to ground in an emergency

I settled into my chair and pulled out my phone. I left a message for Sorren, knowing that he was probably sleeping since it was still daylight. He's old enough that he can stay awake as long as he's out of the sun, but vampires need rest just like everyone else.

After that, I called Father Anne. "We're going to need your help," I told her after we got past the greetings and pleasantries. "Found a hidden witch's workshop that needs a strong cleanse and maybe an exorcism."

"Sounds fun. When and where?" she asked without hesitation.

Father Anne is an Episcopalian priest, but she's also a member of the St. Expeditus Society, a secret group of clergy who deal with the dark side of the supernatural. She's had my back more times than I can count.

I told her about the house and its history and made sure to include the creepy tapestry.

"I think I know where that house is," she said when I finished. "To be honest, it always made me uncomfortable."

"I guess if we do our job right, maybe it won't anymore."

"Charleston will still have plenty of haunted houses. They're not exactly an endangered species," Father Anne replied. "Did Teag go with you? Remember that we need to keep him from getting roughed up before the big day, or the wedding pictures won't be memorable for the right reasons." Father Anne had promised to officiate at Teag's wedding, and I knew she was excited about it.

"That did cross my mind. You know he won't put up with being sidelined."

"I understand, and Anthony probably would too. But if he shows up at the wedding looking like he lost a bar brawl, we won't be able to explain it to the mundanes," Father Anne cautioned. "Worse, the gossips will blame Anthony."

I sighed. "If I could put him in bubble wrap until the ceremony, I would. But he won't stand for it."

"I guess Rowan can always touch up any bruises." Father Anne mentioned our witch friend.

"I'm going to call her next. And she'll probably tell me the same thing you just did." I chuckled.

"Remind Teag that he and Anthony need to get me the final version of the vows they want," she warned. "Otherwise, I'll just say 'do you?' and we'll have the shortest ceremony in Charleston history."

"Teag and Anthony might not mind, but their mothers would probably have something to say about it." I tried to picture the aftermath.

"It's coming up fast. I just got my wedding robes and stole back from the dry cleaners so they'll be fresh. I'm counting on you to nag him to make sure the details are done. That's what best friends are for," she snarked.

"I'm on it. And it's not 'nagging,' it's 'project management.'"

Father Anne Burgett didn't look like most priests I'd met. She wore her short hair spiky, preferred Doc Marten boots to flats, and had a tattoo sleeve of St. Expeditus on one arm. Father Anne could recite several different exorcisms from memory, hold her own against a vampire in a fight, and banish troublesome ghosts without breaking a sweat. We'd made it through some situations together that still gave me nightmares. Teag never even considered any other officiant, and Anthony agreed.

I wasn't sure how Anthony's wealthy, South-of-Broad family would react, but that wasn't my problem.

When I ended the call with Father Anne, I dialed my favorite necromancer. Archibald Donnelly ran the Briggs Society, and with his wild white hair and muttonchops, he looked like an adventurer who escaped from a Victorian potboiler.

"Cassidy! How good to hear from you. To what impending catastrophe can I attribute this call?" Donnelly's voice was hale and hearty. Everything about the man was bigger than life—including his ability to raise the dead.

"Dark magic workshop and a cursed or possibly possessed tapestry," I told him. "I'm putting out the bat signal to call the usual suspects together."

"Smashing. Sounds like fun. Might you be needing a home for that tapestry once it's liberated?"

I smiled. "I was just going to ask if you had room at the Briggs for another piece of art."

"Always. We'll find a way to make it behave. Do you know what it does? Kill people? Grant wishes? Read minds? Push people into another dimension?"

He sounded like he was joking, but I knew all those scenarios were possible.

"We don't know yet. I'm hoping that you and Rowan can help us figure out just how dangerous it is before we move it," I told him. "Something brought bad luck and tragedy to the original owner's family, and at least one person disappeared from the house. It's not the only creepy supernatural object in the workshop, and it might not be to blame for everything."

"Always better to assume the worst and be pleasantly surprised. Of course I'll come. Sounds delightful."

CHAPTER TWO

Donnelly and I chatted for a few minutes more before I promised to keep him in the loop as we made plans. That left me one more call before I tried to pin down a date.

"Hi, Rowan. Are you up for some shenanigans?" I greeted the witch when she picked up the call. Rowan's a powerful practitioner, and she's helped us out of quite a few dangerous situations.

"Sure. Life was getting boring. What's up?"

I told her about the house and the secret room, as well as the tapestry. The long pause when I finished made me check to make sure the call hadn't dropped.

"The Grantham house?" Rowan finally said.

"You know about it?"

"I didn't know about the room, but it doesn't surprise me. The Grantham family was rather infamous in certain circles."

"Nefarious witchcraft?"

She snorted at my description. "That's as good a way to put it as any. The coven still won't speak their name."

"That bad? Wow—what did they do?"

"It's not remarkable for a family to rise to wealth and prominence thanks to a talented witch. Most of the old families in the city rode a broomstick to the top of the social pyramid, so to speak," Rowan replied. "That generally gets a pass as long as they follow the rules. Keep the magic under wraps. Share the spoils. Protect the coven, and don't strike at other members. The Granthams weren't good at playing nice."

"They had a long run of bad luck. Was it their fault or paybacks?" I asked.

"Hmm. Depends on who you talk to. Probably some of both. They were notoriously arrogant, so overreach likely factored into it. Then again, plenty of people would have loved to see them take a fall. Let's just say no one shed tears at their comeuppance."

By the time I finished, I had an idea of when everyone could get together at the house, depending on Zimmerman's availability. I didn't expect Sorren to join us, but I knew he would want to stay in the loop.

Maggie returned to the front of the shop, where she and Teag were busy serving customers.

Since they didn't need me, I poured a cup of coffee and decided to do some digging into the notorious Grantham family.

Charleston's upper crust liked to keep a fairly low profile except for charity events and ribbon cuttings. In the old days, cozy relationships with the newspaper and television stations could control the story, but now that social media exists, it's harder to throttle uncomplimentary information.

I spent the next hour sorting through old newspaper articles, photos from the charity balls, wedding announcements, and awards for business success. Once the family burst onto the social scene with a windfall that landed them in the moneyed set, they had been seen in all the right places.

Lee Harris Grantham, who started the dynasty, made his money in shipping—not uncommon given Charleston's seafaring past. It's a dangerous and unpredictable business, and many men have lost everything to pirates or storms. From a single ship and a middling cargo business that he inherited, Grantham built an international fleet that managed to prosper despite the Civil War and two World Wars, as well as the other conflicts of the era. That alone put him ahead of most of his contemporaries.

As abruptly as fortune shone on the family, its glow faded. The past fifty years saw business and personal setbacks, including family squabbles, legal troubles, and health problems. The house passed out of family control when Ada McIntosh Grantham, the lone surviving heir, died well into her nineties. She left what remained of the family fortune to her cat and several local charities.

Not long before, Grantham Shipping was sold to a multinational cargo company, consigning the family to a historical footnote.

Lee's meteoric rise certainly could have been attributable to magic as opposed to sheer luck and timing. Not every breakout success was hocused, but some kind of supernatural deal or interference played a role in more situations than most people would suspect. For people hellbent on amassing a fortune, no price was too high to pay, even if they suspected it wouldn't last forever.

Amid the triumph came a lot of personal pain. The gossip columnists reveled in missteps, divorces, and reports of questionable behavior, as well as at least one suicide. The Grantham family, for all its charitable donations, didn't seem to have gained the goodwill of their social peers. Considering that the people who earned their place South of Broad were, by and large, ruthless business people or politicians, it said something that the Granthams weren't accepted into the fold.

An article about the "Grantham curse" caught my eye. Most of the piece was scurrilous, but the writer pointed out a string of early deaths in the Grantham line due to accidents, sudden illness, or strange circumstances, and wondered whether it was a "cosmic reckoning" for the family's sudden success.

That was as close as I'd ever seen a columnist suggest someone made a deal with the devil.

Teag stuck his head in my office. "Do you and Kell have plans for dinner? Want to get pizza? Anthony's working late."

"So's Kell. Pizza sounds fantastic." I realized how hungry I was and surprised the afternoon had passed so quickly. "Can Maggie join us?"

He shook his head. "I asked. She's got pickleball tonight."

We closed up and wished Maggie good luck in her game.

"Thanks, but my group just plays for fun. We aren't out for blood, like some of the leagues. All the articles make it sound like this game for mild-mannered old folks. 'Mild' my ass! Some of those retirees will shank you in a heartbeat," Maggie confided.

Teag and I closed up and set the alarms; then we drove to dinner so we could each head home from there. We've been going for so long the staff knows our usual orders and the manager treats us like old friends.

We got our usual table all the way in the back so we could talk. There are high wooden dividers between the booths to add more privacy.

Teag ordered mushrooms and peppers on his half of a large pie while I got hamburger and onion. We added sodas and fried pickles and then sat back and waited for the feast.

"Getting any wedding jitters yet?" I asked. For being two weeks out from the big day, Teag seemed remarkably calm to me.

"No—but that's largely because Anthony hired a wedding planner to micromanage everything." Teag grinned. "It makes sense—he's busier than usual at the law firm trying to clear his calendar for the honeymoon, and our hours are unpredictable. I think it also made his mom feel better knowing a professional was handling everything."

Anthony Benton's family was wealthy, owing to the law firm where generations of Bentons had handled the problems of Charleston's elite with skill and discretion. They were part of the South of Broad crowd, although Anthony was down-to-earth, and his family seemed equally normal when I met them.

"Are you okay with that?" I wasn't trying to pry, but Teag is my best friend, brother-from-another-mother, ride-or-die, and I wanted him to be happy.

"Every time Kim hands us another checklist or timeline, I'm so glad I don't have to figure it out myself. She's got it all down—tux fittings, flowers, cake tasting, venue walk-through. I can't imagine doing it without her."

"Anything new?" I had to admit, the wedding plans had me excited to see how it all came together. "And Father Anne said to tell you she needs your vows ASAP."

Teag rolled his eyes. "I know. I'll see if Anthony can work on his tonight. There are just a lot of moving parts. But all the choices have been made, everything is booked and reserved, and the honeymoon is set up. Now it's just nerves and family drama."

"Cold feet?" I teased, although I knew better.

"Definitely not. Although I understand why people elope, even if their mothers never speak to them again."

"Having mom trouble?"

He shrugged. "Not really. Just trying to navigate so there aren't hurt feelings. My mom is *very* aware we don't come from the kind of money Anthony's family does. She doesn't resent it, but that means that there's a definite difference in experience and perspective."

"You said that tactfully." I gave him a no-bullshit look.

"Anthony offered to do a no-frills, simple wedding to keep the focus where it belongs—on the ceremony. His mom is on a mission to make sure that her gay son gets all the hoopla and honors her other kids got—whether Anthony wants it or not. The whole thing with St. Philips just made her more determined."

The historic church where Anthony's family had been members and donors for generations and which was the site of a century of baptisms, weddings, and funerals had changed affiliation to avoid same-sex weddings or gay clergy. That meant Teag and Anthony couldn't get married there.

Anthony's family promptly renounced their membership and yanked their sizeable endowment, declaring that if Anthony wasn't welcome, the rest of them didn't need to go, either. Given the family's prominence, the decision made the news and ruffled the city's social circles.

"That's better than her being opposed," I pointed out. "And maybe by raising awareness, something good will come from it. Sometimes all it takes is one person standing up for what's right to make a difference."

"I know." Teag sighed. "But both of us just wanted a nice, quiet wedding with our favorite people. It's stressful enough under normal circumstances."

"How's your mom doing?" I knew that his father had passed away a few years ago, and his only brother was an extreme introvert.

"She's excited, happy, and a little nervous. The Bentons have been lovely to her, but she's still self-conscious, although I think that's coming from her and not them," Teag admitted as the pizza was delivered and the server refilled our drinks.

"Do the moms get along?" I asked as we pulled slices with gooey cheese from the pan to our plates.

"They seem to. Anthony's family is very down-to-earth despite their money. The moms haven't spent much time together, but they found common ground on television shows and music, so they've got something to talk about."

"Gotta start somewhere." I cut a bite of the too-hot pizza.

We focused on eating for a while, comfortable with silence. When we finished, we sat back and waited for the check.

"Is there anything I can do to help?"

"Take us to Vegas to elope?" Teag joked.

"I mean, if you really want to—"

"*Both* mothers would kill us." Teag's eyes widened. "But I am glad we're doing the small service for our crowd. That's the 'real' wedding for both of us. The other is just for show. And, honestly, the reception is less for our friends and more for the relatives and repaying social obligations."

"That means we just have to throw a better bachelor party for our crowd," I told him. I was in charge of taking Teag out on the town with our friends while Anthony's brothers and colleagues handled his side.

Teag and Anthony were technically getting married twice. Once in a small friends-only ceremony since not everyone from our crowd would be able to attend the "official" wedding, and to cover all the supernatural bases.

The St. Expeditus Society had a compound with a chapel that was heavily warded with supernatural protections. They also gave sanctuary to Beckford Pendlewood and his partner after Beck renounced his inheritance as the heir to one of the Caribbean witch dynasties. Sorren wouldn't be able to attend a daytime ceremony for obvious reasons.

Teag and Anthony had opted to have the second wedding in the expansive ballroom of the fancy boat club on the harbor. It had an amazing view, and the brand-new facility sidestepped the checkered history of many wedding venues in and around the city.

The St. Expeditus ceremony would be small, with just a few of us for witnesses. Father Anne wanted to convey blessings and supernatural protections that would raise eyebrows among the other guests. Wardings were also more difficult when done in a public place while the chapel was already within a sacred and magically protected private area.

"However it works out, it will be perfect, and you'll be married." I hoped my encouragement helped settle his nerves.

"I know. And I realize that it's the commitment in our hearts, not the ceremony, that really matters, but it would be nice not to have the video end up on one of those 'classic wedding screwups' television shows."

"I think you're safe." I laughed. "Pretty sure Anthony's law firm could squash that if it happened, but it won't."

We paid the bill and walked back to our cars. I checked the time on my phone. "Kell should be getting home soon. I hope Anthony isn't going to be too late."

Teag shook his head. "Normally he can bring work home so he doesn't get stuck at the office, but this was a meeting. It shouldn't run too much longer."

I waved goodbye and drove home, happily full and in a good mood.

At a traffic light, I saw a tall, lean figure in a hoodie. When the light changed and my car drove past him, he raised his head, exposing his face beneath the hood. Bluish gray skin pulled tightly over the skull, and black, sunken eyes watched me pass.

I caught my breath, and only the grip on the steering wheel kept my hands from shaking. I didn't know what he was, but I felt certain he'd not just been looking *at* me but looking *for* me.

Between one breath and the next, my world tilted. I saw my house burned to the ground. I knew in my soul that my dog Baxter was missing. My safe place, my fortress, had been overrun, and the loss was more than I could bear.

I gasped and heard a horn honk behind me. The light turned, and I jackrabbited forward, but not before I caught the menace in the creature's gaze. The unspoken threat was clear—but that didn't explain what he was or how I had attracted his attention.

My doors were locked, but I wasn't sure that would stop a supernatural creature. While I'd never heard of a cryptid carjacking, I figured there was a first time for everything.

I spotted him two more times on my way home, always standing on a street corner along my route, following my car with his gaze, looking right at me, although the spots where he stood were too far apart for him to run between sightings.

In the second vision, I sat next to Teag's bedside in a hospital, staring at monitors that even I knew told a harsh truth. Next to me, Anthony struggled to muffle his sobs.

"He promised me he'd be careful. We were going to get married next week."

I came out of the waking dream before the drivers behind me had time to honk, but not before the hooded stranger gave me a madman's smile.

The third time a taxicab careened into my lane, and I had to swerve hard to keep from hitting head-on.

The image cleared, and I realized there was no cab, just a bunch of pissed-off drivers who had to veer to avoid my sudden, wild maneuver. The hooded man stood near the curb and met my gaze with a smirk.

After that, I took the quickest route with the fewest stops to get home and ran between my parking spot and the door to get inside after checking to make sure he was nowhere near.

My Maltese, Baxter, met me at the door, bouncing and barking.

"Hush," I told him, too fondly to count as a reprimand. I was still shaky from the encounters and the near miss, so I picked up Bax and hugged him tight, listening to his heartbeat until my breathing slowed. He licked my nose. Baxter is eight pounds of attitude. Courage of a Doberman; body of a guinea pig. I kissed him and ruffled his hair before putting him down and heading to the fridge to get his food.

A text message let me know Kell was on his way. I texted him a warning about the creature I had seen.

Cassidy: *Keep an eye out for the gray stranger. Hoodie, grayish skin, looks like a walking corpse.*

He didn't respond, and I figured he was driving, but I hoped he would check messages before he got out of his car.

I got Bax settled with his dinner and went to change into sweatpants and a T-shirt. By the time I finished, Kell was letting himself in the door, and Bax was going nuts again.

"He just ate—don't let him tell you he's starving," I warned Kell at Bax's performance.

"Is that true?" he asked Baxter, who pretended he hadn't seen food in days.

Kell turned to me. "What's this about a gray person?"

I told him about the sightings. "I'm not sure exactly what he is or whether it's connected to the Grantham mansion, but he was definitely stalking me."

He pulled me close. "I'm glad you're okay."

I enjoyed feeling safe in his arms. "Thanks. I'm sure we'll figure out what's going on. It just kinda freaked me out."

"Understandable. Please don't take chances, Cassidy."

"I'll be careful." I couldn't promise not to take risks, given what the Alliance does, but I could certainly do my best to be smart about it.

"Did you eat?" I asked after stretching up for a kiss.

"We ordered in while we worked on the edits."

I could smell onions on his breath. Kell's day job is video production, but his passion is paranormal investigation, and he runs SPOOK, the Southern Paranormal Observation and Outreach Klub, which posts their explorations online. Needless to say, our interests fit together nicely.

"Teag and I got pizza. And I heard all about the wedding woes." I needed to get my mind off the gray stranger.

He looked up. "Something wrong?"

I shook my head. "Just the usual nerves and family drama. How's your project coming along?"

While Kell filled me in on his day, I made popcorn and got sodas. When he finished, I caught him up on the Grantham house and the spooky hidden room, as well as the mysterious gray man.

"I know better than to ask, but that room would make a great investigation," Kell said.

"Oh, it totally would—but the stuff in there is bad news, and by the time it's cleansed and neutralized, it won't be nearly as interesting. I'm also guessing that the new owner wants to renovate and flip it, and while people in Charleston are fine with a ghost or two, having a dark witch's workshop might be a step too far."

"Oh, heads would explode over that, for sure," Kell agreed. "But I still want the secret inside scoop when you're done, even if I can't tell anyone. And I'll do some digging to see if I find any sightings of something that matches your description."

I leaned in and kissed him on the nose. "Absolutely. I hope that cleansing the house turns out to be completely boring." In my heart, I doubted that to be true.

We got comfortable on the couch, with Bax between us, expecting his share of the snack. I pulled up the new superhero movie on streaming that we'd been waiting to see, and we cuddled, just glad to be home.

By the time the movie ended, I was dozing on Kell's shoulder. Bax lay upside-down on the couch, feet in the air, snoring.

"I might have to rewatch the last half hour of the movie." I yawned. Bax woke up with a yelp, looking confused. "There was a lot going on today. I'm exhausted."

We took the dishes to the kitchen, and Kell let Baxter outside into the walled garden to do his business. I live in what Charlestonians call a "single house," which has its narrow end toward the street and a porch facing a private courtyard. The main door from the street leads onto the porch, called a "piazza" here.

While Kell let Bax sniff around the courtyard, Sorren called. "Did everything go well at the Grantham house? Are you and Teag safe?"

His concern told me that we were right to be cautious. If the house worried a vampire, it definitely warranted treading carefully.

"We're okay. I'm hoping to get Rowan, Father Anne, and Donnelly out to cleanse the workshop we found as soon as calendars permit."

"I'm not surprised that the workshop exists. I'd expect as much from the Granthams." Sorren has made Charleston his home for more than three hundred years, discreetly disappearing at intervals to hide his immortality. It's a little freaky that he has personal experience with people who are long dead and gone, but the unique perspective is invaluable for what we do.

"You don't sound like a fan."

Sorren chuckled. "I wasn't back in the day. In hindsight—and given the people I met over the next two hundred years—they were worse than some and not as bad as others. They certainly weren't the only family in Charleston to parlay piracy and smuggling into more legitimate businesses and reinvent themselves as pillars of society."

The mention of the Granthams owning "cargo" ships hit a little differently after his comment, and I rolled my eyes at myself for not having read between the lines.

"They also wouldn't be the only ones to get some witchy help climbing the social ladder to fame and fortune," I said in a dry tone.

"Certainly not. But the elder Grantham didn't try as hard to cover it up as everyone else. Either he was bad at politics or just didn't give a damn. The family rubbed people the wrong way. Those who were already the 'old guard' liked to pretend their own hands were clean of questionable businesses or dark magic, and they didn't like a newcomer who didn't even make a pretense of respectability."

My mind went to several newly minted billionaires in the headlines

who, for all their wealth, clashed with the real old-money power play-
ers. *Guess it's the same in every generation.*

"Was that a factor in the family dying out?"

"The society mavens might have disapproved of the Granthams,
but that's never stopped them from marrying off their sons and daugh-
ters to people with money or power." Soren paused. "Frankly, I
suspected it was either a curse or a deal that came due. It doesn't take
too long of a stretch of childless marriages and heirs dying young
before there's no one left."

"What about the tapestry? It was definitely creepy. Teag thought it
looked very old and might be Flemish."

In his mortal life, Sorren had been the best jewel thief in Antwerp,
so I figured he might have some inside knowledge about things from
Belgium.

"Can you send me pictures? There were several Weaver witches
who gained prominence in that region over the years, some more notorious than others."

"Coming right up." I texted the photos. Yes, my vampire boss uses
cell phones and computers and can text. He's quick to point out that
immortals who can't adapt to change don't last long.

"It looks like the style of Rene Taelman," Sorren said. "He was a
gifted Weaver and tapestry designer—and a dark witch with a nasty
reputation."

"Do you think it caused the misfortune for the Grantham family?"

"Possibly. Taelman was something of an arms merchant, trading in
dangerous magical objects that could be weaponized. Some of his
pieces certainly fit that description. I suspect that one of the early
Granthams obtained the piece to use against their enemies, and the
family witches either weren't powerful enough to wield it or lost the
knowledge of how to make it do their bidding."

"Which might account for the room being bricked up."

"That's certainly a possibility. I'm glad you're bringing in Rowan,
Father Anne, and Donnelly. Taelman's work is dangerous. Handle it
cautiously."

"Donnelly's already said he'd take it to the Briggs Society."

"Good. It needs to be destroyed or locked up." Sorren's past experiences with the Weaver's work must have been pretty bad to make him that adamant.

"Rumor has it that someone disappeared from a nearby room in the house. Could the tapestry have done that?"

"It's theoretically possible, although I'm not sure even Taelman was powerful enough to create a portal."

After seeing fallen angels step out of a painting, I took the idea seriously. "Where would it send someone?"

"That would depend on the witch. According to the lore, it could enable someone to travel across town—or drop them in the ocean. Think of it as an unexploded bomb—it needs to be defused *very* carefully. I suspect even Donnelly will want it neutered before it goes to the Briggs—and that's saying something."

Considering the collection of dangerous objects the Briggs Society watches over, a piece that would give Donnelly pause warranted extreme caution.

"If Taelman was the witch who wove the tapestry, he'd be long dead unless he's not human. So did he find a way to live to be over two hundred years old, or did he pass the baton to apprentice witches?"

I pictured Sorren shrugging. "Taelman was old school, taking a single student he could name as a mage heir," Sorren replied. "Apparently, the successors became the Grantham family witches just like some wealthy families have a private physician or financial advisor. It probably also protected the witch from the local coven, who weren't likely to favor Taelman's tactics."

"Would the Alliance have noticed?" The Alliance does a good job protecting Charleston—and the world—from supernatural threats, but it can't keep an eye on every bad actor.

"Maybe not, if the Grantham witches didn't flaunt their magic or cause a major threat," Sorren admitted. "Interpersonal politics is usually not our focus unless it's likely to have bigger repercussions. The magic families are always sniping at each other over one slight or another. We aren't referees. And the covens have their own 'court' system to handle grievances. So something that wasn't apocalyptic wouldn't have caught our attention. I can't recall the Grantham witches ever coming to our notice."

"Do we know who Taelman's successors were? The last Grantham just died, so did the witches remain with the family all the way to the end?"

"You said the room had been closed, so it doesn't sound like it had been in use lately. Maybe the witch could still monitor the tapestry regardless—"

"Or maybe one of the more recent Granthams tried to put an end to the connection. I can't imagine that going well," I said.

"If Ada knew the family line ended with her, she might have wanted to cut off the magic so the tapestry and other items didn't pass to some other unlucky soul," Sorren said. "I will have to make inquiries."

"I'll ask Rowan. Even if the family witch didn't mingle, I'm sure the other witches knew about them." Which made me think of the unsettling incident earlier that day.

"On the way home, I saw something weird." I told Sorren about the gray man and how his appearance multiple times along the route made me feel threatened. "I don't know if it was the same figure or if there were three separate men."

"That's worrisome," Sorren agreed. "There are several creatures that fit that description, none of them friendly. I don't think it's a coincidence that you saw him after being at the Grantham house. Tell Donnelly and Rowan what you saw. I'll look into some possibilities from my end. I think you and the others are perfectly capable of handling this," Sorren added. "You've brought the right people into it. Just…be careful."

"I promise." It's good to be a little on edge in this business. Complacency gets people killed. He asked me to call him when we had done the cleansing, and I swore I'd keep him in the loop.

I thought about what we had seen at the Grantham house and shivered. Even though Teag and I had been wearing protective jewelry— silver medallions and some of Teag's warded woven bracelets—I hoped that none of the workshop's darkness had followed us home.

Just to be safe, while Kell got ready for bed, I burned cleansing herbs and let the smoke waft over me from head to toe, then used a special soap made from plants known for their power to repel evil. I felt better afterward as I crawled into bed and snuggled beside Kell, and I hoped my precautions would be enough.

CHAPTER THREE

I WENT INTO THE SHOP THE NEXT DAY, WAITING FOR FOLKS TO GET back to me on when we could schedule the ritual at the Grantham house. On the way, I stopped at the grocery store to pick up snacks and staples for the break room.

I was a regular, so I maneuvered around the aisles quickly, picking up cookies, power bars, coffee, creamer, tea bags, sugar, sweetener, Raman noodle cups, and microwave pizza. I threw in a couple of cans of nuts and a big bag of chocolate. Even though it's just the three of us, we go through supplies surprisingly fast.

Self-checkout got me through the line fast. I carried two bags out to the car and nearly got knocked off my feet by a man who bumped into me without an apology.

I growled something under my breath, but the man had already gone inside. Still, the incident left me jangled.

"Aw, shit." One of the plastic bags split just as I got to the car, spilling my purchases. Nothing broke, but it was a pain to pick everything up. I stubbed my toe hard when I wheeled the cart back to the corral. Trying to lighten my mood, I ducked into the coffee shop that was next to the grocery store.

"Skinny vanilla latte, please."

The busy clerk took my card and ran it, then frowned. "I'm sorry, but your card isn't working. Do you have cash?"

I had just used the card to buy supplies, but I didn't want to hold up the line, so I dug money out of my wallet. Just then, the barista brought my cup and someone else's drink to the counter. The woman reached for her order and knocked mine over in the process, sending hot coffee cascading over the counter.

"I'm so sorry," she said as the clerk handed me a towel to mop the steaming liquid from my jeans.

"I'm okay," I replied, although I was annoyed that her impatience meant I'd be sticky and smelling like hazelnut all afternoon. The clerk didn't look thrilled about having to clean up the mess, either.

My now-free latte became a consolation prize, and I took a few sips to calm my nerves before I got back in my RAV4. That's when I noticed a big scratch on the rear quarter panel. I swore that hadn't been there before.

"Damn," I muttered. "This is not my day."

At the next traffic light, the RAV stuttered and stalled.

"What the hell?" I'd just had it inspected, so there shouldn't have been anything wrong. I drove carefully, which saved me from a heart stopping moment when the RAV threatened to stall again just as I pulled out into traffic. Taking the car back to the garage hadn't been in my plans, but I didn't have a choice.

"Glad you're back," Teag greeted me, holding the door while I lugged in my purchase.

"I feel like I ran a gauntlet," I limped a little from my sore toe. "Next time I'll pick another store—I swear that one was unlucky."

Teag frowned as he reached to help me with the bags and then pulled back. "Put the bags down and step away," he warned.

I did as he said, wondering what was going on.

"Don't touch the bags. I'll be right back." He left for a moment and came back with the silver tongs we use to handle problem items and a pair of gloves made from spell-woven cloth with silver strands.

"What's wrong?"

"Something in one of the bags has got bad juju." He stared at the groceries like they were a nest of snakes.

"How? I just went to Piggly Wiggly." My eyes widened. "Wait—a man bumped into me on my way to the car. Maybe he slipped something in one of the bags."

Teag poked around with the tongs until he found a small bundle of knotted threads and held it up. "Weaver magic, dark shit. Simple spell, meant to cause bad luck." He gave me a look, and I thought about everything that had gone wrong since the collision with the stranger.

"Can you tell anything about who did it?"

"Want to bet it's whoever the last Grantham witch was? This was a warning—it could have been even more dangerous." I heard anger in Teag's voice. "Unfortunately, I don't recognize the power signature, so the witch isn't someone I already know. Let me put this in the safe, and we can see if Rowan or Donnelly can get more out of it."

"I didn't see the man's face, but there didn't seem to be anything strange about him." I thought back over the incident. "Just seemed like someone who was in too much of a hurry." Now I realized that for the witch to accost me, he must have been following me, which made me queasy.

"He probably used a shielding spell to keep your psychometry from reading him," Teag said. "That's worrisome."

"Now what?" I felt violated, even though I hadn't been seriously harmed—this time. The implied threat was clear.

"Let's see what we can find out and make a plan," Teag replied. We're good about trading off being level-headed when the other person is in a spin. "We'll figure it out."

Teag went to put the knotted twine in the safe. I left messages for Rowan and Donnelly and hoped that now that the danger was past, this might be our lucky break in finding the Grantham's last witch.

It looked to be a slow morning, so once we were open and set for the day I decided to dig for more scoop on the family, and that meant a visit to my friend at the Historical Archives.

Mrs. Benjamin Morrisey knew all the proverbial movers and shakers in the city, as well as the nuances of local history. That meant she also knew all the good gossip and where the bodies—literally and metaphorically—were buried.

I stopped to get us lattes, knowing her favorite flavor, a peace offering because it had been a while since I'd visited.

"Cassidy! What a wonderful surprise. Come in and tell me what's been going on."

Mrs. Morrissey always looked like she had just stepped out of a photo shoot with perfectly coiffed hair, tastefully expensive jewelry, and suits from St. Johns that flattered her tall, thin figure. I knew she had to be in her seventies.

I followed her into her office. The Archives, like so many buildings in Charleston, was in a converted mansion. Brick exterior, large windows, and columns graced the front, along with a lovely walled garden perfect for receptions.

A sweeping staircase in the foyer made a grand first impression. Molded plaster medallions on the high ceilings, aged cypress plank floors, antique Aubusson carpets, and original oil paintings paid homage to the city's storied past. Most of the furnishings were reproductions, although some originals had been returned to the house by the descendants of former owners.

"Now what brings you here?" Mrs. Morrissey gave a sly grin after we had gotten caught up with each other, and she had quizzed me about the plans for Teag's wedding. "Because glad as I am to see you and chat, I'm sure this isn't just a social call."

I held up my hands in mock surrender and laughed. "Busted!" I set my drink aside. "What do you know about the Grantham family history?"

She shifted in her seat on a high-backed Victorian couch. "The Granthams? Does this have anything to do with the mansion selling outside the family for the first time?"

"The new owner called us in to deal with some…disturbances."

Mrs. Morrissey knows quite a bit about what we *really* do at Trifles and Folly. We've intervened more than once when the supernatural posed a risk to the Archives because of a haunted or cursed object.

"Disturbances, huh? I'm not surprised. They have a rather storied history."

Charlestonians speak in code when dealing with touchy subjects. The wording becomes formal, and the word choice makes a suggestion without actually spilling the tea.

I mentally translated "storied" into "chock full of scandals."

I held my latte and leaned forward. "Do tell."

"The patriarch, Lee Harris Grantham, made his fortune in shipping in the early 1800s. The records suggest he dabbled in piracy and smuggling before becoming a privateer. The same could be said of quite a few of the city's founding families, who either came to the colonies with money or clawed their way to the top before styling themselves as newly minted aristocrats." Mrs. Morrissey warmed to the topic.

"Lee Grantham eventually shifted his business to mostly legal cargo. But the family roots came in handy during the Civil War running the blockade. During the World Wars, his ships had an uncanny ability to avoid entanglements."

Somehow she managed to make hundred-and-fifty-year-old news sound salacious. I interpreted "uncanny" as "everyone suspected there was witchcraft involved but didn't say so out loud."

"How did they get along with the rest of the Charleston upper crust?"

Mrs. Morrissey frowned, and then her expression cleared. "Now that the last of the family is gone, there's no one to take offense, so I can speak plainly. From what I saw and what I heard about earlier times, the Granthams, for all their wealth, were not welcomed by the respectable families."

"Surely they weren't the only ones who obtained their money in somewhat questionable ways." I remembered what Sorren had told me.

Mrs. Morrissey gave a demure snort. "Of course not. But the Granthams didn't try as hard to hide it or paint over the ugly parts. And Lee Grantham, the patriarch, apparently enjoyed getting under the skin of people he thought put on airs."

"What's your theory on why the line died out?" I knew what Sorren thought, but I was curious to see what Mrs. Morrissey made of it.

"Ada McIntosh Grantham never married and, if the stories are to be believed, rebuffed every suitor—even from some very fine families."

She continued: "From the photographs, she was lovely in her younger days and handsome as she got older. She gave to charity, maintained the mansion, and walked her dogs around the neighborhood, but otherwise was a recluse. She granted an interview late in life, although up until then, she had been notoriously publicity-shy. When the reporter asked why she never married when she was the last of the Granthams, all she said was, 'It ends with me.'"

"That's not ominous at all," I said, and Mrs. Morrissey nodded.

"I thought the same thing when I read the interview. Then again, Ada hadn't been welcome in all the places where her cohort went to socialize, and maybe she was proud enough not to go where she wasn't wanted. Perhaps she didn't wish that on another generation."

I thought that was a credible explanation, and if it was true, I couldn't blame Ada, although I felt sorry for her despite her wealth.

"Did you ever get the feeling from her donations or other activities that she was trying to make up for the family's actions over the years?"

Mrs. Morrissey shook her head. "No—that wasn't the Grantham way. I believe Ada had given up on winning a popularity contest or refurbishing the family reputation. She gave to causes that mattered to her for private reasons and honestly didn't seem to give a damn what anyone else thought."

Despite the family's stained history, I had a grudging respect for Ada, who knew who she was and refused to apologize or grovel. I'd seen people do far worse to ingratiate themselves.

"Were there any rumors or 'incidents' regarding the mansion?" I couldn't help being curious.

"You mean aside from being haunted like every other self-respecting grand house?" Mrs. Morrissey smiled, and I caught a glimpse of what she had looked like at a much younger age, with bright eyes and a sincere, mischievous smile.

"Exactly."

"Of course there were stories, fueled no doubt because public opinion ran against the Granthams, so no one was likely to rally to defend them. People claimed the family's original wealth came from a deal with the devil, or that there was a witch in each generation, or that Ada was the witch. The usual claptrap."

As I knew, and I believed Mrs. Morrissey strongly suspected, those rumors weren't outlandish.

"Housekeepers begged the milkman to stop at the Grantham house last because they feared the milk would sour. Any misfortune in the neighborhood got blamed on them, from missing cats to sick children," she went on.

"The servants were clearly afraid to say anything, but they were paid well enough that they stayed. Ada had a nurse who took care of her until just before the end. They were of an age, and the nurse passed away first. Ada followed shortly afterward."

I wondered if Ada and her nurse were more than employer and helper. For Ada's sake, I hoped she had found some respite from her lonely life.

"Any sightings of a gray man?"

She thought for a moment and then shook her head. "No, I don't think so. The only 'gray man' I've heard of is the Pawley Island ghost. Sorry."

"Were there any serious allegations—deaths, bad accidents, people gone missing?" I probed.

Mrs. Morrissey sat back straight, legs primly crossed at the ankle. "People didn't like the Granthams, but they feared them. Actually blaming them for crimes would have likely drawn recourse from the authorities, even if law enforcement didn't like the family, either. But there were always whispers. A workman who died under suspicious circumstances, or a cook's son who came down with a mysterious illness, or a traveling salesman who fell down dead right in front of their gate.

"I have no idea if any of the deaths actually happened, and I'm even less sure the Granthams had anything to do with it, but, well, people talk." She finished her latte.

We talked some more, and I promised to visit more often as she walked me out. Then I glanced at my watch and realized time was slipping away before I was due at the Grantham house to cleanse the workshop. I called in lunch for Teag, Maggie, and me and then drove to the shop and hoped I beat the delivery to the door.

MY CREW GATHERED at the Grantham house later that afternoon. Father Anne wore her clerical collar and basic black shirt and slacks, although her Doc Martens and spiked hair definitely set her apart from most clergy in Charleston. Rowan looked like she was heading for a Yoga class in tights and a loose shirt, but I knew she prized ease of motion when it came to doing a banishment. Donnely's khaki field jacket and muttonchops made him look like he was going on safari. Teag and I had just come from the shop and made sure we had plenty of protective charms and jewelry.

I hadn't glimpsed the gray stranger on the way to the mansion, which I counted as a win.

"I've always wondered about the Grantham mansion." Archibald Donnelly gave the large house a stare as if to intimidate the building. "Didn't think I'd get an invitation."

"Hardly a social event." Rowan pushed a strand of blond hair behind one ear. She eyed the house warily like it might bite.

"I always cross the street when I pass here," Father Anne observed. "Bad vibes."

"Before we go inside, we need to tell you about something that happened earlier." I then recounted the man with the malicious knot magic and the gray stranger.

"There are a number of witches in Charleston who probably *could* do a spell like that; there are very few I suspect *would* do it," Rowan said. "Ethics aside, it's well-known that you, Teag, and Maggie are *protected* by Sorren and Archibald—as well as your own abilities. That's enough to warn away any sane witch."

"We can stop by the shop and have a look tomorrow," Donnelly said. "The knots are in the safe, so they won't be troubling anyone. But realize that unless Rowan and I have had dealings with the witch, we won't automatically know his identity from the power signature of the threads—although we'll recognize him afterward."

"I'll take whatever we can get," I told them before returning to the business at hand. "We're grateful to you for coming." Teag nodded from where he stood beside me. "The new owner, Ron, is waiting to let us in. I've briefed him, so he's going to wait outside in his car until you're finished."

Thankfully, Ron didn't ask questions. He seemed eager to get out of the way and scooted from the house after a hurried welcome and effusive thanks.

Rowan chuckled as we watched him leave. "Always nice to know someone *really* wants us."

I led them upstairs, hyper-aware of the house's bad mojo, which felt even stronger than before.

"You weren't kidding about the resonance," Rowan said as we climbed the steps. "I'm amazed anyone could live in the house—or even stay here for long."

They followed me to the doorway of the secret room. Teag and I hung back, allowing them to take the lead. Rowan reinforced the line of salt I had placed when I'd visited before, then handed me a canister to put a circle around myself as Teag carefully stepped into the room to join them. Both Rowan and Donnelly immediately focused on the tapestry. Father Anne remained in the hallway, looking at the family portraits.

"Problem?" I asked.

She shrugged. "I recognize some of the names and faces from the St. Expeditus archive. They weren't just harmless merchants if they attracted the society's attention." Father Anne and I moved to take our places just outside the door, where we could help with the working inside the room and keep anything from getting out.

Rowan said something in a language I didn't understand and flung out one hand toward the wall hanging. For a second I saw a golden scrim cover the piece. Then the light faded, but the tapestry appeared blurred.

"That's a nasty piece of work." Donnelly eyed the wall hanging with mistrust.

"Have you seen anything like it?" Teag ventured a step or two closer until Donnelly threw an arm out to stop him in place.

"It senses your Weaver magic," Donnelly warned.

"I've put a stasis spell on it, but we should still be careful," Rowan advised. "You, especially, Teag. The magic is going to be drawn to your power."

Teag didn't get nearer, but he made motions that reminded me of working a loom, and some of the tension in the air eased.

"I wove a protection around it, but it won't hold forever—and it isn't strong enough by itself to eliminate all that bad mojo," Teag told us.

Donnelly made a slow circuit, muttering under his breath. Since he walked the path widdershins, I assumed he was working a spell.

The temperature in the corridor plummeted. Disembodied voices howled, and gray wisps darted around me before flying upward and disappearing.

Rowan kept her focus on the tapestry. She moved to stand in front of it and began a litany under her breath, and the stasis spell sparked as if the tapestry was trying to get free.

The air around us felt charged like a lightning storm. My touch magic can activate even through the soles of my shoes if the energy is strong enough, and the Grantham house had plenty of emotions, magic, and haunts to trigger my sight.

Even without touching anything else, the vision overwhelmed me. Vignettes from the house's long, unlucky past flashed in my mind. Screaming arguments, slamming doors, and shattered crockery were recurring themes, but slaps, punches, and shoving also showed up a lot.

The Granthams had a history of intimate violence, which I doubted could be wholly blamed on the tapestry. Perhaps whoever practiced witchcraft did so to quell the danger and level the power imbalance.

Looming in the background of the scenes across time was the same gray stranger.

I gasped and put a hand to my chest as the scenes flew by.

"Cassidy?" Father Anne asked, concerned.

I couldn't speak, but I waved her off. At worst I might black out from the intensity of the visions. We couldn't afford Donnelly and Rowan to lose their concentration.

It didn't surprise me that a wave of sorrow followed the scenes of violence. I heard sobs echo in the empty house and felt such an outpouring of grief, loss, and bitter disappointment that I struggled to catch my breath.

Whatever wealth and privilege the family gained certainly hadn't been worth what they endured.

Not all the ghosts had fled or been cast out with Donnelly's first spell. I could feel the weight of their gazes, and the stronger ghosts who made themselves visible stood in silent ranks, watching with baleful, shadowed eyes.

The raw emotions of the home's inhabitants had sunk into the bones of the house, making it a reservoir of their hopes, fears, desires, and enmity deeper than any mold or rot. I doubted it could ever be completely cleansed.

"It's not just a spell," Teag said, and I saw understanding dawn on his face. "There's an entity involved. The gray man?"

Donnelly nodded. "A djinn, I believe. And he's not happy about us spoiling his fun."

Rowan made a slow circuit of the room, muttering and occasionally gesturing over some of the magical equipment. Now and then she withdrew an amulet or a protective hunk of gemstone from a pouch on her belt to deepen her spellcasting. She took a silver chalice from her bag, poured in a mixture of dried leaves and powders, and then lit the contents on fire, letting the cleansing smoke fill the air.

I felt the pressure ease, but only slightly.

The ghosts drew closer, and I was grateful that the salt circle kept them at bay. My abilities were of limited use here, although I hoped the insights gained from my visions would be helpful. But perhaps, while

Donnelly and Teag teamed up on the malicious tapestry and Rowan defused the dangerous magic in the other items, I could make nice with the ghosts. Then Father Anne could bless the space, and we could be done.

"If you want to be free of this place, he can send you on." I nodded toward Donnelly, who was conferring with Teag in the secret room. Normally Father Anne did banishments, but since we had a necromancer, I figured he could do it. "You don't have to stay. The Granthams are gone now."

I felt a shiver as my touch magic kicked in again. Apparently, the ghosts intended to make their case, and somehow their energy channeled through the house to trigger my abilities.

These images were different from the first raw, uncensored vision. I saw grand balls and weddings, formal family dinners, at-home births, and decorous wakes. One of the ghosts, a bearded older man dressed in the style of the mid-1800s, fixed me with a glare.

"Ours." I heard clearly. *"Our house."*

Great. Possessive ghosts. My head throbbed, and I rubbed my temples and blinked my eyes before responding.

"There are no more living Granthams," I told them. "If the house doesn't pass to another owner, it will be torn down, destroyed. All your history will be lost and forgotten. No one will remember you, and your family name will pass from memory."

Their voices sounded like the rattle of dry leaves as they argued among themselves, just below the threshold of my hearing.

As my sight cleared, I got a better look at the spirits. From their clothing, I guessed they were family members, not servants or unlucky workers. Their outfits spanned more than a century, all of them the height of fashion in their day and accented with expensive jewelry.

I'd never seen a group who looked more miserable. Clearly their social position and affluence hadn't made them happy.

"If you stay, you cannot bother the living, or he will return and force you to leave." I gestured to Donnelly. It's best not to speak names around the dead. Names have power.

"We cannot move on," one of the female ghosts said.

Thanks to my magic, I sensed the deep emotions behind her words. Shame, hidden guilt, pride, and entitlement. Petty grievances over slights long past. Raw fury. And beneath it all, fear of what the afterlife held.

They know they were terrible people, and they're afraid of a reckoning.

"I can't fix how you lived your lives or what kind of karma you've got coming for you. If it would ease your burden, our priest can offer a prayer of reconciliation and remorse to smooth your path."

"We have no reason for remorse, no desire for reconciliation," the old man snapped.

Clearly, according to the ghosts, all the unhappiness that had occurred within these walls was someone else's fault.

"Then prepare to have your ghostly asses booted out," I told them, in no mood to argue.

The spirits surged forward, rushing toward me, faces twisted with rage. The salt barrier held as they threw themselves against it, and I hoped it could withstand the onslaught.

I wasn't unarmed. I had an old wooden spoon that served as an athame, charged with the emotional resonance of years of baking with my grandmother. An antique walking stick that once belonged to Sorren's maker, Alard, served as a weapon in more than one way. The stained dog collar wrapped around my left wrist summoned my spirit protector, the ghost of Bo, my late golden retriever. I shook my wrist, and Bo appeared beside me and wagged, ready for action. The wooden spoon slipped into my hand from beneath my sleeve, and the walking stick hung from my belt.

I couldn't identify some of the noises from inside the room, none of which sounded vaguely human in response to Donnelly's measured chant and Rowan's quiet, authoritative spell-weaving. Teag's magic worked silently as his fingers traced invisible patterns in the air.

While the silver, onyx, and agate protective jewelry I wore would do a lot to keep me safe, I didn't feel like putting it to the test. But I sensed on a level deeper than words that Donnelly and the others had reached a critical point in their countermagic, and I dared not distract them.

Perhaps the ghosts knew that as well and attacked me to keep the others from breaking the hold the spirits had held over the house and its occupants.

I knew several banishment spells, although I wasn't sure they would work against so large an angry gathering of revenants.

Father Anne stepped between me and the ghosts and spoke the incantation. "Be gone, fell spirits and angry ghosts. Depart from this place and trouble the living no more."

I closed my eyes so that the spectacle of dead faces pressed against the salt's protective scrim didn't make me falter.

"I banish you, restless spirits and vengeful ghosts. You are no longer welcome among the living. Your place is with the dead and buried, and your souls must move on to their recompense. By all that is holy, I abjure and command you to leave this place!" Father Anne spoke with the full authority of her ordination and deep belief.

She pivoted quickly into a third invocation as I felt the energy in the corridor roil around me.

"Depart from here, unwholesome spirits of the dead. Remove your energy from this place. I cast you out, and your welcome is withdrawn. Go to your final rest and no longer vex the living."

Her voice grew stronger and louder, and the air stirred in the hallway as the temperature dropped until I could see my breath.

A new onslaught of images assaulted my mind. This time, I witnessed death. A fall down the stairs and from a window. Gunshots and knives. More than one hanging. A figure engulfed by flame.

The visions did not permit me to look away. I knew with certainty what I saw were murders, suicides, and a few tragic accidents. I saw mothers weeping over babies and children, lovers bereft over a lost partner, grieving and angry siblings, and more than once, the smug satisfaction of a killer who knew his deeds would go unpunished.

It took everything I had not to throw up, and only the fear that my vomit might disturb the salt line kept me from losing my lunch.

A blinding flare of purple light flashed behind me. Donnelly shouted words I didn't catch. The ghosts vanished, and the room warmed. My vision faded, although the headache didn't. I dropped to my knees, trying to catch my breath.

"Cassidy? Are you okay?" Teag asked.

Father Anne remained in place between me and where the ghosts had been until she had assured us they wouldn't return. Then she turned and helped me stand.

"Yeah. I think so." I managed to get to my feet, but the throbbing in my temples made me woozy.

"The ghosts are gone. They won't be back," Father Anne said.

"I sent the spirits and entities that were trapped in the tapestry on to their next destination, as well as the ghosts who tried to remain." Donnelly dusted off his hands with satisfaction. "It's definitely djinn magic, so I suspect that the tragedies came about from cursed wishes."

I thought of the deaths I had witnessed in my vision and shivered once more. "I saw…more than I wanted to see." I knew Teag would understand. He gave me a side hug, and I realized how cold I felt.

"I've neutralized the magic in the other paraphernalia," Rowan added. "What's left is inert. I'll take the spell books. They shouldn't be left lying around. Otherwise, the room is just a room."

"I'm going to walk through the house and do a blessing with incense and incantations." Father Anne took a censer from her gear bag and lit the incense. Soon, the air smelled of benzoin, frankincense, and myrrh. After thoroughly blessing the secret room and hallway, she ambled off down the corridor, swinging the censer toward one side and the other.

"If the workshop was closed off, what happened to the family's witch?" I asked when Rowan returned.

"According to the covens, the most recent witch associated with the Granthams was Laroque Shaw," Rowan said. "He was the protégé of the previous witch, who died ten years ago. Shaw isn't welcome in the covens because he has no compunctions about dark magic. He's a loner and keeps a low profile. The problem is, he's powerful enough to cause real trouble, so no one wants to challenge him unless the situation is dire."

"Did he have a falling out with Ada Grantham? Because if the room was closed off, it wasn't actively being used, and it seems to have been walled up for a while," Teag observed.

"Ada was a recluse, and since the coven was never on good terms with the Granthams, I suspect they took a 'no news is good news' approach," Rowan replied. "If there was a falling out, I didn't hear about it, and no one said anything when I asked. But if so, then Shaw might have been angry and adrift for a while—with a djinn on speed dial."

I looked at the tapestry. The image had faded to shades of gray, lacking the sparking energy. "What about the djinn?"

"The djinn itself wasn't in the tapestry," Donnelly said. "It just used the tapestry's magic to grant cursed wishes. So if someone did 'disappear' nearby, I suspect they made a wish to go away and not be found, and the djinn made that happen. I doubt it went well for them."

I thought about the Grantham family's wealth and fame, coupled with the tragedies and unhappiness my visions had revealed. "Cursed" didn't seem like a strong enough word for the misery those granted wishes had caused.

"What does a djinn look like?" I reminded them about the gray stranger.

Donnelly's bushy eyebrows drew together like thunderclouds. "After what we've seen here, I'm sure that's a djinn. I didn't like to hear that Shaw might have been following you—I like it even less for a djinn to be on your trail."

"How do I get rid of it?" I was both glad to have my suspicion confirmed and uneasy at the same time.

"Your normal protective charms and wardings should keep the djinn at bay, and I can look into amulets that work specifically against those creatures," Rowan said. "As for Shaw—you should be safe in your warded places, but outside those, you'll need to be on guard and take more precautions."

"I suspect that both Shaw and the djinn see you as a threat," Donnelly replied. "Keep your distance, stay in warded places as best you can, wear your amulets, and realize that djinn can possess people, so it can change forms."

"Do you think Shaw and the djinn are working together?" Teag asked.

"Possibly," Donnelly replied. "But no telling whether the witch is controlling the djinn or the other way around. From the age of the magic in the tapestry, my bet is that the djinn is older and more powerful, so the witch might be in thrall or a willing accomplice."

"With the owner's permission, we can clean out all of the witchy stuff and do another cleansing," Rowan gathered the remaining spell books and placed them in a tote made from fabric Teag had woven with protective magic. Donnelly removed what remained of the tapestry and slipped it into a warded fabric sleeve to take to the Briggs Society for safekeeping.

"I'll tell Zimmerman that the house is un-haunted. That might lower the cachet, but with luck, the people who move in will have a chance at being a lot happier than the Granthams."

"I've done one round of blessing." Father Anne rejoined us. "I can always come back if more are needed. Some stains take longer to fade."

We walked out together. I could already sense the difference in the house's energy. It didn't feel fresh or clean, but a good cleansing and blessing helped a lot. The oppressive shadow was gone, as well as the sense of being watched. I hoped that whoever moved in could shift the vibes and make the grand mansion a decent place to live.

I stopped by Ron's truck. "The hidden room has been cleansed, and we're taking the cursed tapestry to be destroyed. The dangerous ghosts are gone, so the only spirits who are left want to be here and don't intend to cause trouble."

He looked gobsmacked. "Your people did all that?"

I felt a surge of pride and smiled. "Sure did. Call if you need anything else."

Rowan and the others were waiting for me near our cars.

"The tapestry had its own defensive magic, so I countered that while Archibald dealt with the djinn's spell," Rowan said. "And I 'powered down' the rest of the relics and materials. There was a lot of dark stuff in there that shouldn't have fallen into untrained hands. As for the spell books—I'll go through them to see what's there and make sure they're properly protected."

"The tapestry didn't just have magic woven into its fabric; it had layers of protections and wardings," Teag said. "Whoever created the wall hanging was a very skilled witch as well as a master weaver. I'm in awe of the skill and repelled by the way they used it."

"I haven't run into a djinn in a long time," Donnelly mused. "I think we should pay a visit to Amir Moradi and see what he knows about it."

I looked up, recognizing the name. "The rug shop owner? Do you think he called the djinn?"

Given what we do, I thought I knew who the other magical merchants in town were. I'd heard of Moradi's antique kilim and Persian carpets, but not that he had abilities.

"Moradi's always been reputable," Donnelly replied as we walked. "He's descended from a long line of Persian Weaver witches. I don't think he's the one controlling the djinn, but if there's someone else involved, he might be able to point us in the right direction."

Rowan and Father Anne headed home. Donnelly put what was left of the tapestry in an iron and silver containment box until he could get back to the Briggs Society, then agreed to go to Moradi's rug shop with us.

~

DESPITE THE TREASURES INSIDE, the storefront for International Carpets wasn't impressive. Then again, the shop had been in Charleston for nearly two hundred years, so it had nothing to prove. Moradi's ancestor founded the store thanks to family connections in shipping and rug weaving, taking advantage of Charleston's port to bring in carpets from around the world.

I remembered visiting once with my parents when I was a child and letting my imagination take flight, dreaming of magic carpets and grand castles. Piles of gem-hued, tasseled rugs stacked everywhere filled the air. The smell of wool tinged with the scent of incense clung to the clothing of the man who had shown my parents around. As they debated what to buy, I climbed atop a tower of carpets and daydreamed about flying to faraway locations.

Although it had been years since I had visited the store, I felt a thrill of excitement when the brass bells above the door rang, like we were entering a place where anything could happen.

Not entirely unlike my own Trifles and Folly.

Teag paused just inside the doorway.

"You okay?" I looked at him with concern.

"Yeah." Teag had a wistful expression. "A lot of these carpets are still hand-woven. That bakes in a certain amount of energy, even if the weavers don't have magic. I can sense that, and it's a bit like walking into a crowded room full of conversations."

"Archibald! What a wonderful surprise." Amir Moradi spotted us and made a beeline. He reminded me of an older version of the mysterious warrior in *The Mummy*, with dark eyes and black hair shot through with strands of silver.

"Amir. Always a treat to see these lovely rugs," Donnelly replied.

Moradi embraced him, then turned to us. "You've brought friends. Somehow I doubt this is a social call." He signaled to an associate to oversee the showroom, then led us to his office in the back. "To what do I owe the pleasure?"

We found seats, and Moradi poured cups of strong Turkish coffee, which he served in demitasse cups with sugar cubes. I paused to breathe its fragrance, full of cardamom, cloves, and anise.

The shop owner listened in silence as Donnelly recounted our experience with the tapestry at the Grantham house. Teag and I jumped in from time to time to add details. For now, I left out our suspicions about Shaw and the djinn.

"Merciful heavens! That's quite a tale. One I would doubt from anyone else," Moradi said when we finished. "Are you thinking the tapestry came from my shop?"

Donnelly shrugged. "We don't know. It wasn't purchased recently.

The house was built in 1822, but the carpet felt much older, and we have no idea how it ended up there. And then there's the matter of the djinn."

"Do you have a photograph?" Moradi asked. Donnelly withdrew his phone and showed him the tapestry.

Moradi caught his breath. "*The Idyll*. I wasn't sure it was real."

"You're familiar with the tapestry?" Teag asked as we leaned forward, intrigued.

"I thought it was a legend. Everyone in the rug business has heard of it, but no one claimed to have seen it for at least a hundred years. Outside living memory." Moradi appeared transfixed by the photo.

"What do you know about it?" I asked.

Moradi finally tore himself away from the picture and sat back in his chair. "The story I heard may not be the truth, and it may not be the only tale, but it is a starting point. Several lifetimes ago—centuries, generations—a master weaver lost the love of his life to illness. Mad with grief, he started to work on a tapestry and labored day and night, barely eating, sleeping at his loom."

He paused to sip his coffee. "His friends tried to make him rest, but he refused. He worked like a man possessed, and some of the neighbors feared that was actually the case. Stories circulated about a 'shadow man' who visited at night, a creature that was a silhouette without a body. They worried it was a demon or a djinn, but the weaver wouldn't pause to talk."

Moradi smiled, clearly enjoying having an audience for his tale. "When the weaver finished his work, he had a tapestry of the highest craftsmanship, with lush and vibrant colors and such depth that it looked as if someone could step inside. He said it was of a special place in the forest where he and his beloved enjoyed walking, their special haven. The man hung the tapestry on his wall, and his friends hoped it had eased his pain."

"Did it?" Teag was clearly drawn into the story.

"Yes, and no. Visitors to the house swore they heard branches rustling and birds chirping when they walked near the wall hanging. His housekeeper quit because she said there were glowing eyes watching her from the trees. The weaver grew gaunt and pale. He never left his house or strayed far from the tapestry. Just before he died, he told his friend that the 'shadow man' told him that when he finished the piece, he could be with his lover again."

"But the shadow man didn't mention they'd be joined in death?" I said.

Moradi nodded. "Exactly. Despite that, the tapestry was so beautiful that one of the neighbors stole it to sell it. He came into a windfall—and later lost everything. The tapestry passed through many hands, but the story remained the same. The piece would bring great fortune—and then terrible misfortune. And so it seems to have come to the owner of the house. That is the legend—but I have always thought it was romanticized."

"How so?" Teag asked.

"It fits the fairy tale format too closely," Moradi replied. "I heard a different version, but it isn't nearly as good a legend. A powerful Weaver named Rafe Taelman used dark magic to create a tapestry that would help him leech energy from his victims and wield control over them. He passed that knowledge to his successor."

"Was the shadow man a djinn?" I asked.

"That would fit the tale," Moradi replied and made a gesture of warding. "It's possible that Taelman might have struck an unholy bargain with such a monster."

"You've been in town and part of the supernatural community for a long time," I mused. "Do you know who became the Grantham's most recent witch?"

Moradi shook his head. "No, I'm sorry. I did not have a reason to pay them close attention."

I sipped my coffee and thought about the legend. I'd heard similar stories about cursed objects that came into our possession at Trifles and Folly, so I didn't have difficulty believing. I just marveled that the Granthams had possessed it for so long.

"Did the tapestry come with a djinn woven into it somehow?"

"Stories about magic lamps notwithstanding, I don't think such beings can be contained by mere objects without their consent,"

Moradi said. "But it could function as a threshold where the line between our world and the djinn's was thin enough for him to hear and grant the wishes of the unwary."

"Which apparently included the entire Grantham family," Donnelly said with a sigh. "What happens to the djinn when the tapestry is destroyed and magically bound?"

Moradi shrugged. "Djinn are mostly immortal, so they won't die unless they're killed in one of several very particular ways. If the djinn's threshold closes, I imagine the creature finds another feeding ground."

He refilled our cups. "The Briggs Society is the best place for such a piece. No doubt it has caused enough misery." He muttered a protective phrase under his breath.

"Any ideas how the piece might have come into the Grantham family's hands?" Donnelly asked. "We don't know for certain, but their luck turned golden around 1820."

"I don't believe it came from my shop," Moradi said. "Much like Trifles and Folly, we have a greater calling to remove harmful rugs or tapestries from circulation when we come upon them. Others are not so scrupulous. Have you considered the possibility that the djinn itself might have matched the Granthams with the piece?"

I had, and that made me nervous. "You said they're immortal unless killed in certain ways. Could the djinn still be alive after all these years? And still in Charleston?"

"Yes, the djinn might well still exist. As for remaining in town— Djinn stay where they can feed," Moradi said. "If necessary, they can possess a willing servant to help them."

"Would the djinn be aware that we broke its control over the tapestry?" I asked.

Both Donnelly and Moradi nodded. "Very likely," Donnelly said.

"Almost certainly," Moradi agreed.

"Have there been other recent issues with bad tapestries?" Teag asked.

Moradi thought for a moment. "Not that I've heard about…but I do not hear everything. Then again, a djinn wouldn't be limited to using a tapestry unless it simply favored that medium. All kinds of objects can be cursed."

"Getting rid of the Grantham tapestry required a rather epic battle," I said. "If we happen upon something else, is there an easier way to neutralize it?"

"We have a silver mesh net," Teag reminded me. "And I can weave magic into a rope net and make a sack out of fabric with protections woven in. Would those help to contain another wall hanging if we find one?"

Moradi nodded. "Probably. I'm sorry I can't be more definite, but it depends on the strength of the curse. I suspect that the Grantham tapestry had an especially strong spell on it. The djinn no doubt saw a chance to feed for generations."

I thought about the other old money families in Charleston and wondered if any of them rose to prominence thanks to deals of one sort or another. I didn't doubt that was the case for some, and my mind supplied a short list of prominent people whose questionable ethics would lend itself to such things.

I knew that witchcraft played a role in some of the largest fortunes, either in the past or up to current times. Charleston might bill itself as the "Holy City" for the number of churches, but witchcraft, Voudon, and Hoodoo have always played a big role beneath the surface.

We thanked Moradi for his time and coffee, deep in thought as we went back to our cars. Donnelly followed us, and Rowan was already waiting when we arrived. They followed us to the break room, and Teag used the silver tongs to bring out the knotted rope.

Rowan and Donnelly took a half-step back reflexively and eyed the rope with suspicion.

"Definitely dark magic," Rowan confirmed. "I don't recognize the power signature, but then again, I've never dealt with Laroque Shaw."

"I have." Donnelly frowned as he looked at the rope. "Not for a long time, but he was memorable for all the wrong reasons. I think it's very possible that's who made the hex rope. If so, it's a warning—he's capable of doing much worse. Be careful, Cassidy. Until we settle this matter, it's reasonable to assume Shaw sees you as a target."

"I'll try to find out if anyone knows where he's gone to ground these days." Rowan made a gesture of warding. "There are bound to be rumors. Be careful, and make sure you keep all your charms and amulets close."

They left with promises to be in touch soon. I slumped against the counter in the break room.

"Thoughts?"

"I'm not accepting any tapestries as wedding presents." Teag raised an eyebrow.

"I think that's wise," I replied.

CHAPTER FOUR

"I MIGHT PUT A MORATORIUM ON ANYTHING WOVEN—LINENS, BEDDING, that sort of thing." Teag grew serious. "People don't realize how much energy can glom onto things if they aren't sensitive to it."

"I get it." My touch magic made accepting gifts dicey, even when well-intentioned. New items could pick up dodgy resonance from their surroundings, and vintage pieces could be a real problem.

"How's everything going with the wedding?" I was eager to change the subject. I still wasn't quite sure what to make of the whole djinn issue, but I needed a break.

"I'm going to be very relieved to *be* married," Teag replied. "The *getting* part is stressful."

"Something go wrong?" I was ready to jump in if they needed my help with a reservation or vendor.

"No—at least, not yet. But there are a lot of details, and keeping it all straight is complicated, even with a wedding planner. Anthony and I are trying to be chill about everything, but his mom is stressing big time."

"You usually get along with Mrs. Benton," I pointed out.

"I do. She's very sweet," Teag maintained. "I think she's just gone into 'wedding mom' mode, which should be an official psychological diagnosis. Not in a bad way—she just wants everything to be perfect so we aren't disappointed by something going wrong. And I think she's overcompensating, feeling defensive on our behalf because there are people out there who discriminate."

"Anyone who refuses to bake a cake for a Benton is living dangerously." Benton Connor Hawthorn is one of the oldest and most prestigious law firms in Charleston. Anthony is one of the youngest partners. They wouldn't even have to sue. Once their Country Club friends heard about a slight like that, catering and party orders would dry up. Definitely a fuck-around-and-find-out situation.

"I'd rather have a nice quiet ceremony than prove a point," Teag said. "His mom's always been protective of all the kids, and she hates it when people are unfair or small-minded. I'm grateful for how fierce she is, and at the same time, I keep hoping we can avoid bloodshed. There is no wrath like that of a mother whose child is scorned."

"Are Anthony's famed negotiating skills helping keep the peace?" Teag's fiancé had a gift for brokering resolutions, whether it was about a damaged purchase or an incorrect credit card bill.

"Fortunately, the wedding planner deals with all the vendors. We come in to approve the menu, decorations, and cake flavors. It's her job to keep any snafus from surfacing. I don't envy her. We're paying her very well, but I hope she goes on vacation afterward to de-stress," Teag said.

"And your mom is holding up?"

"Supportive—and a little lost," Teag replied. "We try to include her in the details so she knows everything that's going on. It isn't that she wants to be hands-on. She just worries about not doing something that she's supposed to as one of the mothers of the grooms."

I thought about how traditional bride and groom weddings had defined roles and responsibilities for both the couple and their families. Plenty of people chose to ignore tradition and do as they pleased, so Teag and Anthony were in good company forging their own path.

"Everything you've shown me looks wonderful," I reassured him. I'd been thrilled Teag had asked me along to walk through the venue and go to a cake tasting. Helping to plan a wedding was much more fun when it wasn't your own, and you didn't have to pay for it.

"Thanks. Anthony keeps reminding me that all that matters is at the end of the day, we're married. I try to keep that in mind. It's funny—it's our special day, but I keep worrying that I'm going to let someone else down. People get weird about weddings."

"Just say the word, and I'll drive you both out of state under cover of darkness," I joked.

"Some days that sounds like a great idea," Teag admitted.

"Okay—tell me a couple of good things about all the planning. Drama goes with weddings, like icing goes with cake. What's going right?"

Teag grinned. "I haven't shown you the tuxes!" He thrust his phone at me. "Look!"

He and Anthony posed in the photo wearing black tuxedos in an updated style. The cut flattered both men—not hard to do since they're handsome—and accentuated broad shoulders and trim waists.

"Swanky," I said. "You both look amazing."

"I've only ever rented tuxes before," Teag confessed. "I think Anthony's owned one since he was about twelve. But we bought these, and the fit is totally different. At least with Anthony's work events and the Bentons' social circle, I'll have chances to wear mine again."

"Everything still on for the big night this weekend?" Maggie and I had plans to take Teag out for a great evening in lieu of a bachelor party. We had tickets to see his favorite indie band, reservations for dinners and drinks in the party room at a local fish camp that's a favorite of Teag's, and several more surprises. I knew Anthony's brother had plans for a private dinner cruise for his brothers, cousins, and close work friends that included a premium tasting for expensive scotch, cigars, and imported cheese.

Personally, I thought our plans sounded like more fun. Especially since the signature cocktail at the fish camp was a potent concoction called "swamp water," and I had a limo hired to drive us all home.

"I'm looking forward to your wedding so much," I told him. "And in the meantime, it's going to be my sanity-saver when I need to think happy thoughts."

When it came time to close for the night, Teag insisted on following me home in his car. We warned Maggie to be extra careful and headed out.

"Stay on the phone with me," Teag said. "That way if anything weird happens, we're already talking."

For the first few blocks, neither of us saw anything unusual, so we chatted about the shows we were watching. I took a deep breath, and hoped that the weirdness was done for the day.

I glanced to the side when we stopped at a light and caught my breath. "Teag, do you see him?" The gray stranger stood on the corner, staring at us.

"Yeah."

In my rearview mirror, I saw Teag move to get out of his car.

"Don't you dare," I told him. "You don't have weapons, and we don't even know if we can hurt him."

"Drive around aimlessly. See how long he follows us. Maybe we can piss him off." Teag reluctantly agreed not to chase the djinn.

Instead of taking the next turn, I went straight and so did Teag. Sure enough, two streets ahead, the stranger showed up again. Then I went left, just for the hell of it, and Teag followed. Once again, after a couple of blocks, the gray man appeared on a corner.

"If I keep going around the block, think he'll catch on?" I was annoyed and a little weirded out.

"Sounds like fun. Let's see."

I went around the block once, then twice. Teag stayed on my tail. Next I circled a two-block area. The gray man showed up on the first pass but not the second.

"We should quit before we get a ticket for cruising. But we're going to take the long way back."

"How do you feel?" Teag asked, and I knew he was thinking about how the car's wardings were weaker than at the shop or house.

"Edgy," I admitted. "Bad gut feeling, like something is going to happen. And a sense of...menace." It took me a second to find the right word, but that summed it up. "I don't know whether it's magic or intuition or my imagination, but I can't help thinking he's trying to scare us off his trail."

"I think you're absolutely right," Teag agreed. "So you've got to be extra careful. For some reason, the djinn is focused on you instead of the rest of us. Promise me you won't take chances."

"Promise."

THE NEXT MORNING, I took a circuitous route to the shop but didn't spot the gray stranger. I wasn't surprised that Teag insisted on meeting at my place and following me. The protectiveness warmed my heart.

Maggie greeted us with a wave when we walked in since she was ringing up a purchase. Teag and I ditched our things in the office and returned to the shop just as the customer left.

"How did it go?" Maggie asked. "Tell me everything!"

There wasn't anyone else in the store, so we took turns filling her in. Maggie's pretty stalwart, and she's backed us up despite not having paranormal abilities by making sure we had food and medical supplies ready for afterward.

"Wow! I've always wanted to go inside that mansion—now I'm glad I didn't," Maggie said when we finished. "So you really think it's a genie behind everything?"

I laughed. "Djinn. Not exactly like what you've seen in movies. Not blue, and doesn't live in a lamp."

"Disillusioned, once again," Maggie said faux-dramatically, putting her wrist to her forehead as if to swoon.

We laughed because a djinn isn't the strangest thing she's heard about since working at Trifles and Folly.

"There's also a bad witch involved. So be extra careful," I warned her.

Fortunately, the day went smoothly. I didn't hear back from Rowan or Donnelly, so I figured they were working their contacts for information. We all walked out to our cars together after I locked up.

"Big plans?" Maggie asked.

"Kell and I are going to order delivery from that new Cajun place and watch a couple of movies on streaming. He's been working late, and we haven't seen each other for a couple of days because he's had some out of town shoots, so we haven't had a lot of downtime. He's working on a big video project for the day job and a couple of paranormal investigations. Never a dull moment."

For paranormal investigators, Charleston, with all its haunted locations, was the gift that kept on giving. Kell's corporate videos paid the rent, but his passion was documenting supernatural activity. We always had a lot to talk about.

A spell keeps a parking place at the curb open by the door to my house, courtesy of Rowan. The house and property are heavily warded, thanks to several friends from various magical traditions. The shop is protected as well as Teag and Anthony's place and Maggie's house. Stopping people from using their supernatural abilities to take advantage of everyone else has made some enemies, so the wardings are important. I feel like I can finally relax once I'm inside.

Baxter barked up a storm as I unlocked the door. I swept him up in my arms and held him so we could see eye-to-eye, all eight pounds of indignant potato.

"I don't believe a word you're saying," I told him, but one look in those shiny black eyes always melts my heart.

I put Bax down and unloaded my purse, bag, and coat, then stepped out of my shoes. Bax followed me into the kitchen, clearly hoping for treats. A glance at the time told me Kell should be coming home soon, so I plumped the couch cushions to be ready for our movie marathon and set the table for dinner.

Kell and I had been living together for a while now, and despite some initial apprehension, things were going well. Since we were spending so much time together anyhow, the shift wasn't very noticeable, other than Kell not needing to go home to get clean laundry. Bax was already used to Kell and graciously accepted him. Now that Kell knows the full truth about what we do at Trifles and Folly, I no longer have to hide that side of myself, and there was nothing keeping us from taking that next step.

Bax ran to bark at the door while Kell let himself in. He stopped immediately when Kell scratched his ears.

"How did things go?" Kell came up behind me and wrapped his arms around my waist, pressing against me. I leaned back and let my head fall into his shoulder.

"Everything at the shop was quiet. But Teag, Father Anne, Rowan, Donnelly, and I had a throwdown with ghosts and a cursed tapestry at the Grantham mansion." I pulled up the take-out menu on my phone.

"Are you okay? Did anyone get hurt?" Kell knows things can get rough doing what we do.

"We're fine—no thanks to everything that was trying to mess with us. But the cursed piece is gone, the bad ghosts were sent packing, and the ones that are left agreed to be on their best behavior."

"So it's still haunted? I've always wanted to see inside. The ghosts are legendary." He sounded like a kid at Christmas.

"*Legendary* would be a good word for it." I pressed the send button as I finished our usual order. "It took all five of us. And while we handled that particular problem, the witch and the creature that created the curse are still at large."

"Creature?"

"Djinn. Wish-granting demon. Much scarier than in the movies." I turned around to kiss him and appreciated feeling warm and safe as he brought his arms up to pull me close. "Plus a dark witch who might be stalking me."

"I don't like the sound of that."

"Neither do I, but Rowan and Donnelly are working on figuring out how to find him. We've gone up against worse." I didn't want him to worry.

"I'm glad everyone's okay." Kell stroked my hair. "Maybe I'll take that house off my bucket list."

"Good idea."

After how crazy the past couple of days had been, I was happy to let Kell do most of the talking at dinner. He told me about the new sales video he was creating and then gave me the blow-by-blow details on SPOOK's latest haunted house outing. He and his group are responsible investigators, and they don't tempt fate by going after dangerous supernatural phenomena. When in doubt, he checks with me, and I run the location past my sources.

"What's next with the djinn and the witch?" Kell gathered the dishes while I got rid of the take-out containers.

"Teag is digging to see if there have been any recent strange deaths or weird incidents of bad luck now that we know what might be behind them. It feels like playing catch-up, and that always makes me nervous."

"Djinn are practically immortal, right? I'm sure they've learned how to cover their tracks not to be obvious. You're probably not the first hunters who have come after them."

"Good point. But that makes it creepier, especially since Moradi says djinn can possess people. If he stuck to curses that weren't spectacular and strange, we might not notice." That possibility scared the bejeezus out of me.

"Do you think the djinn is possessing the witch?"

I thought about his question. "I guess it's possible, but where's the advantage? The others seem to think it's a dicey arrangement between two partners who don't trust each other."

"Just mentioning the possibility. I don't like that the witch got close enough to you to hex you. You could have gotten hurt." He tugged me tighter against him.

"I'll just have to be extra careful until the situation gets settled. I will be—I promise." Kell couldn't do anything about the danger, and while I appreciated his concern, I didn't want him to worry needlessly.

"I love you. Please don't take chances."

"Love you too. I promise I'll be careful." I snuggled closer into him.

❧

I DIDN'T SLEEP WELL. Dreams meshed all the cartoon genies I'd seen with a more threatening version that could turn into a wraith or a dragon. When I woke, heart pounding and sweat-soaked, I was amazed that I hadn't disturbed Kell.

Knowing that I couldn't go back to sleep, I slipped out of bed and went to make myself a cup of tea, hoping I could at least calm my nerves. Since it was the middle of the night and too late to contact anyone else, I texted Sorren.

Cassidy: *You awake?*

Sorren: *Yes. But why are you?*

Cassidy: *Couldn't sleep. Weirded out by the last case.*

Sorren: *Want to talk about it?*

Cassidy: *Please—if I'm not interrupting anything.*

Sorren: *Being a "creature of the night" isn't really that exciting.*

I could hear his dry humor as I read his response. My phone rang a moment later.

"What's up?" Sorren asked.

"What do you know about tapestries and djinn?"

"More than I'd like to, unfortunately. What's going on?" He sounded concerned, which is never a good thing.

I gave him all the messy details of the banishment at the Grantham mansion and told him our suspicion that the djinn would seek new prey now that its food source with the dysfunctional family was cut off.

He stayed quiet as I told him about the djinn following me, the hex knots that were probably from Shaw, and the sense of impending danger I felt.

"Djinn aren't all-powerful, but they definitely have abilities mortals don't, and they're nothing to fool with. I don't like the way this one has focused on you."

"The thing is, the Granthams were already gone by the time I came on the scene. And I wasn't actively involved in breaking the tapestry's spell at the mansion. Donnelly says the djinn wasn't still in that tapestry. So why is it focused on me?"

"One explanation might be that their types of magic scare it more than your psychometry, so it sees you as an easier target, wrong as that might be," Sorren said. "Or it could be that, for some reason, your magic worries it most of all. This requires more study."

"Do you know anything about Laroque Shaw?"

"Only the name and reputation. You think he was the most recent Grantham witch?"

"Looks like it. Now we need to find him—and stop him and the djinn. Do you think the djinn plans to stay in Charleston?"

"It's probably already got its claws into a new crop of victims," Sorren agreed. "Djinn are sneaky bastards. They don't offer a cross-roads deal in exchange for your soul. They just gradually leech a victim's energy and feed off the misfortune until there's nothing left—however long that takes. And while they like rugs and tapestries, they can bespell any object, particularly pretty baubles. Djinn are old and ruthless."

"We're still trying to figure out where it's going to go after the Grantham family," I said. "What was your experience with tapestries?"

Sorren sighed. "I'm Belgian, and Flanders is a region of Belgium, at least it is now. Back when I was mortal, it was the source of the finest tapestries in the world. Flemish wall hangings graced many of the castles and noble houses of Europe during the thirteen and fourteen hundreds. Some of those were cursed or haunted."

"Why am I not surprised?"

He ignored my sarcasm. "One particularly famous—and very large —piece was called the *Apocalypse Tapestry*, based on the Book of Revelation. It had ninety huge panels, all filled with terrifying scenes of monsters, plagues, and battles between angels and demons.

"Now, most of the tapestry hangs in a cathedral, but it's incomplete. The Vatican secretly removed the missing pieces because they were cursed. Over time, the Alliance obtained the panels and neutralized them. They're hidden at the Briggs Society, inert but too dangerous to return."

"Wow. I've heard of that tapestry, but obviously not the whole story." I am always blown away when Sorren shares a piece of hidden history. I don't envy him his immortality, but the history geek in me loves his stories.

"Moradi says he doesn't know where the Grantham tapestry came from, but he's going to see what he hears from his contacts," I told him.

"Amir is a good man. I've worked with his family for generations, just like yours," Sorren confirmed. "I'm sure he's heard about Taelman and recognizes his work, but that doesn't fully explain how it came into the Grantham family's possession."

"Do you think the djinn will move on since it lost its big energy source with the Granthams?" The family's drama could have fueled a long-running mini-series, so it didn't surprise me it could keep a supernatural creature fed.

"Charleston would be a rich food source," Sorren observed. "Plenty of wealthy people with a lot of secrets and rivalries. Djinn draw their power from greed. Nobody is completely immune since down deep, all humans hunger for more than they need, but some people are far more driven by covetousness than others."

"Any tips you can provide for killing or banishing a djinn would be welcome. I have the awful feeling we're going to have to confront it sooner or later." Voicing my fear eased the weight I'd been carrying.

"Djinn are considered a class of demons. That makes them immortal in the truest sense, not just long-lived. So they can be weakened, trapped, and banished. Deeply inconvenienced if you kill the person they're possessing, but they're almost impossible to completely destroy. Which is where the genie-in-a-bottle stories come from," Sorren replied. "And while we think of them as granting wishes, they can also create nightmare scenarios, bringing people's deepest fears to life. Either way, they feast on the energy."

"I'm all for stuffing it into a lamp and handing it off to the Briggs Society." The last time we dealt with a wish-granting creature, a Korean bottle-demon, trapping it had nearly gotten me killed.

"I agree. And Archibald will help in any way he can. You have the right team for this. Just—watch your back. I'll help in any way if you need me."

"Thanks. Just hearing me out helped."

"Go back to sleep, Cassidy. You need the rest."

Part of my family's long association with Sorren means that I'm immune to his glamor, so while his voice has the ability to whammy other people, it doesn't work on me. Even so, I yawned, feeling tired now that my thoughts had stopped spinning and relieved at his validation.

I crawled back into bed. Kell murmured something in his sleep, acknowledging my return without actually waking up, and I snuggled close to him. Most people wouldn't think that having a heart-to-heart with a vampire would be a mood lifter, but Sorren's age and perspective grounded me.

I slept fine all the way to morning.

~

TEAG BEAT me to the shop the next day, had a pot of coffee brewed, and had already drunk half of it.

"What's up?" I asked. "Please tell me you didn't have a lover's spat with Anthony."

Teag looked up from where he sat with his laptop at the breakroom table. "Nope. He had to go in early for a meeting, so I was already up. Wanted to do some digging online, and I think I've found another strange death that might be our kind of thing."

"Our kind of thing?"

"Djinn." He turned his computer so I could see the screen. "I think the djinn was expanding his territory even before the Grantham family died out. In each of the past two years, there have been a couple of odd deaths among people who were avid collectors or had a rapid rise to the top. That would mean the djinn started granting wishes to other people before Ada Grantham died."

"Interesting." I poured a cup of coffee and came to sit next to him. "Anybody we know?"

"Not personally, but according to Anthony, the victims moved in the social circles of Charleston's fine art community. Museum donors, gallery crawl regulars, that sort of thing. I'm going to see if I can find any record of acquisitions and where those came from," Teag said.

"Find anything more about Shaw?"

Teag grimaced. "Even on the Darke Web, he keeps a very low profile. Understandable since he's a witch and intentionally difficult to trace. From a couple of comments, he seems to have parted ways with Ada Grantham just before Ada's death—so about a year ago."

"That narrows the timeline," I mused. "Shaw was on the Grantham payroll, and the djinn drew life energy from the tapestry and the mayhem it caused. Shaw lost his patron, so he would have needed to find another way to make money. The djinn had nothing to draw on when the house sat empty."

Teag nodded, following my train of thought. "What did they do after that? And why do they see you—maybe all of our gang—as a threat?"

"I don't know, but we need to find out. Stay on it, and I'll open the front." I took my coffee with me since we're usually slow early in the day, and I moved through the opening routine mostly on autopilot.

I understood the passion for collecting pretty things, although I was fortunate to be able to buy what caught my eye for resale out of the store's money. Being around the pieces in the shop meant I didn't feel like I needed to take them home. Most of the decorations in my place were inherited when I bought the house from my parents after they moved away. The few that I had purchased or received as gifts were carefully checked for unwelcome "hitchhikers."

We made sure the pieces we sold weren't hexed, jinxed, or otherwise encumbered. Many other places that sold antiques and collectibles weren't as careful or didn't have our know-how. Most people never considered a piece's energy before buying it. Sometimes, that worked out okay. In other cases, they might feel a drag or negative vibe and not know where it came from. In the worst cases, bad mojo led to tragedy.

The bells above the door chimed the moment we were officially open. I looked up, surprised. A woman I had never seen before entered. She looked to be in her mid-fifties, and judging from her haircut, manicure, and clothing, well-off.

"Are you Cassidy Kincaide?"

"Yes. I'm the store owner. How can I help you?"

As she came closer, I saw shadows beneath her eyes that defied concealer. She seemed sad but determined.

"Mr. Moradi said I should talk to you." She looked around. "Can we speak privately?"

"Let me get my associate to watch the front." I went to fetch Teag and explained the situation. He closed his laptop and quickly came to take my place. I escorted my new guest to the break room and offered coffee, which she accepted gratefully.

"How can I help you?" If Moradi sent her, I had an inkling of what the problem might be.

"I'm Stephanie Cochrane. My husband, Jim, loved to collect art. We both did. We bought one of our first pieces, a rug, from Mr. Moradi and several others over the years. We also did the gallery crawls and were patrons of the art museum. That's how we found new artists and works."

She had referred to her husband in the past tense, and from her appearance, I suspected the loss was recent. Grief clung to her despite the careful grooming and expensive perfume.

"About a year ago, Jim spotted a piece at an exhibition that he took to right off. I wasn't keen on it—it gave me a weird feeling—but he was so in love with it I agreed to buy it as long as he put it somewhere I didn't have to see it every day," Stephanie continued. "So it went in his study."

"What kind of piece?" I found myself holding my breath.

"A tapestry of a river," she replied. "Well-crafted, pretty scene, but somehow it left me cold."

"Did it come from Mr. Moradi's shop?" I suspected I knew the answer.

She shook her head. "No. It was a private exhibition in a gallery. I don't recall the artist's name, but it should be in our records if it matters. Jim was so happy when he took it home. He said it was a lucky charm."

Uh-oh.

"We had been doing well up to that point, well enough to drop a bundle on art," Stephanie went on with a self-conscious chuckle. "But around that time, Jim's career caught fire. Promotions. International travel. Large bonuses. Awards. It was quite a whirlwind. He was a hard worker and good at his job, but even as it was going on, I remember thinking that it seemed to happen so quickly."

"Did your husband…change…in any way after the windfall?"

Stephanie paused, and I wondered how much she had picked up intuitively. "More responsibility meant more stress, so that was to be expected. We had a good time even so. But as time went on, Jim got more nervous, like he was expecting something bad to happen. It didn't —we had a charmed life."

I tried not to wince at her wording since she had no idea how true that was.

"Jim was an extrovert, but he got quieter, introspective. His health was good—I made sure he had his checkups. It wasn't like he was depressed," Stephanie continued, searching for the right words. "More like he was taking stock of his life. I've heard about mid-life crises, but it seemed a bit early for that and things were going so well."

I found myself holding my breath since I suspected I knew how the story went.

"These last few months, Jim seemed…jumpy. I don't know how else to say it. I asked what was wrong—we always were honest with each other, and before then we didn't have trouble talking things through. But he either didn't know or couldn't say." She blinked away tears.

"I tried to get him to see a therapist, and he just laughed and said they'd think he was crazy and how would that help. I thought that was odd, but I didn't press."

Telling a therapist that you'd made a supernatural deal for good luck probably wouldn't go well. I had to agree with Jim on that.

"Did his behavior change? You've spoken of him in the past tense. I gather he passed."

She blinked rapidly, and this time a tear escaped. "Yes. Just a week ago."

"I'm so sorry for your loss."

Stephanie ducked her head. "Thank you." She pulled a tissue from her designer purse and dabbed her eyes before going on with her story.

"At the end, he rarely left his study. I would try to coax him out for meals or to go to bed or just to watch a movie and find him sitting there staring at that damned tapestry. When I did get him to leave, he always made his way back there. The last couple of days, he barely slept."

I could hear the guilt and grief in Stephanie's voice, along with bewilderment. Much as I sympathized with her loss, I forced down a stab of anger at Jim's selfishness.

"Did you ask why? What it was about the tapestry?"

"Jim was always a logical, rational person. That's why he did so well at his job. He was passionate about art, but not irrational. Very grounded. Which is why his response bothered me so much," Stephanie continued. "He told me that the tapestry spoke to him."

"Spoke? Like it evoked emotions the way a poem 'speaks' to us, or did he actually hear voices?"

Stephanie twisted the tissue in her hands. "I wish I knew. He stared at that thing like it was a window to another world. I was really considering an intervention because I was afraid he was having a mental breakdown, but then he had a sudden, massive stroke and died. He was only fifty-five."

"Something made you seek out Mr. Moradi and come here. How do you think I can help?"

Stephanie lifted her head and set her jaw, gathering her composure. "Maybe this sounds crazy, but I don't think Jim's death was natural, no matter what the autopsy said. I think that damned tapestry had something to do with it."

"Is that what you told Mr. Moradi?"

She nodded. "Yes. After Jim died, I pulled all the paperwork. We had to keep it for insurance, so it was easy to find. It had the name of the person who sold us the piece, as well as the name of the artist. I couldn't find any trace of them online. I know they existed. I went to the gallery show where Jim saw the tapestry for the first time. I was there when he spoke to the artist. But I can't find anything about them now."

"I'd like to get both names. I might be able to find out more through…professional sources. But I don't think that's why you came today."

"I've heard good things about your shop, and I've also heard that if you've got a problem with something that isn't exactly…natural… Trifles and Folly can help," Stephanie said. "I'd like you to come to the house and have a look at the piece. It's hanging in the study, although I refuse to go in that room since Jim died. That's where we found him—"

Her voice caught, and I went to fetch her a bottle of water, which she sipped gratefully.

"Maybe I'm just losing my mind. But if there is something *off* about the piece, I need to find out what to do about it. I want the goddamned thing out of the house. I'm sure it had something to do with Jim's death, even if I don't know how. And if it really is dangerous, then it needs to be destroyed before it ruins someone else's life."

"This is going to sound like a strange question, but did you ever glimpse a strange man with grayish skin?"

Her head came up sharply. "How did you know?"

"We think that…creature…caused the harmful magic in the tapestry," I said as gently as possible. "It's kind leech energy off people's emotions. Eventually, they can drain the life out of a person."

She paled. "Jim never admitted to seeing it, but I did. More than once, out in the garden near the window to Jim's study. One second the yard was empty, then he'd be there and then gone again. I thought it was a trick of the light, except that it happened more than once. Oh, God. Do you think that if I'd done something—"

I shook my head. "There's nothing you could have done. That sort of being is old and powerful. You weren't prepared to stop it, and you just would have gotten hurt too."

She choked back a sob, and I reached out to pat her arm. "We can come take a look. Just tell me when and where."

CHAPTER FIVE

Which is how Teag and I ended up in one of Charleston's upscale neighborhoods once the shop closed. While the Cochrane house wasn't South of Broad, the homes in this area commanded a high selling price. Stephanie had been telling the truth that they were well off.

"Thank you for coming." Stephanie greeted us at the door. She had changed into a top and leggings that looked more comfortable than her earlier outfit.

"I hope we can help," I told her and introduced Teag. "We brought equipment to help us deal with the tapestry. Neutralizing it is likely to cause damage. I would recommend having it removed from the house. I can arrange for specialized storage so it can't hurt anyone else. Are you okay with that?"

Stephanie nodded. She clutched a coffee cup and I thought I caught a whiff of Irish whiskey, which I didn't begrudge her. "God, yes. I can claim damage on the insurance or just eat the cost. Anything to be rid of it."

The house seemed large for one person, but I didn't see evidence of anyone else living there with Stephanie. From the yipping coming from the kitchen area, she at least had dogs.

"Sorry about that. I put the pups in the laundry room so they wouldn't be underfoot."

"My Maltese, Baxter, definitely makes his opinions known when there are visitors," I told her. "I completely understand."

She led us down a hallway and stopped in front of a door. "This was Jim's 'man cave.' He got to decorate it however he wanted, and I got my craft room just the way I like it. I haven't been able to face going inside since he passed because of that awful tapestry. I'm so ready to be done with it."

"Why don't you hang out in the kitchen and have another cup of coffee?" Teag suggested. "We'll give a shout if we need anything."

Teag and I had a gear bag with everything we thought we might need to vanquish the tapestry. I hoped that Rowena and Donnelly had been right that we could handle it on our own.

He held the silver-coated net in one hand. I had a canister of salt mixed with iron filings and the spelled rope net. Both of us wore our protective charms.

"Ready?" I asked.

Given Teag's Weaver magic, I was definitely the backup here. My job was to keep him safe so he could shut down the dangerous piece and get it packed up safely. We had brought a special bag woven with spells, silver threads, and soaked in salt to take the tapestry to Donnelly.

At this rate, the Briggs Society would be acquiring a roomful of new art.

"Let's go." Teag turned the doorknob.

The lights came on automatically, revealing a comfortable, wood-paneled room. Two leather armchairs and a matching couch angled toward a large screen television that hung above the fireplace. The faint smell of whiskey and cigar smoke still hung in the air. A tournament-quality poker table, retro-styled jukebox, and classic pinball machine rounded out the furnishings.

The walls held a variety of memorabilia from sports teams, concerts, and pop culture, which I knew could be as expensive to collect as any artwork. A painting of a sailboat graced one wall, along with a collection of framed photographs of a man I assumed was Jim posing with celebrities.

The tapestry commanded attention in the center of the wall opposite the television. The scene showed a river running through a rocky area beneath a willow tree. While the depiction was beautiful, to me the water looked cold and dark, and the shadows beneath the tree seemed ominous. I stifled a shudder.

All my amulets and protective jewelry didn't completely mute the menace of the tapestry. I had my athame, just in case, and Bo's dog collar, but I left the walking stick in the car since I didn't want to burn down the nice lady's house. I hoped I didn't need to use any of the weapons, but I'd learned the hard way to be prepared.

"Cover me," Teag said.

As we stepped through the door, Teag raised one hand and shouted a spell. I was right behind him and put up a salt barrier inside the entrance to trap anything inside this room.

Teag ran forward and tossed the silver net over the tapestry. A flare of purple light from the weaving lit up the room, and a vengeful shriek made my ears ache.

The wall hanging glowed green with a sickly inner light. I sensed the tension as it struggled against Teag's magic. What I could pick up of the room's resonance made it clear that the tapestry had infused the whole room with its attractive poison, lulling its victim like the poppies had in Oz.

A streak of light broke free of the tapestry's prison, narrowly missing Teag, who jumped aside, but the cadence of his invocation never faltered.

Another bolt came closer to the mark, making Teag stutter the next line. I hurled salt onto the tapestry, then dodged closer and added the spell-woven rope net on top of the silver. The purple light muted but didn't vanish. A low hum of distant, angry voices came from the piece, and I felt certain they weren't wishing us well.

The purple light flared and faded. I watched Teag's concentration as he fought a silent battle for control. More murmured words strengthened his hold.

"What do you make of it?" I asked Teag in a hushed voice.

"It's giving me the same vibes as the one at the other house. And I think the djinn knows we're here."

Stephanie said that her husband heard voices come from the wall hanging. I listened closely and made out a dull hum, like a radio playing in another room. The rich detail of the weaving made me think I saw movement in the river and the tree branches—maybe I did. My gut feeling said to get the hell away from it and not look back.

I tried to avoid staring directly at the tapestry, although I felt it trying to attract my attention. I could have sworn that I heard the birds chirping and water rippling. Darker things lurked in the shadows, where I glimpsed glowing yellow eyes. When I closed my fist around my agate pendant, the sounds receded but didn't completely disappear.

Another streak of light shot from the tapestry. I knocked Teag out of the way and dropped to the floor, hoping to avoid the worst of it. I felt a burn on my shoulder and gritted my teeth against the pain.

Images flashed through my mind, fast and brutal. *Teag and Anthony, bloodied and unmoving in a car wreck. Kell, shot by a squatter in an abandoned house. My parents, dead in a plane crash. Bax, escaping out the door and into traffic. Even Maggie, pale and wan in a hospital bed. Everyone I loved hurt or gone.*

"It doesn't have to be like this," a voice hissed, like the rasp of sand over stone. "Just leave me alone."

The images faded, leaving me gasping on my knees. I had the feeling Teag had been calling my name.

Teag stalked toward the wall hanging, jaw set, expression fierce. He shouted the next part of the spell, eyes blazing.

"I'm okay." I shakily got to my feet, knowing his anger was sparked by the attack on me.

Teag didn't waver, spitting out the rest of the words and throwing a new layer of protection on top of the two containment nets. I couldn't help with this part, and I worried he would drain himself with the effort, but all I could do was hang back and help clean up afterward.

He shouted the final words with triumph and thrust both hands, palms open, toward the wall hanging. Tendrils of smoke seeped from beneath the nets and warding.

"Don't burn down the house," I cautioned. I don't know whether he heard me. The tapestry glowed like embers beneath the protections, flared red once, and then faded to black.

"Is it done?" I didn't trust the tapestry, but I figured Teag could sense its power.

He waited, cautious, and then nodded. "Yes. Although you better believe I want to lock it down in those containment bags, just in case."

When nothing else happened, we both let out a long breath. Teag pulled out the special bags, and I took out two pairs of long tongs—one silver and one iron. Together, we carefully maneuvered what remained of the tapestry—still wrapped in the nets—into the bag without making skin contact. When Teag tied the sack shut and said a spell over it, I felt the resonance in the room shift dramatically.

"Are you all right?" Teag sounded worried.

I nodded, still shaky. "The djinn sent a vision. Everyone dies."

"Djinn lie." He met my gaze. "They aren't all-powerful. And the more we weaken him, the less of a threat he poses. Don't let him spook you."

I took comfort from Teag's words and his certainty, but the djinn had planted a seed of doubt and fear, and I prayed it couldn't be used against us.

"I think we've figured out the answer to our question," I said. "Shaw went into the cursed art business to make money, and the djinn used the artwork to create a link to victims he could drain. Evil—but sorta brilliant."

Stephanie was waiting outside the door, wide-eyed. "Is it over? Did you kill it? My God, I can already feel a difference."

"I'm not sure that 'kill' is the right term, but we neutralized the bad magic," Teag said. "We'll make sure that what's left of it never hurts anyone else."

"For the next few days, it might make you feel better to do some cleansing rituals," I told her. "If you're religious, ask someone to bless the house. Burn candles and protective herbs. Do a deep cleaning, and use a broom with natural fibers to sweep out the bad vibes. Washing the floor with Four Thieves vinegar and water will also help."

"Just so you know, we didn't pick up on anything else of his collections having bad mojo. So you can tackle those when the time is right without any surprises," Teag spoke up.

I felt for her, having to deal with all of this on top of losing her husband.

"Thank you," Stephanie said, and now that the danger was gone, her grief shone through. "I wouldn't have known what to do."

She walked us to the door and thanked us again. Teag put the containment bag in the trunk which was lined with protection symbols, and slammed the lid.

"Thoughts?" I asked as we pulled away from the curb. I watched for the djinn as Teag drove, but this time he wasn't stalking us on street corners. Maybe he figured he had already made his point.

"Just hoping there aren't a ton of other killer wall hangings out there." Teag gave a nervous laugh. "And I thought my grandmother's macrame decorations were bad!"

"Let's put the bag in the safe, and I'll call Sorren. He can come pick it up and get it to Donnelly."

Teag's phone rang. "Anthony? What's up?" He frowned as he listened. I couldn't make out the words, but the torrent of frustration was unmistakable.

"Okay…slow down," Teag said. "Start from the top. Cassidy and I are in the car, so I'm going to put you on speaker."

"Hi, Anthony," I said, not sure whether I belonged in the conversation.

"Hi, Cassidy. Sorry to interrupt." Anthony was unfailingly polite, even when he was down to his last nerve.

"No problem. We just finished up a situation, and we're on the way to the shop," I assured him.

"Talk to me, babe," Teag said. "Do we have a real emergency, or do you just want to strangle someone?"

Anthony let out a long sigh. "Nothing's on fire, no one's dying. And I'm not on the brink of murder. Is it too late to elope?"

"Your mother will hunt us to the end of the earth," Teag replied. "Even WITSEC couldn't save us."

"Yeah, I was afraid you'd say that. I love her, and I know she just wants to give us the 'perfect' wedding, but I'd go with 'good enough' and have some sanity left." Anthony sounded worn out.

I saw Teag take a deep breath to prepare himself for calming down his partner. "Tell us what's wrong, and we can brainstorm a solution."

Anthony was silent for a moment, and I figured he was doing some deep breathing.

"Wagu beef and sea bass," Anthony said finally.

"What?" Teag looked confused.

"Mama wanted Wagu beef sliders and sea bass kabobs for passed hors d'oeuvres," Anthony replied. "Partially because we did that for my brother's wedding—and she's obsessed with making things 'equal'—and also because she just likes sea bass."

"Supply chain problems?" I ventured.

"Something like that." Anthony sounded ragged. "The vendor had committed to the right quantities, but he just called to say he couldn't promise the full amount, so the caterer is scrambling, the wedding planner is stressed, and Mama definitely sounded like she could use a martini."

Teag hid a smile, and so did I. The frustration was real, but no one was going to die, and I had no doubts that their wedding would be beautiful—and the talk of the social page—even without the sea bass.

"Do you think your mom will get over it?" Teag asked.

"Eventually. Underneath it all, she's usually very practical. This isn't the first child she's married off, so she should be used to the drill by now," Anthony said. "Or maybe that's the problem since I'm the last to tie the knot. Some weird empty nest thing?"

"Have you talked to the wedding planner?" Teag seemed to know exactly what to say to help Anthony regain control.

"Yes. Kim called me after they met with the caterer. Not exactly carrying tales, but letting me know how 'important' the menu items were to Mama and asking me to see if I could get alternatives from her just in case another vendor doesn't come through," Anthony said. He didn't sound quite as freaked out as when the call started.

I bit back a chuckle. Anthony regularly handled major criminal cases in court, with an impressive streak of wins. Teag was a real-life monster hunter. But all it took to wreak havoc was a glitch in the catering menu and all hell broke loose.

"Did anything else go wrong?" Teag prodded.

"The monogrammed cocktail napkins are late," Anthony admitted. "Not exactly the end of the world. We can substitute plain if necessary, and you and I will have enough fancy ones when they do come in to last until our fiftieth anniversary."

"We'll just have classier barbecues and shrimp boils," Teag said in a reasonable tone. "Not the worst thing."

"Apparently the photographer pointed out that with all the windows at the marina's ballroom, and at the time of day we're doing the ceremony, the light might not be great for some of the important shots the way they originally planned to set up the room," Anthony went on.

"Can't they just move things around?" Teag asked.

"That's what they were planning to do, but then the chef overheard; he was concerned about changing the traffic pattern through the tables for the serving staff," Anthony continued, and I really wanted to buy the poor guy a drink to settle his nerves.

"That sounds like a 'first world' problem to me," Teag said. "They do a lot of weddings at the marina. I would have thought they'd have it down to a science."

"So did I. But apparently the chef is fairly new, so he is still trying to make his mark and impress the members, and he doesn't want to risk messing up," Anthony said. "And the photographer has a lot of experience, but he's not the one who the marina recommends, so he hasn't shot the venue a million times to know what's what."

"Someone the wedding planner wanted?" I guessed.

"Yeah—and he's probably fantastic. But I thought he and the chef were going to come to blows," Anthony admitted.

"Okay—fist fight averted," Teag said. "What else?"

Anthony was quiet for a moment. "The Hansons turned down the invitation—with a side of hellfire."

"What?" Teag went from calm to furious in zero to five seconds. I tried not to get absorbed in the drama.

"Yeah, I'm surprised and disappointed too. Mama's really hurt. She and Dad socialized a lot with them over the years, and she thought they were friends. Apparently not. She says that they never said anything when I came out—maybe they thought it was a 'phase' I'd outgrow—but marrying the love of my life is a bridge too far."

"No Wagu beef for them!" Teag declared in an exaggerated accent, and I knew he was trying to lighten Anthony's mood.

"I think this whole thing has been eye-opening for Mama and Dad because it's the first time they've ever really seen what happens and felt it themselves," Anthony said. "They thought their friends were 'not that sort.' Mama forgets that some people make nice because being connected benefits them."

"I'm guessing the Christmas card list is getting whittled down?" Teag asked.

Anthony managed a wry chuckle. "There are definitely people moving from the inner circle to the outside fringe. It won't get said out loud or show up right away, but certain folks will drop off the invitation list for the annual fish fry or the Christmas cocktail party. And if I know my mama, it will all be done so politely that they'll have frozen solid before they ever realize it had gotten colder."

"Is she okay?" Teag asked, concerned.

"She will be. Mama's tough. And so far it's only a few people who decided to get on a soapbox. But still, I can tell she's hurt and disappointed and at the same time mad as hell on our account."

Anthony laughed. "She's also having a sign made for the reception stating that on behalf of the folks who were invited and couldn't attend, my parents are making a large donation to several LGBTQ charities in their names. Mama always gets the last word."

I definitely fell a little in love with Mrs. Benton at that.

"Anyhow—I need to get back to work," Anthony said. "Thanks for letting me vent."

"Any time," Teag and I said in unison and chuckled.

"I'll pick up something yummy for dinner," Teag promised. "Give your mom a hug for me."

I tried not to eavesdrop at the murmured endearments as they ended the call. Sometimes they were so sweet it made my fillings ache.

Teag huffed as he put the phone back in his lap.

"No," I said.

He frowned. "No, what?"

"No, you can't send hex bags, cursed objects, or pissed-off ghosts to the Hansons or anyone else—and you definitely can't put a root on them."

"Spoilsport."

"It's their loss," I said as he maneuvered in traffic. "Not only are they going to miss out on the Wagu beef and sea bass, a fun reception, and your parents' friendship, but there'll be other people who'll notice and not say a word, but they'll draw back too. Look at the bright side —now you know their true colors."

CHAPTER SIX

THE NEXT MORNING, I FOUND TEAG IN THE BREAK ROOM AND A HALF-empty pot of coffee.

"Is coming in early a new habit? Is Anthony okay?"

Teag put his mug down and blinked at me as if the caffeine hadn't helped to wake him. "Anthony's fine. The mama drama got settled, the marina agreed to rearrange the tables, and he had to start early again today. Probably run late too. So here I am."

I put my things in the office, poured a cup of coffee, and went to join him at the table. "Find anything good?"

He took a long drink from his cup, then nodded. "Yeah, I think so. I cross-referenced a bunch of things, and I might have come up with a partial list of the djinn's recent victims. Two people had large lottery winnings. One got a huge legal settlement. A guy went from middle manager to CEO. A few others won awards, got unusually large promotions, or a bestselling first book."

"How did you link them to the djinn and not just a fluke of luck?" I went to stand behind him, staring over his shoulder at the screen.

"Once I found the people in the news, I made up a reason to call them on the pretext of a possible credit breach and confirmed they had all bought 'textile art' from that same defunct gallery." Teag looked extraordinarily pleased with himself.

"Clever. Possibly illegal, but still clever."

"That eliminated the people who were just unusually lucky," he continued. "I gave the others a line about possible forgeries and got their addresses, leaving the door open for us to 'confirm authenticity' and get the tapestries away from them."

"Good move. What now?"

Teag yawned and stretched. "I need sugar." He reached into a bag from a local donut shop, something he must have picked up on the way.

"Is that maple bacon?" I inhaled the scent.

"It absolutely is—and there's one in there for you because I'm an awesome best friend."

I hugged him. "You totally are. Thank you for indulging my need for a sugar rush." I realized I hadn't asked Teag a question that had been on my mind.

"Why tapestries? Why not paintings or carvings or some other kind of art?" I asked through a mouthful of donut. We've run into bad magic attached to artwork, jewelry, and other possessions, and I wondered why the djinn preferred a certain type of object.

Teag considered for a moment before answering. "I believe that all original art retains some resonance from the artist. Weaving is a very hands-on creation and one that has always been linked with magic. The work lends itself to making spells part of the fabric, and additional words of power can easily be blind stitched as well."

"Back in the day, tapestries were huge and lined the walls of castles. Do you think djinn used them to feed?" I reconsidered what I knew of history. I also remembered the evil Weaver Sorren had mentioned and figured it probably made sense for the djinn to stick to wall hangings.

"Some tapestries, probably. A lot of them depicted battles or uprisings, which would be like an all-you-can-eat buffet for a djinn," he replied.

I thought about that and how there never seemed to be a time without a war or natural disaster going on somewhere. "If djinn can cause wars, why bother with petty domestic drama like at the Grantham house?"

"From the legends I've found, not all djinn are super powerful, even if they are relatively immortal. There's a lot of debate over whether djinn were all created when the world was new or if some come into being now and then if the conditions are right." Teag made a face. "Unfortunately, the old stories don't agree on how that works, and I'm pretty sure some of the poets just made things up."

"I was thinking about what I said yesterday about people showing their 'true colors,'" I paused to sip my coffee. "People's wishes and what they're willing to pay for them fall into that too. If someone wants money and power or status more than anything else, that's what's really important to them, even if they put on a good front."

Teag nodded. "And while I think anyone can be seduced with the right offer in a moment of weakness, djinn can't save lives or bring people back from the dead, which cuts out a lot of desperate people. I'm betting that if someone who had a chronic illness wished for health, the djinn would only keep the disease at bay for a while, not actually heal them."

"Which is why they're regarded as a type of demon, because they don't actually help people, and pretending is cruel."

"If the djinn has been in Charleston for long, it's probably aware of Sorren and the Alliance," Teag speculated. "The Alliance doesn't usually get involved if it's someone making bad personal decisions unless it has the potential for causing large-scale harm. So the djinn might have been able to co-exist. But maybe it's powered up somehow or gotten ambitious."

"Or with the Granthams gone, the djinn and Shaw have a new game plan," I pointed out.

"Rowan and her coven keep a close eye on what the other witches are doing after that dust-up a while back," Teag said.

Covens jockeying for power and practitioners with lesser magics who were excluded from covens got into a big confrontation over who controlled magic in Charleston and whose magic counted. I'd thought they had worked out their differences since they didn't end up burning down the city.

"I'll talk to Rowan," I volunteered.

"Thanks. I'll keep digging to see who else might have a djinn-tainted tapestry, and then we can figure out what to do about it," Teag said.

I heard the front bell chime, so I knew Maggie had arrived. "I'll go help Maggie open, and then Alistair at the museum asked me to see their new display. You'll never guess what it's about."

"Tapestries?" Teag asked with a laugh.

"Got it in one. And not just any tapestry. *The Apocalypse Tapestry.*"

He frowned. "I thought that was in a castle or a cathedral in Europe."

"It is, and the missing panels are secured with the Briggs Society. But this is a multi-media, immersive, interactive projection display that makes you feel like you're in the tapestry's world," I quoted from the advertisement.

"So it's fancy pictures of the piece but not the real thing?"

"Yep. There've been a couple of traveling exhibits like that for art by Monet and Van Gogh. I didn't go to those, but the reviews were good, and people seemed to enjoy them." This job makes free time scarce, and when I'm not saving a corner of the world, I really love just being home with my boyfriend and dog.

"Be careful," Teag said. "You're warded here, and in the car and at home, but out in public, anything can happen."

"I promise," I told him. "While I'm there, I'll ask Alistair if he knows about privately owned tapestries in town."

Up front, I helped Maggie take jewelry out of the regular safe—not the one we used for cursed items—and freshen the displays. Once that was done, I headed over to the Lowcountry Museum.

I greeted the receptionist, who recognized me and waved me through. "Mr. McKinnon said to send you back. I'll let him know you're here."

I thanked her and walked farther into the museum's lobby, taking in the posters for upcoming exhibits and lectures. Museums have always been one of my happy places, along with libraries. It feels like anything could happen when I'm surrounded by books or historical objects. Of course with my touch magic, I have to be careful. I learned that the hard way when I got whammied by an exhibit and passed out.

Fortunately, it's been a long time since that happened, and I've gotten better control—most of the time.

"Cassidy! Thank you for coming!" Alistair greeted me while we were still half a lobby apart. He looked like he was picked by Hollywood casting to be a museum curator—early sixties, white hair, trim build, and a wardrobe of seersucker for summer or tweed for winter. "I can't wait to show you the new display!"

"And I can't wait to see it," I told him with honest enthusiasm. I've helped Alistair out more than once when an object on exhibit carried a curse or a ghost. Since the touring display wasn't the actual tapestry, I hoped this would just be a fun outing.

"Have you ever heard of *The Apocalypse Tapestry*?" he asked as we walked together. I remembered what Sorren had told me and gave a condensed version, leaving out the part where he remembered the piece from back in the 1400s when he was still mortal.

"Very good! We can skip all the signs then," Alistair congratulated me. He gets almost giddy when they get a new installation, and his enthusiasm is contagious. "Then let's get right to the dishy stuff. There are nineteen missing panels out of ninety, and all sorts of legends about what happened to them."

"Oh?" I tried to look innocent since I knew where they had been stashed on magical lockdown.

"Some say they were carried off during the Black Plague, or taken during the Crusades, or looted by one cash-strapped noble or another," he confided. "Of course, those are the plausible explanations. The more fantastical ones are even more intriguing."

"Oh, yeah? Fill me in." I loved stoking Alistair's excitement about the displays. He lights up like a kid on Christmas, and I appreciate anyone who is passionate about their favorite subject.

"Of course, none of these can be proven," he said. "But they make great stories. One version says that the missing panels pleased the Devil so much he took them to hell to hang in his throne room."

"Interesting. I hope it's climate-controlled so they don't burn up," I joked.

"Good point! Another story says that a group of warrior monks stole the missing panels because they were cursed and hid them in a blessed dungeon so they wouldn't hurt anyone."

My smile froze, and I wondered if the St. Expeditus Society might have been involved. After all, somehow those panels went missing and were spirited away to the Briggs Society.

"Monks or the Devil. Plenty of imagination on display." I hoped I sounded off-handed. "What else?"

"They get wilder," he warned. "Some say Vlad Tepas—the Impaler of Dracula fame—wanted them, or the Marquis de Sade, or Madame Bathory."

I knew all the infamous names and didn't doubt they would have coveted the dark magic of the tapestries. "What do you think?"

Alistair sighed. "My realist side wars with my inner romantic. Other much less sexy accounts say that during hard times, some of the less popular or darker-themed panels were used for floor coverings or horse blankets. There's probably some truth to that."

I wouldn't have wanted to be around the dark panels, but I hated to hear of artwork being destroyed without good cause. If a panel could be used as a horse blanket, it didn't seem all that evil to me.

Before I could comment, Alistair stopped in front of the entrance to the exhibit. "This is the first time we've used the new projection technology, and I'm honestly blown away by the possibilities," he gushed.

"It's what they use to do those fantastic light displays on the castle at Disney World." His eyes went wide with wonder. "The computers map the walls or building, and then 'wrap' the images around it. The details and textures are mind-blowing. Come on—you need to see for yourself."

I followed him into the museum's largest exhibit hall and stopped. My mind knew that it was four bare walls, but my eyes saw the vibrant colors and fanciful images of the famous medieval tapestry all around me.

"Magnificent, isn't it?" Alistair murmured next to me. The room had benches scattered throughout the area so people could sit and appreciate the grand scale and intricate details—or maybe gather their wits after being assailed by dragons, monsters, and battles. A few patrons sat, taking in the display.

"The walls aren't completely flat," he confided. "There are three-dimensional panels here and there that recreate stonework, towers, and other architectural details from castles and cathedrals. That makes the tapestry feel more real, so it's not just a picture."

"I'm impressed." I had heard friends rave about seeing the technology elsewhere, but I didn't grasp how different it was from just projecting a picture onto a screen. I felt like I could reach out and touch the individual threads in the tapestry, and I could see how the figures gained depth with the fabric's texture.

"It's amazing how vibrant the tapestry is after seven hundred years." Alistair had the tone of someone utterly besotted with what they were seeing. "And I have to admire the imagination of the weavers—or else wonder what they were smoking. Some of those monsters are really scary!"

I turned in a slow circle, awed by the scale, overwhelmed by the detail, and swept away by the epic soundtrack that meshed perfectly with how the images faded in and out. The real tapestry was huge, made to hang on castle walls. Projected here, the panels were even larger, with surprisingly vivid colors. Knights, dragons, horses, demons, angels, and fantastical beasts morphed from one scene to another, looking three-dimensional thanks to the technology.

They were jaw-dropping now, and I imagined that they must have been even more astounding to the people of their time who hadn't been jaded by movie special effects. I just hoped I didn't run into any of the horned devils or many-headed, winged creatures.

As Alistair and I talked, I realized that most other patrons had left the room. One man remained on the bench, sitting quietly, seemingly mesmerized by the images. He wore a long coat with the hood over a baseball cap, which struck me as odd since it was fairly warm inside the museum despite the chill outdoors.

Alistair and I made a slow circle of the room, and I felt certain the stranger was watching us. He didn't move, but I sensed his attention. With the hood raised, I couldn't see his face. The longer we were in the room, the more my gut told me that the stranger was bad news.

Alistair went on about the technology behind the exhibit and his desire to bring more touring shows to the museum, given how well-received this one had been. Despite my interest, I couldn't get my mind off the stranger and tried to come up with a reason to move closer and get a better look.

"I appreciate the details, and the presentation is absolutely astounding, but could we stop at your office? I've come across something I need your opinion on," I finally said.

"Sure," Alistair agreed. "I know the display can be overwhelming the first time you see it. We've had a few people report feeling dizzy or like they're having an out-of-body experience."

My gaze went immediately to the stranger at that, picking up red flags in Alistair's comment. The man sat completely still, but I knew instinctively that he was watching and listening.

Dizzy. Feeling woozy and disconnected. That would fit if something was draining energy. It's a perfect set-up because if someone passes out, it'll be blamed on vertigo from the moving images. Exactly the kind of place the djinn could hunt and siphon off energy without raising suspicion.

My heart rabbited, and I knew I needed to get out of that room and away from the creepy stranger.

"I'll have to bring Teag back—I know he'll be impressed." I appreciated Alistair's personal tour and shared his excitement over the exhibit, but right now I needed some space away from the guy in the hoodie to regroup.

"Come on—I'll make us both a coffee." He gestured for me to walk ahead of him.

I intentionally chose a path that took me past the stranger. His hands were in his pockets, and with his head angled, I couldn't make out his face. Then he glanced up, just for a second. Gray, leathery skin stretched tight over gaunt features and pale lips. I thought I saw a spark of red in his black eyes.

He smiled, exposing sharp, yellowed teeth, and met my gaze.

The djinn.

He wanted me to see him. Somehow he knew I hadn't come prepared to fight him and wouldn't risk innocent bystanders. The smile taunted me, dared me to do something about his presence, and acknowledged that this time, he had outmaneuvered me.

I blinked, and the museum disappeared. I stood on the edge of a cliff over an abyss so deep I couldn't see the bottom. An irresistible voice whispered in my ear, "Jump," foreign and compelling.

Just as quick, the vision vanished. I staggered, and Alistair caught my arm.

"Wobbly heel," I lied, taking a moment to catch my breath and draw strength from Alistair.

The malevolent gleam in Djinn's eyes promised real danger—later.

Out in the hall, I struggled to keep my composure, weighing my options. I had no weapons and wasn't even sure how to fight a djinn. I wasn't foolish enough to take on something I couldn't win.

Once Alistair and I walked away, I knew the djinn would leave, even if he intended to return later. As a shapeshifter, he could come back looking completely different, although maintaining that appearance would cost energy.

I weighed calling Teag or even Donnelly, then dismissed the idea. Maybe the djinn was trying to lure us into confronting him before we were ready. That would be disastrous.

For now, he passively drained energy from onlookers. But no one had collapsed or died. That meant we had a bit longer to figure out how to deal with the djinn without being pushed into fighting on his terms. It also meant he knew we were after him. We'd lost any element of surprise.

Alistair gushed about how popular the exhibit was, with a strong opening weekend, and I was truly happy for him. I love the museum as both a patron and a member of the community. Alistair does a great job as the curator, and he brings interesting and unusual exhibits to town. Often, he and Mrs. Morrissey coordinate their plans so that the Archive's special events and the museum's go hand-in-hand.

"I'm glad you came to see the display, but it seems like you've got a lot on your mind," Alistair said when he finished filling me in. "What's going on?"

Alistair doesn't know the full extent of what we do at Trifles and Folly. He counts on us to make sure exhibits aren't dangerously haunted or to help if a problem item shows up and wreaks havoc, but he hasn't found out that we sometimes save the world.

"You know how we've run into some haunted and cursed artwork?"

He nodded.

"The Grantham mansion had a tapestry woven with dark magic. We've neutralized it, but we believe it affected the family for generations—bestowing good luck and then taking it away."

"Any magic lamps? Because that sounds like a genie," he joked, then sobered. "Please tell me they aren't real."

I shrugged noncommittally. "Not like in the movies. In real life, it's more like owing a favor to a supernatural Mob boss."

He pinched the bridge of his nose. "Do I want to know?"

"Probably not."

He sighed. "Okay. I'll trust you on that."

"The man in the hoodie sitting in the exhibit room—have you seen him before?"

Alistair frowned. "I really haven't paid attention to individual visitors unless they cause a problem or are wearing something extremely inappropriate—which doesn't happen as often once beach season is over. Why?"

"I don't think he's what he appears to be—and he could be dangerous."

Alistair took a deep breath. "Is he a threat to patrons or staff?"

I weighed how to explain without taking away the shield of innocence that lets normal people sleep well at night.

"He's not a potential shooter or a terrorist. We believe he's a type of creature that leeches energy from people's emotions. A little makes you feel tired. A lot makes you unwell. Too much drains you dry."

"Creature. A real genie?"

"Djinn." I didn't want to lie. "They aren't blue, and they don't sing and dance. This one likes tapestries. It makes sense he'd be drawn to your display. I think he was siphoning off energy as people reacted."

"What can we do?" His hands fluttered nervously on his desk, and he gripped a pen to still them.

"Nothing. Don't approach him. Let us handle it. Once we deal with him, your problem will be solved."

Alistair gave me a look as if he were seeing me for the first time. "This is what you do," he said quietly. "It goes deeper than sending a ghost on its way or cleansing the 'bad vibes' from an antique. This djinn…it's a monster. And you 'deal' with them."

Busted. "Yes. When we have to. That's what the shop has done all along. We keep Charleston safe. It's part of the family business."

He was quiet for a minute. I hated to burst his bubble of normalcy because once someone knows what lurks in the shadows, they never have the same peace of mind they had before.

"It's a bit much to take in. And I promise I won't tell anyone. Just…wow. And, I guess, thank you."

"No thanks necessary. I can bring some charms to put around—discreetly—that might make the djinn less comfortable hanging out here. I don't think he'll call attention to himself by harming anyone and cutting off his food source. The people will feel better after they sleep and eat. It would be good to limit staff time in the room if he's here so they don't get affected day after day."

He nodded, looking shell-shocked. "Okay. I've got to trust you on this, and you've always done right by us. Just—be careful, please."

I smiled, appreciating the sentiment. "I always am."

Alistair insisted on walking me to my car. I didn't see the djinn, and I hoped he would avoid a public attack. I drove away and let out a long breath feeling like I had dodged a bullet.

A text message reminded me to stop by the auction house and pick up a couple of boxes of items Trifles and Folly had bought from a recent estate sale. Since the purchases would fit in the back of my RAV4, I figured I might as well swing by on my way back to the store.

When I got to Avery Auctions, I checked in at the desk. The attendant pointed toward four sealed, sturdy cardboard boxes stacked to the side. "Give me a minute and I can get someone to help you load," he told me.

Being behind the scenes at an auction house is a lot like being backstage at a theater, except all the props and scenery are for sale. I love the glorious mish-mash of furnishings, housewares, decorative items, restoration pieces, and more. While the resonance felt like standing in the middle of a noisy crowd, the wonderful mix of objects was a visual feast.

I signed off on the boxes, and four warehouse workers loaded them into my RAV. The pieces were a mix of fancy glassware, silver candlesticks, and other vintage knickknacks that I knew would sell well. Mostly I remembered that the items at the sale had a good resonance. Sometimes I walk into an estate sale and turn right around to leave because the vibes are so bad. That hadn't been the case with this auction, and I was looking forward to putting the pieces on display.

Mr. Avery waved and came over as I stood at the top of the steps at the loading bay. He was a portly, balding man in his middle years with a penchant for cardigan sweaters that made him look like everyone's bachelor uncle. "Congratulations on your purchases—you have a real eye for gems."

I grinned. "You just say that because we buy a lot of stuff."

"True—but you buy *good* stuff," he replied. "That takes a knack. Some people just go by the manufacturer or artists, even if the individual piece is a real stinker. You've been around the business long enough to tell the good stuff from the dross."

"Thanks. It's always like a treasure hunt. I feel like Indiana Jones."

"Well, I can promise you—no snakes," he teased.

I thanked him and started down the steps, then lost my footing. I made a wild grab for the railing as Mr. Avery lunged to help. That meant I only tumbled a few stairs, but I wrenched my shoulder, stopping my momentum, tore my jeans, and bloodied my knee on the concrete. I plunked down to sit on the bottom step until my heart stopped racing.

"Are you okay? Do you need a doctor? Do you want to sit down and have a cup of tea?" Mr. Avery's concern took the sting out of my embarrassment.

"I'll be fine," I assured him. "I just lost my footing."

"Just rest until you catch your breath." He was actually worried about me, not just afraid of being sued.

I rotated my shoulder gingerly, knowing it would be sore from the abrupt jerk when I had stopped my fall. My knee throbbed, but the scrape wasn't too bad. Advil, ice, and antiseptic cream would fix me up, and we had all of those back at the shop.

When I walked to the car, I assured Mr. Avery that I could drive. We had known each other long enough to know that.

A horn blared as I pulled out of the parking lot. I saw a car coming right at me and swerved. The sedan braked hard enough to leave skid marks, and I held my breath as I feared it would fishtail into me anyhow. The back fender missed my RAV by inches, and the driver kept on going without even slowing down.

My hands shook on the steering wheel, and I figured that the stress of the day was catching up to me. In the next block, scaffolding covered the front of a historic building being renovated. I heard a man shout, and I looked over to see a section of the scaffold fall, coming right at me.

I gunned the engine since there were cars behind me. It felt like one of those movies where the main character is running ahead of a forest fire or an angry mob. I didn't dare look back; just gripped the wheel white-knuckled, floored the pedal, and hoped no one had the bad luck to step out in front of me.

The scaffold crashed to the ground behind me in a tangle of steel and canvas. I pulled to the curb and tried to slow my breathing so I didn't pass out. On top of the near-miss with the other car and the fall down the steps, I was past taking things in stride.

Wait. What are the odds?

Shit. I bet I've been whammied again.

Teag must have heard something in my voice when I called because he immediately sounded alarmed. "What's going on? Where are you?"

I gave him my location and asked him to bring the silver tongs and a containment box. "I think Shaw or the djinn slipped something in the stuff from Avery's. They were already sealed, so I didn't examine them there. I have the list of contents and figured we'd go through the boxes at the shop, but—"

"Stay where you are. Don't move. I'll be right there," Teag ordered.

I did as he said, taking deep, measured breaths and focusing on getting my pounding heart to quiet. Minutes later, Teag pulled in behind me. He must have run every red light on the way to make it that fast.

"You okay?" He gave me a head-to-toe once-over.

"Yeah, but I feel like I'm bucking the odds." I hated that my voice wasn't steady, but I guess I shouldn't have been surprised.

Teag motioned for me to step back as he opened the back of the RAV. He carried the lead box from the trunk of his Volvo and pulled out a box cutter. "Let me do this. If Shaw left another 'present,' it's going to affect me less than you."

I hated being sidelined, but couldn't argue with his logic. I stood on the sidewalk and fidgeted as he carefully went through each box using protective gloves.

"Bingo," he said halfway through the second container. He lifted a complicated tangle of thread, yarn, and twine with the silver tongs. "Got it."

Although I hadn't felt the hex's resonance when it was in the box, now that the piece was out in the open, it radiated malice. As soon as Teag closed the lid on the containment box, the awful vibes disappeared. I slumped against the RAV, feeling the adrenaline rush dissipate.

"Give me your keys." Teag put the containment box in his Volvo. "I'll drive you back to the shop, and Maggie can bring me back here to get my car."

Overwhelmed and shaken, I nodded and got into the passenger seat.

Teag's set jaw and deep frown made it clear he was pissed. "Shaw's watching you. He somehow found out about the auction and knew you'd have to pick up your purchases."

"The auction happened before we went to the Grantham house. There's no reason for him to have even noticed me back then," I protested.

"No, but there's been enough time for him to sense danger and figure out where you've been lately. He stepped up the threat level from the last time. I'm afraid that the next time, he won't miss."

A chill scampered along my spine. The same thought had occurred to me.

Teag escorted me into the shop, and I felt my anxiety ease once I was back inside the familiar wardings. He ducked back out to carry in the boxes, then parked my car in its usual spot.

"Did something happen?" Maggie asked, seeing us return together.

I gave her a brief recap.

"I'm so glad you're safe." Maggie appeared wide-eyed over my recent peril. "Of course I'll drive Teag to get his car as soon as you're steady enough to watch the shop."

I thanked her and went to the back to make a cup of tea to soothe my nerves. Now that I'd had a chance to think about the danger, I felt twitchy. Despite good intentions, I feared it would take more tea than we had in the break room to settle me.

When Teag and Maggie returned, I felt less jittery. Maggie nodded to let me know she was okay handling the store. Teag put the new acquisitions in the break room and stashed the containment box in the safe. Then he opened his computer and poured himself a cup of coffee.

"I never got to ask—how was the museum exhibit?" Teag asked.

"Nice. The projection technology is impressive. Alistair is like a kid on Christmas day."

"I hear a 'but' coming."

I grimaced. "*But* the djinn was there."

Teag's eyes widened. "Are you sure?"

"Yep. And he wanted me to know it was him." I told Teag about the interaction, the djinn intentionally revealing himself, and my conversation with Alistair.

"If the djinn kept to feeding like that, it wouldn't be as much of an issue," Teag mused. "Assuming he didn't binge eat."

"It's still taking something without consent," I pointed out. "People go to museums to relax and recharge. It's not fair to drain their energy without their permission. For some people in shaky health, that could be dangerous even if the djinn is careful."

"True," Teag conceded. "But I bet that's how djinn and psi vamps have existed throughout history. They can look like everyone else, so they go out to a crowded place and siphon off what they need without leaving a trace."

"Probably so." I didn't like the idea of being munched on by monsters without even knowing they were nearby. "What did you find?"

"I did some digging on the Darke Web before you called and found info on djinn that seems pretty credible. I also learned a few more things about the Granthams and found a little on Shaw. Putting the information together, I think the pieces start to come together," Teag replied.

"Okay. Tell me a story." I got comfortable in my chair.

"I went back to the beginning for the Granthams, to their 'big break.' That was a few years before they built the mansion. Lee Harris Grantham had been the struggling captain of a merchant ship. Then he did a cargo run to Africa for spices and 'exotic materials' and brought back a trader who became an unofficial business partner.

"Rumor had it the trader was the son of a chieftain and wealthy in his own regard. The articles called him a 'prince' and said that his connections opened up trade in areas that had previously been closed to Westerners," Teag continued.

"Wanna bet he was the djinn?"

"That's where I'd put my money," Teag agreed. "After that, the family fortunes rose rapidly. Lee cornered the market on spices, materials like ivory, exotic pelts, and unusual foods that could withstand the journey. He added new routes to Asia. His ships had uncanny luck avoiding storms and pirates. Trading partners vied to work with him. He became wealthy, and his single ship grew into an empire."

"What about the witches?"

"There was a mention about Lee hiring a 'financial advisor' from Baltimore—Taelman," Teag replied. "I don't know whether his know-how about finance was real or a way to hide that he was a witch. Between the new 'prince' and the 'advisor,' the Granthams got rich fast."

"Do they mention the cost?"

"Everything seems to have been fine for a while. The bad luck tended to be more personal than professional—family illnesses, losing babies and children, house fires. And reading between the lines, soured relationships," Teag replied. "The financial success stayed, even while everything else tanked."

"That squares with what we've found," I mused. "Anything else?"

"I looked closer at djinn in general. Never had reason to study them before this," Teag replied. "Sometimes a djinn possesses people to get what it wants, but it can also create a persona and maintain that appearance by shapeshifting. It has to be in its true form to feed."

"Interesting. That explains why the guy at the museum didn't look human when I got close."

He nodded. "Djinn can give immersive and hyper-realistic dreams and nightmares, good and bad, and drain people while they are in the dream. They can also produce hallucinations that trap a person while they are awake for a period of time and leech their energy."

"Like that's not creepy." I shuddered.

"Yeah. These guys are bad news," Teag agreed. "And from every-thing I've found about djinn, if the djinn's ally is a witch, the witch is their servant—even if the witch thinks otherwise."

"That sounds like it would be a built-in conflict with local covens," I mused. "Or a chance for the local witchy underdogs to try to get a leg up on everyone else by making a powerful best buddy."

"That occurred to me too," Teag agreed.

I knew we both had dealt with enough coven politics to last a lifetime.

"What's with the tapestries?"

"Djinn can use an object as an anchor that maintains a link to the victim so the djinn can feed without being present," Teag replied. "That could be a piece of jewelry, a painting, an object—a tapestry."

"Super stalkerish," I commented.

"No kidding. From what I found, it's believed that djinn can feed off positive emotions, but they enjoy the negative ones more. So when someone comes under the djinn's influence, they tend to make more and more self-destructive choices."

"Lovely." My snide tone made my opinion clear.

"Isn't it just? The sources said that although most djinn feed from individuals, they can feed from more than one person at a time—for example, everyone in a household."

"Like the Granthams."

"Even then, they're believed to siphon from the individuals, not the group as a whole—unless they're very old and strong."

That brought me up short. "So the djinn that attached itself to the Granthams was probably feeding from one person at a time."

"According to the sources I found."

"The older and more powerful a djinn gets, the more likely it is to be able to feed from a whole crowd at once. What about wars and natural disasters?" My head spun, thinking about the possibilities. "Are they powerful enough to sink a ship or crash a plane and then slurp up everyone's misery? Or start a war?"

Teag grimaced. "Theoretically, yes. There are stories about djinn causing earthquakes or tsunamis or setting two kingdoms against each other to gorge themselves."

"How do we know whether our djinn has enough mojo to start World War Three?"

"I guess we don't—until it happens," Teag replied. "There's no way to tell how old he is, and even age might not directly reflect a djinn's strength."

"Have you talked to Sorren about all this?" My stomach churned thinking about the possibilities—and none of them were good.

"I left him a message," Teag said. "Haven't heard back yet."

"Do we know anything more about the gallery where they bought the pieces?" This whole thing had gotten bigger and more complex than I ever expected. "Want to bet that Shaw had something to do with it as well as the djinn?"

"Turns out it wasn't a standard bricks-and-mortar shop. More of a pop-up that rented like a big old store for a short time. No lease, sketchy paperwork, perfect for fly-by-night operators."

"But the sort of locations that attract an artsy crowd and collectors looking for an 'undiscovered' gem that will get more valuable," I finished his sentence for him. "Shaw could run the business side and get the money he needed, and djinn got food sources with every cursed piece of art they sold."

"Those types of places prey on collectors who are hoping to buy something that's underpriced and then make a killing on the resale," Teag pointed out. "Or they buy into the idea of a 'good luck' piece that will make them rich. I swear that most of the dark magical items wouldn't work if people could stop being greedy."

"What about the other people who bought tapestries, like Stephanie's husband?" This whole situation had gone from dealing with what we thought were a few cursed objects to something with the potential to be so much worse.

"I'm working my way down the list. Made a couple of calls. Both people I talked to today let slip that they really wish they could get a refund because they've had problems since buying the pieces and could use the money."

"Oh?"

"The first guy said he bought a new car when he got a big bonus right after buying the tapestry. Then the car had transmission problems, and he can't afford to fix it."

"That sucks."

"No kidding. The woman said she bought the tapestry as a splurge from an inheritance and spent the rest of the money on a vacation. But she got hurt zip-lining, and now she's got big medical bills."

I hated the cruelty of the djinn. Bad enough to feed off people's random bad luck, but so much worse to cause misfortune and then benefit from it. Shaw was even worse because he wasn't just a monster —he was human.

"I left messages for some of the others, but they haven't called back yet. And I spent all morning digging because I wanted to know more about what we were dealing with before I talked to witnesses." Teag arched his back and stretched. "Did you get any clues about where the djinn might be going to ground?"

"No. And I didn't dare follow him because I wasn't ready for a fight. I think he knew I wouldn't challenge him in public with civilians around."

"I hate smart monsters." Teag sighed. "I wish we knew more about this djinn in particular. It's bad enough if he's causing problems for individuals like Stephanie's husband. But it gets a whole lot worse if he's powerful enough to cause bigger conflicts. It wouldn't have to be a full-on war. Riots, large-scale storm damage, random shooter, wildfires—anything that affects a lot of people at once and makes them angry or afraid is like a buffet."

"So we're back to saving the world again?"

"'Fraid so."

CHAPTER SEVEN

"Father Anne said Mom can stay on the St. Expeditus compound since we're still chasing the djinn, and staying with my brother is never a great option even if he were in town," Teag told me on our way back from talking to another of the gallery's tapestry customers.

"How did you explain that?" Neither Teag nor Anthony had leveled with their folks about the supernatural side of what we do, which was completely understandable. My parents only knew because the shop had been in our family for so long, and even then, I spared them the distressing details when the store passed from my great-uncle to me.

"I told her that Father Anne was a good friend and that the compound offered retreats, so they had nice rooms that weren't expensive. All of which is true," Teag replied.

Of course, the rooms were also within a heavily warded compound for warrior priests trained to fight supernatural threats, but that detail could be easily omitted.

"She was okay with that?" Despite the dangers peculiar to what we do, I hated for Mrs. Logan to miss out on a chance to visit the Historic District or do a little sightseeing.

"She thought it sounded restful." Teag smiled. "Whenever she visits, we do the carriage rides and house tours, so I think as long as I pick up a couple of bags of benne wafers and pralines for her, she won't miss doing the touristy stuff this time—and she'll be protected."

Anthony's parents lived in town, so lodging wasn't an issue for them.

"How are the rest of the arrangements going? Has Anthony's mom chilled out yet?"

Teag let out a long breath. "She's doing pretty well, actually. Having the wedding planner helps. Holding the reception and ceremony at the marina with a full staff used to hosting dinner parties also means there's less margin for error. Way different than trying to do it at the Benton house, even if the weather was good enough to be in the yard."

"I think you and Anthony deserve multiple drinks on the plane just to celebrate surviving the ceremony." I was one of the few who knew they planned to spend that night at a cozy little—unhaunted—B&B and then catch a flight to England for a return visit to a castle on the Welsh border that had become a favorite destination.

"I will drink to your health as soon as the wheels leave the ground," Teag agreed wholeheartedly.

The tapestry owner we just visited hadn't cared for her ex-husband's purchase and relegated it to a sealed garbage bin in the garage as soon as he moved out. That made it easy for us to take it off her hands and get it to a safe place where it could be neutralized.

Unfortunately, break-ups and financial distress seemed to be part of the fallout from purchasing the tapestries after a few prosperous years filled with luxury vacations and high-rolling Vegas weekends. The tapestry reminded her of everything that went wrong, and she happily handed it off without a backward glance.

Now the sealed can lay wrapped in the spelled metal and rope nets in the back of the RAV4.

"Turn left here." Teag pointed to an upcoming intersection. "That's one of the places on my list."

Teag's research had given us some clues about where the djinn might be hiding. According to lore, they liked caves, basements, and abandoned buildings. Charleston didn't really have a lot of underground structures since we came by the "Lowcountry" name honestly, but parts of town definitely had their share of empty buildings in various stages of disrepair that might serve just fine as a monster lair.

"We don't know for sure how close a djinn needs to be to his target to feed, but clearly some distance is okay because he wasn't in the houses with the most recent victims," Teag said. "So I looked at abandoned places that were on the same side of town."

"Find much? Charleston real estate is pretty expensive."

"It's expensive in prime areas," Teag replied. "But you can go from pricy to run down in a few blocks. The places I found aren't in the heart of the Historic District or South of Broad, but a number of them were closer than I expected."

We pulled over to the curb, and Teag showed me a map with addresses circled. "This djinn doesn't abduct his victims, so that means he can crash anywhere that he won't be disturbed. Technically, that could include abandoned houses, but I leaned toward more commercial or industrial areas for privacy."

The old Navy Yard would have been my first pick a few years ago, but the long-promised redevelopment was finally happening, so the area had more activity and wasn't quite as run down as it had been.

"These seemed like the best bets." Teag pointed to four places he had circled on the map. "They're only a couple of miles away from the victims' houses, big enough to hide in but small enough to defend, and they're commercial, so set off a bit without nosy neighbors."

"How did you come up with those parameters?" I couldn't help being curious. "There are plenty of old warehouses."

Teag nodded. "I thought of those. But if djinn prefer basements and caves when they go to ground, then it seemed they'd like a smaller space that would be easier to guard. They wouldn't need a whole warehouse, and those sites might attract regular squatters or illegal activities, which could cause problems. If the djinn is vulnerable when he goes to his lair, he's not going to want to defend a place the size of a city block."

"Good thinking." I studied the map and admitted that these were areas I had no reason to seek out and plenty of reasons to avoid. Nothing looked familiar.

"We don't know how the djinn gets around. These sites are only a block or two from bus routes. Assuming djinn don't drive."

"How did you narrow down the distance?" Teag's research always intrigued me.

"Stories talk about the djinn lurking near the homes of the people they target, sometimes hanging around outside to feed. With the tapestries as a connection, I wasn't sure the djinn needed to visit in person, but I guessed it would be easier to maintain the link by being closer," Teag said. "I could be wrong, but I needed to start somewhere."

His logic worked for me. "So what did you pick?"

"I want to start with the location of the pop-up gallery," Teag said. "I spoke with the rental agent, so we can visit legally. I thought we might pick up something from the resonance, or maybe Shaw or the djinn left something behind we can use." He tapped his fingers on the steering wheel. "After that, an old gas station, a small office, a defunct bank branch, and a dead corner store. I pulled them up online to see pictures. They're all fairly small, more than one entrance but limited windows, and not right next to anything. Easy for the djinn to get in and out, no neighbors, very little street traffic."

I hadn't been nervous before, but now that we were actually going looking for the djinn, my stomach tightened.

"Those would be just a drive-by. We don't stop, we don't get out. I'm just trying to eliminate anything that might not be suitable when we see it in person."

"And then?" I relaxed a little realizing Teag had no intention of going djinn hunting.

"We take what we find and see what Rowan and the others make of it. Then we go after it."

"Do you think it can sense us?"

"We're staying on the public road, which still has traffic. We aren't getting close. And the car is warded. We're not even sure the djinn is home right now. If he attacks us just driving past, he also gives away his location," Teag pointed out.

"Looks like they've packed up shop." We stood on the sidewalk outside the former dress shop that for several months had been transformed into an edgy art gallery.

"Pop-up locations are trendy," Teag said with a shrug. "They're like food trucks. There's a rush of discovery, the thrill of not knowing where you'll find them next, the idea that they could vanish and be gone forever."

The darkened storefront held the empty, featureless space that had briefly been the gallery where patrons mingled over canapes and champaign looking for the next "breakthrough" artist. From what we heard from those who had visited, everything seemed legit.

"Everyone said that the host called it 'his' gallery and was suave and knowledgeable," I said, as Teag used the key we had gotten from the real estate agent on the pretext of looking for space to hold a fundraiser.

"That's what I heard too. Whoever it was rubbed elbows with the well-off clientele and never raised alarms," Teag agreed. "Apparently he dropped all the right names, used the correct technical terms, and hobnobbed with the wealthy patrons like an insider."

The attraction, for collectors, had been the chance to acquire "up and coming" artists before their careers took off when the pieces still sold at bargain prices. The con man had been good enough to deceive seasoned collectors with the right mix of fawning and insider knowledge.

"Anything that looks too good to be true usually is," I repeated the old adage.

Teag turned on the lights, and we stared at the empty shop. The building had been many things in its long life—dress shop, haberdashery, even a fancy hat store. When the storefront didn't sell, the owners tried to cut their losses by renting it out to short-term retail customers who only intended to stay for a couple of months.

"Most of these cons wouldn't work if people weren't greedy," Teag said as we made a careful circle of the interior. Even with the lights on, it felt dim and shadowed.

Attracted to being in the know and hoping to sell later for a big increase, collectors had pulled out their credit cards and checkbooks. The gallery had delivered the artwork promptly, and the djinn had a new slate of victims.

"Did anything unusual happen here?" I couldn't shake the feeling that a trace of evil hadn't been scrubbed clean. "Not just business failures. A murder? Suicide? Missing person? The energy is off."

I was careful not to touch anything, but sometimes the emotional stain is strong enough I can get a reading through the soles of my shoes. "I feel desperation, uncertainty, hopelessness. It's not haunted, but I'm surprised that the customers didn't get dragged down by it."

"Maybe whatever we're dealing with can mask that sort of thing or cast a glamour," Teag suggested. I didn't like the sound of that since the sort of creatures who can do those things tend to be powerful and dangerous.

"It certainly didn't get in the way of the party guests plunking down plenty of cold, hard cash—or credit," I said. "I don't think anyone is going to lose their shirt—or their house over it. The buyers were wealthy, but they still didn't deserve to be scammed."

As suddenly as the gallery appeared, it was gone. Its rent hadn't been paid, no permits had been issued, and the host's meticulous resume fell through as his "references" denied ever knowing him.

The paintings were real but not their provenance, so anyone who bought for an investment rather than because they liked the artwork was out of luck.

"I read the police file," Teag murmured.

I knew that meant he had hacked into the system. His magic and computer talents come in handy. "He scammed the who's-who of Charleston. There are probably more who didn't want to admit they got bilked, but the ones who made a complaint certainly had the wherewithal to get an independent appraisal before buying."

"But where's the fun in that, especially if they were spending 'mad' money," I replied as he made a slow circuit of the show floor. "They weren't going to be strapped for cash even if the investment didn't pay off. They liked how edgy it felt to come to a place that appeared and might disappear, that wasn't their usual, boring, same-old, same-old."

"So the con man wasn't just peddling art—he was selling an adventure," Teag speculated.

"Yep. You know how you read about someone who buys a sketch at a yard sale, and it turns out to be a real Picasso? Or who goes on vacation and picks something up in a flea market in Europe that is a long-lost rare antique? The dodginess and here today, gone tomorrow aspect was part of the charm."

I knew the kind of buyer the pop-up gallery attracted. They wandered into Trifles and Folly all the time. Wealthy and financially secure, the safety of their lives took away the surprises. They romanticized having less and feeling more, taking risks, finding a hidden treasure.

"It probably felt rebellious to buy the paintings without calling their wealth management advisor first," I said with a sigh. I didn't envy or begrudge our clients who were like that. I was glad they didn't have to worry about paying the bills and had money to indulge their fancies and interests.

At the same time, the layers of safety that protected them from the cruel world took away any sense of adventure as efficiently as a helicopter parent. "High stakes" meant betting on a golf game or a poker tournament. "Risky" was staying at a different high-end resort on vacation or trying out a new masseuse.

"The people who got scammed might have been bored, but they aren't stupid. Even though they didn't lose their rent money, they're risk-averse. The paintings were magicked. Maybe the gallery owner had some mojo of his own to lull them into letting down their guard," I wondered aloud.

"Probably," Teag answered. "Maybe it felt like going to an amusement park—you pay money for the thrill of walking on the wild side. A witch would have just needed to nudge a little. *Throw caution to the winds. It's your money—do what you want. You could make a killing, and everyone will be so jealous.*"

We had made a full circle of the first floor and found nothing. "Despite all the security cameras, none of the recordings showed the face of the gallery owner or the host at the receptions." I'd hoped we'd find some clue left behind that might help us put the pieces together. "That's got to be magic."

"The Grantham's witch probably had the mojo, but would anyone have recognized him and put two-and-two together?" Teag asked.

"No one said anything about Shaw in connection to the haunted artwork. Maybe he wanted to keep the local covens off his tail by using intermediaries. That also eliminated consequences once the paintings turn out not to be what people expected," I said.

"That still doesn't tell us who the slick gallery host was."

"If Shaw was working with the djinn, maybe the djinn possessed someone to be their frontman," I said.

"If so, I'm betting they didn't leave him around as a loose end," Teag replied in a grim tone.

The longer we stayed in the empty store, the more my intuition warned me something was wrong.

We made another sweep of the room. This time, we opened closets and peeked into offices. All were empty except for unremarkable basic furnishings. I frowned when I noticed a door on the far side of what appeared to be a staging area.

"Look at the floor." I pointed to a line of dirt next to the bottom of the door. "Whoever cleaned swept up to the entrance, but it doesn't look like they went inside."

I put my hand on the knob, and a rush of bad feelings swept over me. Fear, pain, terror. I stumbled, and Teag caught me.

I took a deep breath to steady myself. "I think we're going to find something really awful inside."

"Do we leave and call the police? Call Donnelly for magical backup?"

I thought for a moment, evaluating the feelings that had caught me by surprise. "No to the police—at least just yet. Let's make sure there's a problem before we get them involved."

"Donnelly?"

I frowned, parsing through the feelings that my touch magic raised. "I'm not picking up on an active threat. Something bad-wrong-awful, but not currently dangerous. I don't think we need Donnelly for this, but it wouldn't hurt for us both to be ready—just in case."

I let my wooden spoon athame fall from my sleeve into my hand. I didn't bring the walking stick because much as it comes in handy, I hadn't wanted to burn down the building. Teag had a net of spell-woven rope and his short daggers sheathed on his belt.

The door was the only one in the interior to be locked. That just confirmed my gut feeling that there was something horrific inside. Teag picked it easily and let the door swing open. He hit the light switch, illuminating a small kitchen.

"Why would anyone hide a kitchen?" I murmured. The room looked as barren and soulless as the rest of the empty space. A table and four chairs had been pushed against the far wall. The cheap coffeemaker nested on the counter above a bottom-of-the-line dish-washer. At one end of the counter sat the refrigerator. Its hum told us the appliance was still plugged in.

"Want me to open it?" Teag asked, and I figured he wanted to spare me any negative resonance. I had a really bad gut feeling, but we had come here to find answers. Reluctantly, I nodded.

A man's badly preserved body tumbled out.

We both gagged at the smell. Someone had turned down the fridge's temperature, but it hadn't been enough to prevent decomposition.

"I think it's the gallery host." I recognized the corpse's clothing from pictures of the gala. "He's been in there a while."

"We were right about the djinn not leaving loose ends." Teag looked queasy.

I had to call the real estate agent and tell her there was a corpse in her client's fridge. That meant the police showed up, asking plenty of questions. Teag and I stuck to our story about looking for event space, and we didn't have to fake our horror over finding the body.

When we were finally cleared to leave, the poor real estate agent was still answering questions.

Neither of us spoke until we had driven miles from the gallery. "That was…" I didn't know how to finish the thought.

"It definitely was." Teag sounded just as rattled. "Now what?"

"Let's see if we can find out who else attended the showing. I'm wondering if there's a list somewhere of people who bought the artwork."

"I'd be interested to know who handled the sales that night," Teag mused. "What kind of records did they keep? Was it cash-only? Cryptocurrency? Either should be a red flag to legitimate collectors, but bored and jaded folks like to pretend to walk on the wild side."

"I want to know where Shaw was during the gallery event and why he didn't attend." I was still trying to make sense of how the salesman for the night ended up dead. "I've got a theory."

"Try me."

"Shaw knows the artwork is dangerous and more likely to react to his magic if he's nearby. He doesn't want to freak the mundanes, so he uses a proxy—the dead guy who emceed the event. To make sure everything goes as planned, the djinn possesses the guy. But the longer the djinn is in control, the harder it is on the guy's body, burning him out. The djinn vacates the corpse, and Shaw leaves him behind like so much trash," I speculated.

"Awful, but possible," Teag agreed. "It's the best story we've got. I'd like to know how often Shaw was around the gallery when it was in business."

"The cops can run a trace on the dead guy."

"Which I can hack into," Teag said.

"It would be helpful to know who was here—and who bought art. I bet Mrs. Morrissey and Alistair could work their contacts and find out."

"The so-called artists weren't supposed to be famous or have much of a track record," Teag recalled. "That's what made the showing so exciting—and such a gamble. People might have reached out after the fact to Alistair to see if the museum knew the provenance of what they bought."

"That's where Mrs. Morrissey might come in handy. Rich people aren't going to like admitting that their new piece of art wasn't what they thought it was. They got conned. It's going to stick in their craw."

"Want to bet Alistair gets some calls from donors as well, looking for second appraisals?" Teag asked.

"Buyer's remorse," I replied. "I can let them know that there are some dangerous forgeries out there and see if they'll pass along the names of people who contact them."

Maggie handled the store while Teag and I sleuthed. She's worth her weight in gold. Sorren and I make sure she's well-compensated.

"I want to know all the juicy details," Maggie said during a lull when the shop was empty. "Sounds like a humdinger from the little I've overheard. Not that I'm eavesdropping." She gave a mischievous grin.

We kept very few secrets from Maggie, only the ones that might put her in more danger than what came just by associating with us. She's got nerves of steel and a passion for seeing bad guys get what's coming to them, even if justice has been delayed by a lifetime or two. Lucky for us, the supernatural side of what we do doesn't bother her.

Turned out Mrs. Morrissey and Alistair had already gotten calls from long-time donors and patrons who regretted their impulsive decision to buy at the pop-up gallery. I concocted a reason to call—saying that as the owner of Trifles and Folly, I wondered about the attractiveness of the pop-up sale model.

"Boy, did I get an earful," I told Teag after I had talked to them. "Buyers are unhappy that the pieces sold for inflated amounts when the artists are unknowns. I was right about it being gambling with art. There's no one to get the money back from, and the museum and historical archive can't buy them."

"If the gallery only took cash or crypto, I'm guessing they might not have gotten receipts that will hold up under IRS scrutiny if they try to donate the pieces," Teag said. "We don't want the art here at the shop, but I'm wondering if there is a way we can take 'unwanted' art for store credit."

"Hmm....that has possibilities. We wouldn't be out the cash—

although I'm sure Sorren and Donnelly could cover expenses if necessary."

"The buyers get something for their trouble, and we can 'donate' the art to the Briggs Society for Donnelly to get rid of," Teag added. "We don't need to match what they paid for the piece because by now they know the art is nearly worthless, so salvaging anything helps them save face."

"And the South of Broad crowd likes to shop here, anyhow. We might take a temporary hit to the bottom line for a good cause." I fret about profitability, and we usually operate well into the black. Sorren sees the shop primarily as an avenue to stop supernatural evil, so he's less concerned about the balance sheet, although he appreciates our efforts.

"Make it an invitation-only offer, and it only goes out to the people who got taken advantage of by the pop-up gallery," Teag suggested. "They have to bring an original invitation to be accepted. Plays to their ego as they offload their white elephant and take home something nice from the store."

"You're a genius," I told him. "We can design the invitation and write the letter tonight."

A few hours later, my phone pinged. "Mrs. Morrissey sent me a list of the people who talked to her and a few others who didn't but who run with the ones who did. So they probably got rooked too. Alistair said he'd get his list to me tonight."

On one hand, I could make the case that the buyers' greed got them into trouble. At the same time, I didn't doubt that Shaw and the djinn added some supernatural influence to secure new marks to leech money and energy. Helping the buyers out of their bad choices ultimately would weaken Shaw and the djinn, so it fell in line with our mission of getting bad stuff out of circulation.

At this rate, the Briggs Society would be naming a wing of the building after us.

We're handling the "folly" part—which is right in our name.

As the names of the buyers trickled in, Teag put his hacker skills and Weaver magic to work investigating them.

"Are we surprised that in the time since the pop-up gallery sales, every one of the buyers had a streak of good luck and then some calamity?"

"Doesn't surprise me," I replied.

"One guy's stock portfolio got wiped out—and since he had bought on margin with money he didn't have, he lost everything."

"Ouch."

"Someone else got a sexy new girlfriend after a nasty divorce, which went great until she turned out to be a Russian scammer," he went on. "A few of the buyers came into a lot of money and ended up with terminal diagnoses or incapacitating accidents. They might not have lost the money, but they won't be around to spend it. Mrs. Morrissey and Alistair have found about twenty people so far. All of them had a shot of good luck, and then it went south."

I didn't fight the anger that surged through me at Shaw's cruel schemes. Whether or not the victims had been "good" people, they didn't deserve what he did to them. He got the money, and the djinn drank down their fear and pain. There were serial killers I loathed less.

Forcing a calm I didn't really feel, I called Donnelly and filled him in, along with confirming that the Briggs Society would take the "fire sale" artwork off our hands.

"Absolutely. And kudos for coming up with a truly inspired solution," he chortled. "Brilliant. Are you any closer to finding the knave who caused the problem?"

I'm not entirely sure how old Donnelly is. He dresses like a time-slipped Victorian. As far as I know, he's human—but I've never had that confirmed.

He's not a vampire—I've seen him in daylight—but lots of other creatures are long-lived. Or he might have started out as mortal and just had his lifespan extended through supernatural means. Maybe the time the Briggs Society building is "elsewhere" doesn't count for aging. I'm curious, but not enough to pry.

"We'll have to come up with a safe-ish way for them to hand over the artwork to you, but we have time to figure that out."

"I already have a few ideas," Donnelly assured me. "I do love turning tables on the bad guys. Smashingly good fun."

~

FOUR DAYS LATER, we held the "donation' day at the St. Expeditus Society within their wardings and under the watchful eye of Father Anne and the monks. Beck helped with triage since he had seen a lot of dark magic growing up in a witch dynasty.

Nearly everyone on our list showed up. If anyone questioned why we picked such an unusual and out-of-the-way place to do the drop-off, they didn't ask. I suspect that on some level, they could feel the wardings and understood that the compound was the safest place to get rid of their dangerous acquisitions.

With Father Anne's help, we set up a heavily protected tent not far inside the warded gate. To me, the magic felt thick, like a humid day. Most people might feel calm or peaceful.

Teag, Rowan, Beck, and I wore our entire arsenal of charms and protections, as well as spelled linen scarves Teag wove. Donnelly reinforced the wardings and added a few more of his own, as well as a supernaturally protected truck to transport the cursed artwork to the closest place he could "land" the Briggs Society, since the building can travel through space and time.

"I don't know what came over us," an older woman said as she turned over a painting of a young girl. On closer inspection, the feral gleam in the girl's eye would have made me sleep with my door locked if I lived in a house where it hung. "We got caught up in the excitement of the auction, I guess, and the chance to discover a hot new artist."

I remembered her story from our research. She and her husband had a great run on Wall Street that paid for a round-the-world vacation and set them up for life. But within months, the stocks crashed, and the husband caught a rare fever on the vacation that killed him.

"You're not the only one." I did my best to comfort her. "All these people got cheated too—if it helps to know that. I'm very sorry for your loss."

A haggard man was next in line, also toting a piece of artwork. His was a landscape that managed to look menacing and idyllic at the same time. Like the tapestry at the Grantham house, I thought I saw creatures with eyes and sharp teeth barely hidden among the plants.

"We thought it was a lark, you know?" He sounded like he had lost all his fight. "We had brunch downtown at our favorite place and then went over to the tent sale to score a bargain. Always dreamed about being one of the first to 'discover' the next Picasso."

He gave a self-deprecating snort. "We thought we got a real deal. And for the next month, everything came up roses. Until it all turned bad. Got in a car accident that put my wife in a wheelchair. Our dog got sick. Nearly lost the house in a fire. One thing after another. And it all started when we brought that accursed thing into the house. So take it. I don't even need your voucher. I just never want to see it again."

Teag, Rowan, Beck, and I sat behind tables in the warded tent, and we each had a line of people bringing their items for disposal and to get the purchase credit at our store.

Donnelly and the monks took the pieces and moved them to the heavily warded truck so they could be whisked away once the event was over.

I exchanged a look with Teag. We had just started the exchange, and I wasn't sure my heart would survive hearing how much harm Shaw's paintings had done. The buyers might have been foolish or vain, but whatever their failures, the cursed paintings and the djinn had made them pay for their sins many times over.

Thankfully, with four of us handling the intake and giving out the vouchers, the lines moved steadily. I wondered if there were others who had been taken advantage of who didn't live to get our invitation, or who had ended up hospitalized or in a nursing home due to the djinn's curse.

I try very hard not to make the job personal. We go up against absolute evil, and if we didn't keep some distance, the scope of what we do would eat us alive. Usually, I'm pretty good at maintaining professional distance. But this case made that difficult. Maybe it was because we deal with a lot of artwork at the shop, and I know the joy that the right piece can bring to a collector. Using it to destroy lives seemed especially twisted and wrong.

"You okay?" Father Anne asked before she brought up my next "client." I could tell from the look in her eye that she had probably guessed the direction of my thoughts.

"Trying not to feel," I told her. "I don't have time to grieve for them, and thinking about what I'd like to do to Shaw isn't good for my blood pressure."

She gave me a pastoral smile. "Never stop feeling. It's what keeps us human." She put her hand on my shoulder and murmured something that was probably a blessing under her breath. Maybe it was wishful thinking, but the gesture helped a little.

Two hours later, all the art collectors were gone. Donnelly's bespelled truck was full of cursed art, and we had given out a hefty amount of store vouchers, although more than one person offered to pay us to take their paintings.

Father Anne and Rowan cleansed the tent in their varying ways and placed protections on Donnelly's truck on top of whatever he had already put into place. They also cleansed each of us individually with purification spells, holy water, and incense. Maybe it was my imagination, but I felt lighter and cleaner afterward.

Psychic residue is real, and it can be dangerous. It's like stepping in dog poop, only way worse, and I didn't want to carry home any malicious hitchhiking bad juju.

"We'll take it from here." Donnelly gestured to the monks headed for the truck who had offered to help him.

"Let's be blessed and break bread together," Father Anne said. "Two of the oldest ways to send away the darkness."

Two of the kitchen monks wheeled out a cart with hot tea and coffee and a tray of fresh cookies. Teag, Rowan, Beck, and I sat down with Father Anne, Donnelly, and the priests who had helped handle the donors. We talked about what we had seen and the stories we had heard. Just sharing the tragedies told to us helped me get a healthier distance.

"We will lift them up to the light," she promised us. "You've removed a great evil from them, and that is one of the greatest blessings we can give to another person."

I usually thought of myself as more of a fighter than a healer, but I appreciated the sentiment.

"Thanks again for letting us invade your space," I said with a wan smile. "I can't think of anywhere that would have been safer for us—and the donors."

"That's what we're here for," Father Anne replied. "Happy to be of service. And when you find that son of a bitch Shaw, you let me know, and I'll be right beside you for the fight."

CHAPTER EIGHT

Our reconnaissance didn't take long. The four locations were fairly close to each other, and although the neighborhood had seen better days, we weren't the only cars on the road.

The corner store and gas station seemed like long shots because once we saw them, we realized that the big windows made them hard to defend. The other two sites looked more likely, assuming Teag's criteria were solid.

"So much for that." Teag turned the car toward home.

"We need to stop at the museum. I promised Alistair I'd bring some hex bags and charms to make the museum a less friendly place for the djinn to hang out." I'd gotten the items from Rowan and Mrs. Teller, a powerful local root worker.

"Coming right up."

Alistair met us in the lobby, and I handed off the protections. "Put something in each room where it won't get easily noticed or swept up by housekeeping," I told him. "They have no effect on regular people —but they'll make the djinn uncomfortable enough he may decide to go elsewhere."

I knew Alistair would follow through, which left me feeling better about the exhibit. Teag and I kept our eyes open for the djinn, but neither of us spotted him.

"He's a shapeshifter. He could look like anyone," I muttered.

"Still, there should be energy around him. And he has to be in his true form to feed."

We wandered from room to room since Teag hadn't seen the display. Although the tapestry in the projections wasn't the actual woven item, Teag seemed to be just as enthralled as I had been to get a good look at the famous masterpiece up close and in so much detail.

"I can't believe that the colors are still so bright after eight hundred years," he marveled. "And the monsters are kind of like the Muppets on mushrooms!"

Now that he'd said that, I was never going to think of it any other way.

We finished touring the exhibit and walked back toward where we had parked, still remarking on the tapestries' details.

"Teag!" I only had time to call for him before I fainted.

I never saw the car that hit me.

Warning shouts came seconds too late. I glimpsed grillwork, and everything went black.

I woke up in a hospital bed with an IV in one arm. Everything hurt, my throat parched, and I didn't know where I was. A nurse hurried in after I rang the call bell.

"You're at St. Francis," she told me. "What's the last thing you remember?"

My head pounded trying to recall anything, and I just shrugged.

"You were hit by a car, and you've been in and out for the last few hours," the nurse said. "I'll call the doctor and have him speak with you."

"Wait," I called out as she started to turn away. "Is there anyone here with me?"

She shook her head. "No. I'm sorry. Someone called 911, and the ambulance brought you here. They couldn't find an emergency contact in your phone or next of kin."

She went to get the doctor, and I stared after her. What the nurse said felt wrong, but I didn't know why. I sighed and chalked it up to how much my head ached. Maybe I had a concussion.

The doctor walked in a few moments later, a middle-aged Black woman with a nametag that read "Dr. Shelby."

"Good to see you awake, Cassidy," she greeted me.

I managed a smile. "I'd agree, except everything hurts."

Dr. Shelby nodded. "That's to be expected. You're lucky. It could have been much worse."

"Can I have my phone? I need to call people so they won't worry."

Doctor Shelby's expression turned quizzical. She found my phone in the nightstand drawer and handed it to me. "Do you remember their numbers? We couldn't find any contacts when you were brought in."

I looked up, surprised. "But everyone's in there—Kell, Teag, my parents..." My voice drifted off as I called up "contacts" and stared at a blank page. "I don't understand." I searched her gaze, confused.

"I own Trifles and Folly, the antique shop on King Street," I said. "My boyfriend, Kell Winston, lives with me and should be at our house with my dog, Baxter. There should have been an emergency card with contact information in my wallet, along with my insurance card."

The concern on Dr. Shelby's face deepened. "I've never heard of an antique store by that name, and I'm frequently on King Street. The address on your license was an apartment, but the landlord says your lease ran out last month, and you put everything in storage."

"No. That's not right. Please—I need to call my parents. They'll get this straightened out."

I knew Mom's cell phone number by heart. "I'm sorry, that number is not in service..."

Dad's number got the same response.

"I don't understand."

Dr. Shelby gave me a strained smile. "Confusion is very common after an accident like you had. Rest, hydrate, and eat. In most cases, the symptoms resolve on their own."

The nurse left me a glass of water and made sure the television remote was nearby. *"Just ring the bell if you need me. You've got time before dinner—might want to nap a bit more,"* she said and patted me on the arm.

I stared at the door when she closed it and tried not to hyperventilate.

Then I grabbed my phone and searched for my mom's name, choking back a sob when I found the obituary for her and my dad—a car wreck in Charlotte two years ago.

There had to be photos. But when I flicked the app open, there were no pictures of friends or Baxter. Just snapshots of landmarks around Charleston, the beach, and flowers.

Between my racing heart and shallow breathing, I nearly lost my balance and reached out for the bedrail to steady myself, then flinched expecting an onslaught of impressions from the other sick people who had been here before me.

Nothing happened. I couldn't quite remember why I thought something would, but for a second I had been certain that touching the rail would connect me to the emotions of other patients from the bed's past.

The memories seemed so solid and real, but the longer I was awake, the more I began to doubt. I'd heard of people forgetting who they were after hitting their heads, but not about them making up completely new lives.

I sank back into the pillow and blinked hard trying not to cry.

Images and names flashed through my mind. It didn't seem possible that they were all just figments of my imagination. I tried to remember what I was doing just before I was hit by the car, but the details were fuzzy. Shopping? That didn't feel right. Going to work? But what did that mean if I didn't actually own a store? The more I tried to remember, the more everything slipped out of reach, and I let exhaustion take me under.

"Cassidy." I heard a man calling me from a long way away. "Cassidy—follow my voice."

I knew him, even if I couldn't remember his name. I associated that voice with safety, friendship, and protection. Gray eyes. Blond hair.

Someone I trusted. I clung to the sound in my mind and tried to bring it closer.

"I've got you," another voice said, and I had the oddest sense of my soul gripped tight in strong, careful hands.

"Keep your eyes shut and focus on what you see in your mind," the first voice prompted. "We'll bring you home."

None of that made sense, but I didn't question it because deep in my heart, I believed them. Trusted them with my life.

Either I was about to be rescued, or I had gone mad.

In my imagination, I was inside a darkened room. A glowing line appeared on the floor. I felt someone beside me, and although I couldn't see him, I knew he was my guide.

"Follow the line, Cassidy. We won't let anything keep you here, but you have to walk out."

A flurry of noise around me threatened my concentration, but I kept my eyes shut and ignored the other voices that called to me, pleading for me to look at them, say something. The line glowed brighter, and I followed it one faltering mental step at a time. The more steps I took, the brighter the line shone and the more muffled the voices in the room near me became.

"Keep going, Cassidy. You're safe," the first voice had a note of authority beneath the reassurance, which felt strangely compelling.

It felt like I passed through an invisible curtain that sent shivers through my whole body and made every nerve ending tingle. Was this what it felt like to die? I hesitated, unsure.

"Almost home, Cassidy. Keep going. We're all waiting for you."

I imagined myself held tight in a giant's strong hand, led by the glowing line. The darkness faded, growing lighter with each step. I no longer heard the voices from the hospital and hoped that I had made the right choice.

"Cassidy?"

I knew Teag's voice, but I wasn't sure it was safe to look yet, so when a hand gripped mine, I gave it a tight squeeze.

"You can open your eyes now," the first of my invisible rescuers said—and I heard him with my ears, not in my mind. I recognized him now—Sorren.

"She's back," Donnelly said nearby.

My eyes fluttered open and focused on the ceiling in my living room, and seconds later, Baxter shoved his furry face into my field of vision and licked my nose.

"What—" The word came out as a dry croak. Teag put a cup with a straw to my lips, and I sipped the cold water, letting it ease my parched throat.

"Go easy," Teag coached. "You've been out for a while."

"How long?" I managed.

"About four hours." I could hear the worry in Teag's tone.

I turned my head and saw Sorren and Donnelly watching me with concern. "How?"

"You were outside wardings, and the djinn saw an opportunity." I knew from the tension in the way Sorren held himself that he was angry.

"You collapsed just as we got to the car," Teag said, and I realized he was holding my hand. "I didn't think it was something normal, so I drove you home instead of to the ER. Rowan couldn't wake you, so we called Donnelly. Sorren had to wait for nightfall. You scared the shit out of us."

"Kell?"

"He must have his phone turned off on a shoot," Teag replied. "We tried to call, but he didn't pick up, and it wasn't the sort of thing I wanted to leave in a text or a voicemail."

Baxter licked my face frantically, doing his part to rouse me. I reached my free hand up to scratch behind his ears.

"What?" I didn't seem to be able to manage more than a word or two at a time. I still remembered the hospital and the devastating news they had given me. At the time, it seemed so real, but now it was beginning to fade like a nightmare.

"Drink this." Rowan carried a glass from the kitchen filled with a bright green liquid. It looked like Midori and smelled like anise. I braced myself and sipped it, going slowly to get it all down.

"That will help clear your head from the djinn's influence," she told me. "It's the antitoxin to their psychic poison."

I looked to Sorren and Donnelly. "You came for me."

Sorren returned a wan smile. "That's what friends are for. Archibald gripped your soul, and I gambled that the glamouring that usually doesn't work on you might be effective under the circumstances to compel you to listen. I'm glad my hunch paid off."

I realized I was lying on the couch and struggled to sit. Teag helped and then pushed pillows behind me for support. "I thought I was in the hospital. They told me I got hit by a car," I told them haltingly about what I experienced. "It all seemed so real."

"That's how a djinn feeds." Rowan took the empty glass and brought me more water. "They can manipulate the events in someone's life to give temporary good luck and then leech off the good feelings, but in a pinch, they create a hallucination that their target can't break and siphon off the emotions, positive or negative."

"I'm really tired." I felt like I'd pulled a couple of all-nighters.

"To be expected." Donnelly gave me an avuncular smile. "I can assure you, however, that your soul is undamaged and complete, and your lifeforce should be replenished with a little rest, sugar, and good food."

"Thank you," I murmured. "I knew something was wrong, but I had no proof, and no one would believe me." If I had wondered before what made some of the djinn's victims waste away in their own private world, I didn't now.

"You scared the shit out of us." Teag gave my hand another squeeze before finally letting go. "I'm glad you're back."

Now that the shock was wearing off, I remembered that we had tried to reach Sorren before my "incident."

"You got our messages?" I asked him.

"Yes, and the new information is troubling. I had hoped this was an unremarkable djinn, and we could be rid of it fairly easily. What just happened and what you've told me suggests it's much older and gaining power. Now that its convenient source of food is gone and it's gone back to hunting, I suspect it likes the thrill."

"Can a powerful djinn draw energy from the emotions of crowds, not just individuals?" Teag asked.

Sorren paused. "Yes. Fortunately, it's rare for djinn, although there are other creatures that feed on negative emotions from disasters. But this djinn is growing stronger. That means handling him becomes a priority."

"We think we know where it's hiding." Teag's comment reminded me of what we had done earlier that day.

"Don't go after it alone," Sorren responded sharply, and his tone told me he was truly worried.

"We didn't plan to," Teag hurried to add. "But I don't think we can wait long—especially after what it did to Cassidy."

"I agree," Donnelly said. "The djinn knows who you are, and you've become a threat. He won't wait long to make his next move."

"We need to handle this problem while it's still something we can manage." Sorren's words left me chilled. Our friends had a pretty formidable array of supernatural abilities and experience. We've gone up against ancient witches, demi-gods, Petro Loa, all kinds of ghosts and spirits, and some pretty terrifying monsters. This djinn had shifted from monster-of-the-week to big bad.

"How long will it take me to get back up to speed?" I glanced from Rowan to Donnelly.

"I've been sending energy to you, which should help a good bit," Donnelly said. "Rowan's potions and her healing spell will counter any remaining effects. Add a good meal and a solid night's sleep, and you should be right as rain by tomorrow evening."

"If Kell's still out of town, I can stay with you. Anthony's tied up with work all week," Teag volunteered.

"Kell's on another shoot for a big client. He won't be back for a couple of days." I didn't want Kell in the line of fire while we dealt with the djinn. He's backed us up in bad situations before, but he's limited to using weapons to protect himself, and I suspected the djinn was going to take more than silver bullets. Especially after what I had just experienced, I really didn't want Kell anywhere he could become a target.

"Now that you're awake and stable, Archibald and I will check out the locations you suggested for the djinn's lair. I have a few ideas of my own to add to the list. We'll gather materials so that we'll have everything we need," Sorren said.

He and Donnelly took their leave. Rowan lingered for another hour until she felt certain her potion and magic had done their job, then left with strict instructions to call if anything didn't seem right.

Bax hadn't left my side. I wondered what he could sense since dogs are highly intuitive, and I knew he could pick up on emotions and energy.

"Now—food." Teag looked at me with mock sternness. "What do you think you can eat?"

"Let's start with chicken soup and go from there. Cans are in the cupboard by the stove."

Teag handed me the remote, made sure my drink was close enough to reach, and tucked the blanket around me. "Sit tight. I'll heat the soup."

I surfed channels looking for something comforting that didn't require much attention and ended up on the English baking show. Baxter squirmed and flipped onto his back, presenting himself for belly rubs. Even though I knew I was home, safe, inside wardings, and healed with magic, the enormity of what had happened overwhelmed me.

I'd been completely alone, no family, friends, Kell, or Baxter. No Trifles and Folly. Homeless. And it had all felt so real.

Tears pricked my eyes, and I choked back a sob. Bax looked at me quizzically. "I'm okay," I told him and tried to reassure myself too.

"Rowan and Donnelly said you'd have flashbacks for a while, but they thought it would be a lot better by tomorrow." Teag brought a tray with soup, crackers, cheese, and an energy drink to the coffee table. "I've found some cookies for dessert because you definitely need a sugar boost."

Now that the adrenaline had faded, I felt like I *had* been hit by a truck. "Tell me something about the wedding. Cheer me up."

Teag cradled a cup of tea in his hands and sat in an armchair facing me. "We have our last tux fitting this weekend. According to the wedding planner, the flowers and cake are all taken care of, the photographer and DJ are ready, and the table layout is fixed."

"Good to hear. How's Anthony holding up with all the late nights?"

"He's tired, but we're both looking forward to the time off, so it's worth the extra effort up front. But it's making rehearsals difficult."

I frowned. "For the ceremony?"

Teag shook his head. "The wedding dance. The music is going to be Swing and Big Bands, with a jazz trio while we're eating. Anthony and I have a first dance all cooked up—but we need to practice."

The soup felt good on my throat, and I hadn't realized how hungry I was. "That sounds like fun."

"We've taken ballroom dance lessons for a while. It's a nice night out to do dinner and dancing when we can get some free time," Teag said. "Right up there with going to the art cinema if there's something good playing." I tend to forget what a big classic movie buff Teag is.

"I can't wait to see your dance routine, but don't expect more than the most basic moves from Kell and me. I don't know how to dance to anything that has actual steps."

He laughed. "It's easier than people think. Who knows? We might win you over!"

"How are the moms doing? We're in the home stretch now."

Teag leaned back in his chair and took a sip before answering. "They're frazzled, but for different reasons. Anthony's mom isn't going to rest until the reception is over. It's just her personality. I think micromanaging the details helps her let go of her youngest, although we aren't actually going anywhere."

"And your mom?" I had met Teag's mom several times over the years but didn't know her well.

"She's pretty quiet. Anthony's mom has been great about reaching out and involving her, but Mom is fine hanging back and letting someone else take the lead." He sighed. "All the weddings I've been to, and I never realized how much work went into them."

"Everything set for extended family coming into town?"

"I don't really have much, so that's not an issue on my side. My brother was sent to Germany for a client emergency at the last minute —one of those things only the lead engineer can handle. But it's probably for the best. He doesn't do well around strangers, and forcing him to socialize would probably trigger a panic attack. Anthony and I can have a private dinner with him once he's back. I haven't paid a lot of attention to what's going on with all of Anthony's siblings, cousins, aunts, and uncles, but I assume Mama Benton is herding them."

The image of a corgi darting around confused sheep came to mind, making me chuckle, and I had to admit it was perfect. I was glad that Teag was okay with his brother not being there. I knew he loved Conal. It was so unlike the relationship with my brother, which was so bad, I usually claimed to be an only child so I didn't have to explain. I pushed the dark thoughts away.

I finished my soup, nibbled a few crackers, and downed the energy drink. It helped me not feel so jittery, and the memories of the djinn dream were beginning to fade.

"Go back to sleep," Teag urged. "I'm sure Sorren will let us know once he's figured out where the djinn is hiding. You'll want to be ready when we get the chance."

I called Kell and got through this time. "Hey, everything going okay?" I tried not to sound as unnerved as I felt. "I worried when we couldn't reach you."

"We've been doing a lot of editing and dubbing, so I had my phone off. What's wrong?" He's highly intuitive, and I can never slip anything past him.

"That situation with the witch and the djinn is blowing up, and the witch is going after our friends. Please, stay out of town for a couple more days until we get this settled."

He sighed. "I used all the protective items you gave me and warded the hotel room and my car. How about you? Are you safe?"

"As safe as I can be. Sorren, Rowan, and Donnelly are hip-deep in this. I think it's going to be over soon, and I want you out of the line of fire." I know Kell feels guilty sometimes about not being able to help more, but I valued him being an anchor to "normal." And I didn't mind having a valid excuse to take him off the playing field when things got rough. I figured I would tell him about the djinn's attacks once this was done so he didn't worry.

"Please be careful, Cassidy. I love you."

"I promise. Love you too." I ended the call, glad to know he was safe but missing him all the same.

Despite feeling like I had been sleeping all day, I gratefully heeded the suggestion to go back to sleep, hoping that this time when I drifted off, my dreams would be djinn-free.

CHAPTER NINE

"Ron Zimmerman is dead." I looked up from my phone, stunned, and met Teag's eyes as if he could make sense of it. Two days after the djinn's attack, and it looked like the situation was escalating.

"The guy who bought the Grantham mansion?" Teag asked as he and Maggie both came to a standstill.

I nodded. "That was Sorren. He has contacts in surprising places. An ambulance was called to the mansion, and the paramedics found him hanging upside-down from the second-floor balustrade. It's getting written off as accidental since it looks like he tried to climb over the railing, and his foot got stuck when he fell."

"Tried to climb over the railing?" Maggie echoed. "Why would he do that?"

"He wouldn't," I said. "He wouldn't be able to reach the chandelier from there—it would take a tall ladder from the ground floor. I didn't get the impression Zimmerman was suicidal."

"Do you think it was the witch or the djinn?" Teag asked.

I thought for a moment. "My money is on Laroque Shaw. He's angry that Zimmerman bought the house and destroyed the hidden study. Of course, with Zimmerman out of the way, the house will probably end up at auction—unless Shaw intends to buy it himself."

"Do you think Shaw hoped to sucker Zimmerman into a deal like he did with the Granthams and was pissed Zimmerman didn't bite?"

"Maybe. Makes me wonder how many of the old families have a djinn in their closet along with all the skeletons," I replied.

Teag's phone pinged. He glanced at it, and from his expression, I knew it was bad news.

"What?" I asked.

"Remember Stephanie Cochrane—the lady whose husband bought the cursed tapestry? Her housekeeper came and let herself in—not unusual if Stephanie was out and about—and said there was a terrible smell coming from the 'man cave.' The door was locked. She shouted for Stephanie and didn't get an answer." Teag scanned what I guessed was a news article on his phone.

"She called emergency services and they broke down the door. Cochrane was dead—the report says it looked like she had been for 'quite some time.' But it also says that friends reported going out with her just days before, and she was in good spirits," Teag summarized.

"You think Shaw is hurting the people we've helped to make us back off? Or to 'punish' us for interfering?" A chill swept over me.

"I think it sounds likely," Teag replied. "The timing is certainly suspicious. And since the djinn's connection to them was severed, they weren't 'useful' anymore. Shaw may have decided they were more valuable as a warning."

I turned to Maggie. "I hate to ask this, but can you stay in the upstairs apartment for a few days? We'll get whatever shopping list you need and fetch anything from home. But even with the protections on your house, you're safer here. I don't want Shaw to hurt you to get to us."

Maggie's pretty stalwart, but she's also level-headed. "That works for me. I can read and stream movies here as well as there. Thank you."

"Either Shaw isn't very smart, or he thinks he's got aces up his sleeve," I mused. "People in the supernatural community know about Sorren, and they know he protects his own. Shaw might be a powerful witch, but does he really think he can go against a vampire and a necromancer—not to mention several witches—and win?"

Teag shrugged. "Maybe. Some guys inflate their own abilities and minimize everyone else's. He might think that with the djinn along for the ride, he's invincible."

"I'm pretty sure he isn't."

I was even more glad that Kell was out of town and Maggie had agreed to stay upstairs. Shaw sounded like he was out to prove a point and didn't care who got hurt.

My hunch proved true over the next few hours.

My house was thoroughly warded, but that didn't keep a car from catching on fire at the curb just past the end of my protections. Nobody was hurt, and nothing was damaged except someone's Chevrolet, but I took it as a warning even if the police considered it a "faulty battery."

"Someone tried to burn down my rose bushes," Maggie reported when she called me later that night.

"Oh, my God. Did anyone get hurt? What about the building?"

"My neighbor said there was no damage to the building, but I think that's due to your wards. Fortunately, they saw the flames and put the fire out. I lost a couple of bushes, but no one got hurt. There's no way they spontaneously combusted."

I'm sure Maggie was afraid, but if so, she channeled the fear into righteous anger.

"I'll buy you new ones," I promised. "I know that isn't the same, but I'm so sorry."

"Nothing that can't be replaced," Maggie said. "I'm really glad to be in the shop apartment. Catch this guy and call him to account. Avenge my poor bushes."

I promised her we would do just that. When I ended the call, I hugged Baxter for several minutes, needing the comfort.

"Something happen?" Teag came back from the kitchen with a big bowl of fresh popcorn. He's been here enough times that he knows where everything is.

I recounted what Maggie had told me, and Teag listened, frowning with worry. "Do you think Shaw is going after us because, comparatively speaking, we're the weakest of his enemies? Sorren, Donnelly, and Rowan have a lot more firepower, and Father Anne lives on a warded compound with a bunch of warrior priests."

"Maybe." Though I knew we could put up quite a fight despite having less magic than the others. "We're also easier to find. He has to be able to sense the protections, so he's not actually trying to breach them. It's a threat."

We settled in and watched a movie. I'm sure we were both trying not to think about witches or djinns. Even though I wasn't in physical contact with Teag, I didn't need my psychometry to guess his thoughts and worries.

An hour later, Teag's phone rang. I heard Anthony's voice, and I knew from his tone he was upset, but I tried not to eavesdrop.

"I'm pretty sure this is related to one of our cases, not yours," Teag told him after listening for a while. "Once the police and the insurance people are done, go inside, lock the doors, ward the entrance like I showed you, and don't go out again until tomorrow morning. I'll pick you up—my car has more protections than yours."

He listened again, and Anthony's tone sounded upset.

"I know, babe. And I'm so glad you're okay. I'm sorry this spilled over, but sometimes your cases do too. Just make yourself safe and I'll explain everything when I pick you up tomorrow."

I turned away as his voice got quieter and the tone softened. "Yeah. I know. You too. Love you."

He ended the call and pocketed his phone with a heavy sigh.

"More meddling from Shaw? Is Anthony alright?" I asked. Baxter managed to look worried too.

"Our place is pretty heavily warded. But just as Anthony got home, a driver lost control of his car and almost hit Anthony. The car slammed into a fire hydrant, or it would have gone into the wall around our yard. No word on how the driver is. But given the timing, it can't be a coincidence," Teag said.

I'm usually pretty patient, but the attacks lit my fuse. "I'm tired of being a target. Shaw is sending us warnings. The next time, he'll mean business. If we wait for him to bring the fight to us, we won't see him coming. But if we give him a perfect target and draw him out, we play the game on our terms."

He set the popcorn aside. "What are you thinking?"

"I'm the one Shaw has the real grudge against, out of the 'regular' mortals on our team. So, we figure out a way to make it look like I'm vulnerable, and when he makes his move, our team jumps him."

"You want to be bait." Teag's voice went hard, and I saw the tension in his jaw.

"It sounds bad when you put it like that—but yes. That's exactly what I'm suggesting."

"Sorren and the others aren't going to like it."

"Won't know that until we run it past them," I said, too angry not to be a little reckless. "Whether it was Shaw or the Djinn today, he made a pretty good show of telling us he can hurt us and the people we care about. As far as I'm concerned, that's a declaration of war."

I might be strawberry-blond, but that red tint comes with a hot temper when the circumstances are right.

That night, we got Sorren, Rowan, and Donnelly together on a video meeting. Teag and I explained about the attacks over the course of the day.

"I agree that Shaw is trying to force our hand," Sorren said when we finished. I knew how much he hated when bystanders got used as pawns. "He's daring us to declare war."

"We still haven't figured out where he goes to ground," Rowan remarked. "He hasn't been seen around his house in weeks."

"We could play hide-and-seek with him forever, and meanwhile, he'll take potshots at our friends and family. Sooner or later, those will turn deadly," Teag said.

I knew he didn't like my plan, but he's pragmatic and forcing Shaw into the light beat chasing him in the shadows.

"So you want to change the game and give him a target," Donnelly rumbled. "Is that it?"

"Got a better plan?" I shared Teag's reservations. I usually didn't take unnecessary risks, although in our business, that's a relative statement. I don't grandstand, and I don't need glory.

But I meant what I said about not liking our friends and loved ones being drawn into this mess against their will and without the magic to defend themselves. We still weren't entirely sure what Shaw's game was, whether he really thought we would back down and leave him alone if he made threats or if he was tipping his hand to promise vengeance if we continued to pursue him.

The thing was, I didn't trust him to keep his end of a bargain even if we did let him go—which we couldn't after all the people he killed. He would just take advantage of the leeway our "deal" provided and then circle around and attack us anyhow.

His kind were predictable. So I gambled that he expected that of others. Maybe we could get an advantage by doing the unexpected.

"You make a good case," Sorren admitted when I laid out my logic. "Are you sure you weren't a lawyer in a past life?"

"Maybe. I like legal dramas on TV." I kept my tone light, although the subject remained deadly serious.

"What is this plan of yours, and how would we figure in it?" Donnelly rumbled.

"And how do we manage to have him show up for a fight without putting civilians in danger—and ending up in videos on social media," Rowan asked.

"I have to do the appraisal that came in on items for an estate sale in a mansion out on Ashley Road." The street ran near the river and was home to many grand old homes. "So—I go. Apparently alone, at a set time. Of course, you'll already be in position. Shaw takes the bait and figures it's a golden opportunity. And then we jump him."

"There are all kinds of holes in that plan," Teag said.

"It's loose," Sorren objected. "Will there be other people there? Shaw won't hesitate to cause collateral damage."

I shook my head. "No one but us. I've worked with the estate sales company before. I think the owner will work with us if I explain that I've gotten threats and we're trying to draw out the stalker.

"It's not just about what happens inside the house," Donnelly fretted. "You have to get there and go from the car to the house. Shaw could strike before you ever get inside, where we can't protect you."

Rowan frowned as if she was figuring out options. "I could have the coven in place along her route to observe and provide a warning. I'm not sure they could go head-to-head with Shaw, but they certainly have the power to fuck up his plans."

"You're gambling on Shaw wanting to toy with his target instead of just eliminating the problem," Sorren protested. "What makes you think he won't attack from a distance when you show up before we could even intervene?"

I grimaced. "I can't guarantee he won't. But what we've seen of Shaw suggests he's got a colossal ego. Blasting me from a distance without getting to say his villain monologue doesn't seem narcissistic enough for him. I think this has gotten personal for him."

"I think you're right." Donnelly gave an apologetic glance to Sorren. "So far, Shaw has shown himself to be vain and egotistical. He wants to believe that Cassidy on her own doesn't pose a threat."

Rowan gave a crafty smile. "We can work with that. Especially if we are nearby but out of sight."

"What if part of getting there early is having some surprises planted that I can trigger with my wand or the walking stick that won't draw his attention? If I can hold his attention and still defend myself, that gives the rest of you a chance to ambush him. Preferably without destroying everything at the estate sale," I added.

"I can get aerial photos, and we can map this out," Teag said. "We already have the floorplan and layout of the house, although if things go as planned, Shaw never needs to set foot inside."

"It's too risky." For all that Sorren is willing to take big chances himself, he's very protective of Teag and me, sometimes too much for my liking. He says that we break too easily, and he's lost too many friends along the way. I understand, but sometimes I still chafe at his caution.

"So is waiting for Shaw to decide where and when to strike next," Donnelly said.

I figured Donnelly and Sorren had plenty of these arguments over the decades.

"I think we can manage this to reduce the risk," Rowan said carefully. "Archibald is right. Letting Shaw pick the when and where is like Russian roulette. We can't keep Cassidy safe every second or lock her up. This brings Shaw to us, and we handle him."

I liked her phrasing. "Handle" had a very final sound to it.

"I will reserve judgment until I know the full plan." Sorren sounded annoyed. Somehow, pissing off a six-hundred-year-old vampire seemed safer than the alternatives in this case.

"Thank you," I said. "I promise I won't be foolhardy. But we have no idea who else Shaw will target to clean up his loose ends or draw us out. We can't afford to find out the hard way."

I felt guilty about Ron and Stephanie's deaths. Maybe Shaw would have killed them anyway, even if we weren't involved. But I had the feeling that his sadistic streak knew their deaths would hurt us, and he intended to weaponize those feelings against us.

That made me angry, and while I knew I couldn't defeat him one-on-one, I hate bullies, and I wanted to be part of his downfall.

"I'm in," Donnelly said, and Rowan echoed his agreement. "Send us everything you know about the location, and we'll figure out a plan."

That changed what Teag and I were doing for the evening except for the popcorn. We opened our laptops and booted up while Teag made another batch. I turned off the streaming movie in favor of music and brewed a pot of coffee since it was going to be a late night digging into the history of the house I was supposed to visit.

In the old days, rice plantations created vast fortunes. Homes along the Ashley originally fronted the river, not the road, and had their grand entrances facing the water to receive guests who arrived by boat.

Connaster House wasn't as famous as some of its sister plantations that had long ago become historic landmarks and opened their doors to the public. Instead, it had remained in the family, much like the Grantham mansion, passing quietly from one generation to the next.

Unfortunately, grand mansions are expensive to maintain, even with historical status. The newest generation didn't want the burden of upkeep or the responsibility to deal with the plantation's past since the rice that created the family's wealth was farmed by enslaved individuals.

A historic preservation group had purchased the home to maintain as a museum and wanted some but not all of the family possessions. Anything "too modern"—which meant Twentieth Century to present—was tagged for sale, while the older pieces would stay with the house.

Trifles and Folly often gets called in to appraise estate sales. The owners want to validate the provenance of objects, get a fair market value, and ensure the pieces aren't haunted or cursed.

As far as I knew, the Connaster family kept whatever magic it employed under wraps, so I wasn't worried about another secret archive like at the Grantham house. A place without a reputation for haunts or bad luck usually isn't packed with dangerous or spooky objects. Normally, it would be an easy appraisal.

We checked, but the Connasters did not appear to have close ties to the Granthams. That meant Shaw was unlikely to have anticipated a possible showdown there so he would be scrambling for advantage, just like us.

Over the next few hours, we came up with a plan. We needed to get Sorren, Rowan, and Donnelly into the estate without attracting Shaw's notice. That was dicey because we couldn't be positive when Shaw would pick up on my appointment and stake the house out himself. Since Shaw had magic of his own, he was likely to notice if spells were placed nearby.

We decided that Shaw probably wouldn't keep a round-the-clock vigil. That meant Donnelly and Rowan could slip in overnight and set whatever traps they wanted.

I would time my visit to be near sunset. Sorren could use speed and glamour to get to the mansion without alerting Shaw. Teag would accompany me since his magic is largely defensive. Together, we've fought off some pretty heavy hitters. Once Shaw made his move, our allies would swoop in, cutting off his escape.

As plans went, it wasn't too bad given the circumstances. But we all knew that nothing ever goes the way it's supposed to.

"There's still time to change your mind," Sorren said. I knew he was going along with the effort unwillingly, preferring to be part of the assault and therefore in place if anything went wrong.

That didn't reflect a lack of confidence in our abilities. Sorren had been around long enough to lose people he cared about because details didn't work out. I knew he cared about Teag and me more like grandchildren than colleagues, and I appreciated it. But we all had a part to play, and I was done with letting Shaw call the shots.

"Do you think he'll show?" Teag asked as I drove up the long lane toward the mansion.

"Yeah. I think he's spoiling for a fight." I wasn't sure why I felt so certain, but I was unable to shake my impression. "The question is, will he come alone or bring the djinn along?"

Teag considered for a moment. "Honestly? I think he'll come alone. He's overconfident of his own abilities—he's strong but not invincible. And I don't think he'll expect us to have backup because he wouldn't do it that way."

Even alone, Shaw was a threat. We knew he was a powerful witch, but we didn't know his limits. Then again, he had never gone up against us, either individually or together, so he didn't have any idea what we could do.

The Connaster House wasn't as opulent as many of its Ashley Road neighbors, although it definitely qualified as a "mansion." It was a two-story, white wood house with wide porches on both levels and a dormered roof, looking out over a large lawn with lovely gardens. Unlike some of its larger "cousins," the house didn't have barns or other dependencies besides a garage, but I didn't know whether those had disappeared over time or had never been present.

Old houses bear the energy resonance of the lives that have played out on their stage. Even if they aren't actually haunted by ghosts, they can retain emotional stains that make visitors feel edgy or melancholy.

The Connasters had been wealthy but stayed out of politics so they weren't as famous as some of their neighbors. Since the house had been occupied until just lately, it hadn't been turned into a tourist attraction or museum like many of the others on this road. I wondered if Shaw had "business" with the Connasters through the years. If not, this was unfamiliar territory for him and us, making the playing field a little more even.

I had keys to the house, and I knew that Teag had hacked the security cameras so we saw Shaw drive up and hide his car—either he wasn't worried about being seen or didn't think to tamper with the technology. Rowan, Donnelly, and Sorren had their own ways to deal with pesky recordings and obscure their arrival.

My hope was to settle the fight with Shaw outside so that we didn't damage the mansion. I also liked the idea of a wide-open lawn where it was harder to hide weapons.

"Here we go." I opened my car door and left it open as a potential refuge. My athame—the old wooden spoon that had belonged to my grandmother, charged full of strong emotions—was in my left hand. An old dog collar was wrapped around my wrist. In my right hand, I had a walking stick that could channel fire. I had protective amulets and woven braids from Teag that held textile magic, and I hoped they would be enough.

My intuition tingled, telling me that something was not as it seemed. I couldn't pick up anything with my touch magic, but I had learned a long time ago to trust my gut.

"You have gotten in my way." Shaw seemed to appear between one breath and the next.

"Impressive parlor trick." With a shake of my left wrist and the jangle of dog tags, the ghostly form of my late golden retriever, Bo, appeared by my side. Goldens might be lovey, but they're fiercely protective and big enough to make a point. Bo lowered his head, bared his teeth, and growled.

Teag came around to stand slightly behind me, watching my back in case Shaw brought friends. For now, Sorren, Donnelly, and Rowan stayed hidden.

"Why can't you just stay out of my business?" Shaw snapped. "I'll leave you and yours alone. Give you a cut of the deals if that's what you're after. Your family ignored me for years before you came on the scene—and so did your pet fang."

I registered the insult to Sorren but figured he would have the chance to respond in person later.

"Your deal with the Granthams was a private matter. Seems like you and your genie have gone freelance since you lost your meal ticket." I suspected Shaw had a short fuse, and I wanted to provoke him so we could give him a beat down and make him go away.

I didn't think it would really be that easy, but I was angry enough that I was ready for a fight.

The sun sank low, but the security lights lit the lawn and house brightly enough to read a book in their glare. I hoped that gave Sorren a chance to get in position, and provided cover for Rowan and Donnelly to move away from the mansion.

"Your family and your vampire have always been high and mighty, trying to tell everyone else what they could do with their power, making yourselves the law. What I do is none of your business," Shaw spat.

"You killed Ron Zimmerman and Stephanie Cochrane. The Alliance protects Charleston. That makes it our business." I knew if I could just get Shaw monologuing, we could attack as a unit.

"So what if I did? I gave them what they wanted and they weren't grateful. None of those greedy bastards are ever grateful, so eventually I have to put them in their place."

Something felt off. I couldn't place what didn't seem right, but Shaw himself wasn't what I expected.

I leveled my athame at Shaw and had the walking stick for backup. "Give yourself up, stop getting people to sell their souls to you, and stand trial before a Tribunal."

Shaw laughed. "Or what? I didn't come to negotiate. I came to give you a message."

Sorren burst from the darkness beneath a stand of trees, moving too fast to follow. He collided with Shaw and knocked him to the ground, pinning him with undead strength and keeping a hand over the witch's mouth.

A circle of flame ignited around them in the grass, and I saw Rowan had left the shelter of the mansion and entered the battle.

"*Revelare*!" Donnelly commanded, striding down the steps of the mansion like he owned the place. He's a scary guy when he goes full necromancer on someone's ass.

Sorren sat back and pulled his quarry to sit up.

Donnelly's command made the face of the man in Sorren's grip melt and rearrange under a strange purple glow until the shifting ended.

The prisoner looked nothing like Shaw.

"Who are you?" Sorren gave the man a tooth-rattling shake.

In the stark glow of the security lights, it was clear that the only thing the man had in common with Shaw was his height and general build. He was older by a decade, with a gaunt look that suggested too little food and too many other substances.

"Asa Hopkins," the man admitted. "Please don't kill me. He…he made me do it. I'm supposed to give you this." He took out an envelope from his shirt pocket.

"Open it and read it out loud," Sorren said, and I felt certain he was using his vampire compulsion on Hopkins, who complied without arguing.

"This was your last warning. Get out of my way," Hopkins read.

"I guess Shaw didn't feel poetic," Teag quipped with a grim expression.

"Tell us what happened," Sorren commanded.

The rest of us stayed outside the fiery ring, on alert in case Shaw took advantage of Hopkins as a distraction.

"I owed money." Hopkins looked twitchy and terrified. "This guy told me he'd pay off my debts, but I had to do a job for him. He'd put a spell on me so I looked and sounded like him. He said he would send me where I needed to go and tell me what to say. That's all I know."

I looked to Rowan. "Tell him what to say?"

She cocked her head and seemed to look more closely at Hopkins. "There are 'ventriloquist' spells that let a witch speak through another person from a distance. I think Shaw cast a glamour on him and then used him like a magician's dummy to threaten us."

Donnelly nodded. "I can pick up the trace energy of Shaw's magic. I believe she's right."

"So Shaw realized it was a setup?" I asked.

Rowena shrugged. "Maybe. Perhaps he just wanted to hedge his bet. Or he might not be ready for a fight and wanted to stall for time."

"What do we do about him?" Teag nodded toward Hopkins.

Before anyone could answer, the man seized in Sorren's grip, shaking and gasping, frothing at the mouth. Sorren let go and backed away. Hopkins convulsed, and Donnely knelt next to him, placing a hand on the man's chest as the imposter fell still.

"He's dead," Donnelly said. "He was gone before I touched him. I think Shaw set some kind of trigger to avoid leaving a witness."

"I thought something seemed off, but I wasn't sure what was wrong," I admitted. I had been so certain this was the best ploy to catch him. In the back of my mind, I still believed we should try something like this again.

"I sensed Shaw's magic, but it was the glamour, not the real thing," Rowan said.

"By the time I realized the soul was wrong, it was too late," Donnelly said.

Sorren looked to me. "You really did have an appointment to do an appraisal here?"

I nodded. "Yeah. Although the last thing I want to do right now is stay and go through that house."

"I'll get rid of the body," Donnelly volunteered. "Maybe if Sorren and Rowan stay behind, you can still do the appraisal, and we can make sure Shaw doesn't circle around."

"Thank you." I hated that my voice shook, but I'd had my share of battle for the day.

Teag and I made quick work of going through the items the auction house set aside for us. I tagged a few as having bad energy to be cleansed later and dismissed the rest as old but not particularly valuable and neither cursed nor haunted. Teag's touch magic backed up my impressions.

"I'll send them an email. They can bring the pieces that need a cleansing to the shop—those aren't terribly dangerous but shouldn't be in circulation," I told the others, snapping photos of the questionable objects.

"Thanks for everything," I told Rowan and Sorren as they walked Teag and me back to the RAV4.

"All part of the job," Rowan said.

"Goes with the territory," Sorren acknowledged. He looked me in the eye. I'm immune to his glamour except in extreme circumstances, but since he rarely gives me a direct stare, I knew he wanted me to listen. "Be careful. Shaw will strike to kill next time."

"I understand." I appreciated his protectiveness. "Will do."

Even so, Sorren and Rowan followed us back to my house, and I sent them off with a wave as we went inside.

A glance at my watch told me it would be dawn soon. Teag made up a bed for himself on the couch as Baxter ran between us, barking. I had the feeling he was yelling at us for leaving and welcoming us back all at the same time.

"See you later in the morning," I told Teag, who replied with a mock salute.

I thought that the events of the night would keep me awake, but I barely brushed my teeth and changed into my pajamas before I sprawled on the bed with Baxter beside me and fell into an exhausted, dreamless sleep.

CHAPTER TEN

"Shaw's disappeared." Teag turned away from his laptop in annoyance. "He hasn't shown at any of his usual spots—or his house— in several days. His car hasn't moved or been on any traffic cams. There's no activity on his credit card or bank account. No calls made or data used on his cell phone. He's gone dark."

Teag's hacking abilities often crossed into dubious legality. I still remained amazed at his ability to find information, even though I knew his Weaver magic helped him weave random data into answers.

"Can we do a tracking spell?" I brought my cup of coffee over and sat next to Teag.

"I asked Rowan. She tried, but she thinks he's got a deflection charm helping him evade notice. She says he's 'slippery'—as in the magic can't hold onto him long enough to pin down his location."

"Maybe we need to try again to draw him out."

Teag gave me a look. "Whatever you're thinking about doing, I don't like it."

I stared right back at him. "He's dangerous on his own and doubly so working with the djinn. If we pick the time and place for the fight, it's on our terms."

"Didn't we try that once? It didn't work."

"This is different."

Teag sighed. "I'm going to regret asking, but what are you thinking?"

"We check out more of the places we thought the djinn was hiding. Maybe Shaw's with him."

"That's a terrible plan," Teag said, and I could tell he was worried. "We don't know for sure how powerful Shaw is, but he's desperate, so he's not going to hold back. He's made it clear that you're a threat. You've had warnings. He's going to try to kill you the next time."

"I know."

"Cassidy—"

"That means he'll show up this time."

"He's a witch. He can do magic from a distance. We don't know if he's got something that belonged to you as a focus point. He doesn't have to be in sight. You could put yourself at risk—maybe get badly hurt—for nothing."

I had considered the risk. I just didn't have a better idea.

"What's our alternative? Believe me, I'm not crazy about being a target. But how else do you propose to get him to show up? You and Donnelly and Rowan would be watching. I wouldn't be alone. And I'll have my athame and the walking stick and Bo. I won't be defenseless."

"If Shaw has a deflection charm good enough to make him 'slippery' to Rowan's magic, then even Donnelly might not spot him before he can strike," Teag countered.

"If the djinn is close to being strong enough to feed from a disaster, then the clock's ticking. Look at all the harm Shaw and the djinn did just with their 'art sale.' I'm afraid if we wait, they'll get even more powerful and harder to stop—and more people will die."

I hadn't expected Teag to like the idea. I'd even hoped he would come up with something better. From the set of his jaw and deep frown, I knew how much he hated the plan—and I sensed his frustration at not having a better option.

"Have you talked to Rowan and Donnelly? Can Rowan get any help from her coven?"

"I haven't mentioned it to them because I wanted to run it past you first," I admitted. "I know we tried something similar, but I think Shaw is likely to be more desperate now. As for the coven—I don't know. The more witches involved, the more possible it is that Shaw will sense that it's a trap."

"I hate it—but I don't have a better idea, and the longer we wait, the stronger the djinn gets," Teag said, clearly annoyed. "Let's talk it over with Rowan and Donnelly and go from there."

ROWAN AND DONNELLY hated the plan just as much as Teag did—but no one had a better idea.

So I ended up letting myself into the empty office and hoping no one saw how much my hands shook. I had my athame up my sleeve and the antique walking stick clipped to my belt. Bo's dog collar wound around my left wrist, and I took comfort from the jangle of his tags.

Teag, Rowan, and Donnelly watched from several vantage points, hidden by charms to keep Shaw from noticing their magic.

The door swung open at my touch, and I stepped into the musty foyer. The office had been closed after the owner's death and felt cold and empty.

I locked the door behind me, figuring that Shaw would find a way in. I didn't need to be surprised by anyone else. My hand rose to the agate necklace at my throat. Bracelets of silver, onyx, and braided spelled string also held protection. In the pocket of my jeans, I had an ancient agate spindle whirl that amplified my touch magic. My jacket pockets held salt and iron filings, in case Shaw could manipulate ghosts. I'd left my deflection charm at home since this time, we wanted Shaw to find me.

Between one heartbeat and the next, Shaw seemed to appear out of nowhere with a cocky smile I wanted to wipe right off his face. Whatever distraction he had used was a good one since I doubted even he could just "poof" himself from one place to another.

I took a step back into the main foyer. Last night, Rowan had hidden hex bags around the first floor, dormant spells until she triggered them—a bit of insurance. We weren't sure how much effect they would have on Shaw, but we figured they might at least sap his strength.

"We've been looking forward to meeting you." Shaw moved slowly toward me. I saw a spark of blue light in his eyes and realized we had made a big mistake.

We.

Shaw had allowed the djinn to possess him, making him double the adversary we expected.

I jangled Bo's collar and felt the energy shift as a ghostly golden retriever appeared at my side. Bo snarled, baring his teeth. My athame slid down under my sleeve into my hand.

"You've been quite an annoyance." Shaw barely gave Bo a second glance. If he registered that the wooden spoon in my hand was a wand, he clearly didn't see it as a threat. "Should have known when to mind your own business."

"That doesn't run in the family," I replied. "Was the pop-up gallery your idea? Or are you just the body, and the djinn is the brains?"

Poking the bear probably wasn't smart, but I didn't want to stand here and glare at each other all night. I also hoped that if Shaw focused on my smart-ass remarks, he might not notice the hex bags. He had tipped his hand when he became visible, so I hoped Rowan, Teag, and Donnelly knew the game was on.

"My partner says your pain was delicious," Shaw said with a creepy smile. "He wants seconds."

"You can both go to hell." I raised my athame and blasted Shaw with a bolt of power. It took him by surprise, and he dodged—right into Bo's lunge. Bo might be a ghost, but he's got real teeth, and he got a good bite on Shaw's forearm before being shaken loose.

Shaw flung out his hand and sent me tumbling, but I came up in a crouch and promptly fired off a second salvo with my wand. This time my quick reflexes surprised him, and I hit him in the shoulder making him curse and fall back several steps. I didn't know whether being possessed by the djinn would increase his strength, but I knew the bond would eventually weaken and tax his reserves if we could keep him busy long enough—without me getting killed.

Shaw tried to throw me around again, but I dodged as Bo attacked, sinking his teeth into Shaw's thigh. Bo backed off before the witch could strike him. I managed to avoid getting tossed around. I rolled and came up in a different spot, getting in another blast before I threw myself out of the way before Shaw could retaliate.

Hosting the djinn might tire Shaw, but he could borrow the creature's energy. I was on my own and likely to fade faster, so I really hoped my friends showed up soon to back me up.

Come on, come on, I silently urged my witchy friends.

Both doors slammed open at the same time. Donnely stormed in from the front as Rowan swept in from the back, already chanting. Teag followed with the silver net in hand.

That cost Shaw precious seconds of focus. I sent a controlled stream of fire from the walking stick, careful not to set the house on fire.

Shaw screamed and clearly forgot to stop-drop-and-roll. As he flailed, Donnelly and Rowan closed in. Bo circled Shaw, head down, growling.

Donnelly thrust out his hand and clenched his fist, freezing Shaw in place and extinguishing the flames.

"He's possessed by the djinn!" I shouted.

Rowan neared the crescendo, and Teag stepped up, ready to throw the silver net, Shaw screamed. His body arched backward, and his features contorted in agony. I watched in horror as Shaw's body shriveled. Teag lunged forward to cover him with the net, but just before he made contact, a plume of blue light streaked from Shaw's open mouth and vanished through the ceiling.

Shaw's emaciated corpse fell to the floor, looking like he had aged a millennia.

None of us moved for several seconds, frozen in shock. Unsure the danger had passed, we stayed alert, ready to fight at the first sign of threat.

"He's dead." Donnelly relaxed from a fighting stance. "His soul is gone—and so is the djinn."

Rowan finished a binding spell to assure Shaw wasn't suddenly "reanimated." For good measure, Teag kept the body covered with the silver net.

Bo's ghost looked up at me, and I ruffled his ears before he vanished.

I watched Shaw's corpse like he might suddenly jump up and attack, but as moments passed without incident, I finally let myself believe the battle was over. Just in case, I kept my athame trained on the body.

"What happened?" My voice was quiet, although it was just the four of us.

Donnelly moved closer and ran the flat of his hand just above the body from head to hips. "Shaw was using a lot of magic, probably borrowing energy from the djinn. He didn't count on all of us ganging up on him and putting up such a fight. When it became clear he was going to lose, the djinn stole Shaw's remaining magic to give itself enough power to break free and escape."

"The djinn is still out there?" Teag asked.

"Unfortunately, yes," Rowan replied. "We didn't expect the djinn to be here, so we weren't prepared to trap it."

"It's loose—but it's wounded." Donnelly rose from a crouch next to the body. "The djinn lost a lot of energy breaking free. It'll strike easy targets to replenish itself, but we've bought ourselves time. Until the djinn recovers, it won't have the power to cause a disaster. We have an opportunity that we're unlikely to get again."

That meant we needed to find where the djinn went to ground and go after him in his lair while he was weakened. If the creature had the chance to regroup, it would take its vengeance on us and wreak havoc to power up even more.

"What next?" I felt a little shaky now as the adrenaline crashed.

Rowan moved around the space, gathering her hex bags. "We should rest, eat, and go tonight. We don't dare let the djinn have more time."

"I agree," Donnelly said as he and Teag made sure we had left no other evidence behind. As I kept watch, Teag bundled Shaw's body in the silver net. He and Donnelly carried the corpse out the back door and put it in the trunk of Donnelly's Lexus.

Only then did I finally believe Shaw's threat had ended. "I'm not sure anyone will miss him, but we need to get rid of the body," I pointed out.

"I'll take it back to the Briggs Society," Donnelly said. "The remains will be secured so that there's no chance they can be used again." Since he was a necromancer, I took him at his word.

"Take five hours to recover," Donnelly said. "It will take the djinn longer—we dealt it a blow. Then we'll finish this."

Teag looked as tired as I felt. I called Maggie and asked her to close up, letting her know we were hot on the trail of the djinn. I left out Shaw's death so Maggie had plausible deniability in case someone started asking questions.

"Congratulations," she told us. "I'll handle things here. Get your second wind and kick that djinn's ass. You can tell me all about it tomorrow."

BY THE TIME we all gathered to fight the djinn, I not only felt much better—I was furious over the unnecessary deaths and what the creature had put me through. I clung to that anger, letting it overwhelm any remaining fear.

I'd only dealt with the djinn for a short time and felt devastated in its wake. That stirred my pity for the Granthams and those who had been in the demon's thrall much longer. I wanted to make sure no one else shared that experience and make the djinn pay for the harm it had caused.

Especially now that I knew it could feed off happy emotions just as well as sad ones, but found grief and fear to be "tastier." This wasn't about denying a creature the means to survive. Its tastes veered toward cruelty, and in my book, that meant it lost the live-and-let-live free pass to go about its business.

As it turned out, Teag and I were only partially right about where to find the djinn. Sorren and Donnelly were able to track him to the salvage yard behind the defunct gas station we had checked. I guessed that made sense if the creatures not only preferred abandoned places but also ones that were dirty and cluttered.

"He knows we're here," Sorren murmured as we entered the old junkyard.

Rusted chassis and random car parts littered the space. Saplings and weeds grew up between the metal carcasses. The owner had long ago left the rotting hulks to the raccoons and rats.

The site had been listed for sale for years—futile since the listing admitted that remediation was needed to deal with all kinds of chemical leaks. Oil, gasoline, transmission fluid, and God only knew what else had seeped out of the broken vehicles through the years, fouling the land.

That squared with the lore, which said djinn preferred "unclean" places. Since Charleston's cemeteries were hot tourist attractions, they were rarely empty and always meticulously kept. But this salvage yard held poison and secrets.

I walked among the junkers, careful not to touch anything. They all had stories. Some bore the scars of collisions in their twisted steel and shattered glass. Others had been used up and cast off by the side of the road. No telling how many had been repossessed or surrendered from owners who died or grew too old or sick to drive.

The yard's previous owner, "Big Bobby" Baucom, had been a shady character with ties to drugs, gangs, and organized crime. I figured that explained why the salvage yard gave off a skeevy vibe.

Glancing around again at the wrecked vehicles, I wondered how many hid bloodstains and maybe even a body or two locked in trunks.

My touch magic kicked in through the soles of my shoes, picking up powerful and tainted energy. This was a burying yard of a different sort, a cemetery where no one mourned the dead. A sense of gloom pervaded the heaps of scrap metal and tangled steel.

I could usually read a lot about a person from their car.

People spend more of their lives than they realize behind the wheel, under all sorts of circumstances in every mood and season. Excited vacationers, frustrated commuters, lost tourists, and weary salespeople all left their mark on the vehicles' resonance. It might not rival the prime feast of a terrifying dream, but I suspected the residual energy could sustain a hungry djinn for quite a while.

The burned ruin of the owner's house hunkered up front near the misshapen chain link fence. When Baucum died, the property had been caught in legal limbo due to the lack of a will and the needed hazmat cleanup. That probably qualified it as liminal space, a place "between," which would also appeal to the djinn.

"Where do we even begin to look?" I scanned the heaps of metal.

The wind whistled around the wrecks, and the scurrying of small critters put my nervous system on high alert. This was a sniper's paradise, and it was a toss-up as to who was hunting whom.

"Stay close," Donnelly warned. We all carried even more protections than usual: charms, amulets, salt, iron, silver, hex bags, and bracelets made from spell-woven cloth Teag had fashioned. Rowan had spoken wardings over us, and Father Anne blessed us. It would have to do.

Despite bright moonlight and a few still-functioning security lights, a pall hung over the salvage yard. I caught a glimpse of motion out of the corner of my eye and pivoted, unsure whether I saw the shadow of a cloud reflected in old chrome or the silhouette of a creature that could change shape at will.

He's toying with us.

We stood in one of the few open spaces between the office and the first row of junked cars. Teag and I hurried to lay down a salt line as a perimeter while Rowan walked widdershins around the area, reinforcing protections. They might not hold off the djinn, but they would prove useful if he influenced other spirits or creatures.

Teag had his silver throwing knives, part of his martial arts discipline. He was a competition-level fighter, but most of our adversaries weren't vulnerable to his blades. The djinn was, and Teag came prepared.

I had a machete and a shotgun with salt and iron rounds, in addition to my athame and walking stick, and Bo's collar around my left wrist. Rowan, Sorren, and Donnelly might have knives for backup, but their magic and abilities were their best weapons.

Teag unfolded a metal frame from which he hung a piece of material he had woven, about three feet square. I knew he'd been working on it since we recognized the djinn's threat. The yarns had been colored with dyes made from protective plants, spun with the *seithr* magic of ancient Norse *seidrs*. Containment spells and incantations were part of the warp and woof. Binding sigils and runes had been embroidered on top, and the knotted fringe held additional spells.

One thin thread hung below the others—a one-way entrance for a spirit to enter the weaving.

Sorren placed the frame outside the circle and stood beside it, taking a calculated risk to stay outside the area protected by Rowan's magic.

Rowan marked sigils in the dirt and lit candles at the quarters. She started a low chant, and I saw the air sparkle as she raised the same sort of protective dome over us that sheltered us at the Grantham house. Most of her role tonight lay in maintaining the dome against attack. I didn't envy her the task.

My athame was ready in my hand.

"Come out, come out wherever you are," Teag sing-songed in a whisper.

A crash made us all flinch as a stack of three crushed cars fell over. All around the salvage yard, the sound repeated as pile after pile tumbled, and I suspected it was a show of power from the djinn.

Sorren prowled around the outside of our warded dome, lithe and lethal. He's usually so good at hiding his nature as an apex predator that it's easy to forget how dangerous he is. The djinn ignored that warning at his own peril.

The sound of breaking glass and crunching metal made me wheel in alarm. Sorren moved so fast he was difficult to track, but I knew he intended to harry and herd the djinn toward our "outpost." In the glow of the security light, I saw two silhouettes moving faster than human speed and quickly lost track of them among the shadows.

Donnelly's incantation made the hair on the back of my neck rise. A cold wind swept through the salvage yard. Metal trembled as if something beneath the stacks of cars and components struggled to be freed. The air around us dropped from chilly to frigid enough for me to see my breath.

Misty spirits rose from the poisoned ground and the twisted chassis. Animated corpses crawled out of the wreckage. Some might have been killed in accidents, but the wounds borne by others suggested a violent death and secret burial.

"Find it," Donnelly told them. "Bring it to me."

The ghosts flitted off to search for the djinn while the zombies shambled along the narrow pathways to herd it toward us.

Teag and I stood ready to protect Donnelly and Rowan so that their magic wasn't interrupted. We weren't as bulletproof as Sorren, so we didn't dare chase the djinn through the salvage yard, and our magic worked differently, better one-on-one. Sorren might not need our protection, but Donnelly and Rowan were deep into their spells, vulnerable if the djinn found a way to breach the dome. Teag and I wouldn't let that happen.

I wondered how much Sorren and Donnelly had discussed strategy because the vampire incorporated the extra help from the ghosts and zombies while taking charge of the direction. Vampires are speedy, so he darted in one direction and then the next, hemming the djinn into the path he wanted, using the slower spirits and zombies to keep the djinn from straying.

The djinn hurled pieces of cars at Sorren and the zombies. Quarter panels, wheels, and fenders flew through the air and crashed to the ground. The creature threw some debris our way, forcing Rowan to send more energy to the protective dome.

I watched and waited for an opening. Bo's ghost prowled the confines of the dome, letting everyone know he was on the job. I alternated salvos of fire and force whenever the djinn came into range.

Then Sorren ran at the djinn directly, tackling him. They struggled, equally matched, tossing each other around like rag dolls. I gasped, knowing that despite being immortal, Sorren still felt pain. The impact from his body hitting the old wrecks made me fear for his safety.

Rowan couldn't keep the dome strong all night, no matter how long Sorren could battle the djinn or Donnelly could marshal his undead forces. The strain showed on her face, and now and again, she wobbled on her feet. Teag sent his energy into the fabric trap in an attempt to lure the djinn closer. So far, the djinn kept his distance, and whatever damage he might have taken from killing Shaw had not made the creature a less formidable opponent.

Sorren rose from where he had been thrown, bleeding from a gash on his forehead. His torn and bloody clothing made it clear the djinn's attacks posed him a threat. Getting impaled through the heart with a scrap of steel or decapitated by a sharp-edge piece of wreckage would cause damage even Donnelly could not heal.

We couldn't maintain the stalemate forever. That spawned a reckless idea, crazy and daring, that might just bring the battle to a close.

I saw the djinn hurl Sorren into the side of a bus and advance on him with a piece of rebar held like a lance.

"Cover me!" I yelled to Teag, and I stepped outside the protective circle.

"Cassidy!" Teag shouted, too late.

I grabbed the blank tapestry he had woven with one hand while the other still held the walking stick; the athame was tucked into my sleeve. Making contact with the fabric, my touch magic flared to full strength, picking up on Teag's resonance, the worry that had gone into weaving the piece, and his hope that we would all come through the battle safely.

Come and get me, I thought at the djinn, raising my head in defiance as I still kept contact with the tapestry.

Now that its prize was within reach, the djinn reached me in a blur of motion and laid a hand on my shoulder.

His magic warred with my protective amulets and the pull of the tapestry as I fought to retain control. The djinn clearly intended to possess me, and I didn't know how long my will or my amulets could hold out or whether I could somehow manage to force him into the woven cloth.

Bridging the space between the djinn and the tapestry put me in a dangerous position, but I couldn't let my friends down.

I heard its gloating, inhuman voice in my mind, taunting me with threats and horrible promises. I knew my will alone wouldn't suffice, but I had no intention of dying or becoming the djinn's host.

We will work miracles together, a voice, rough as snakeskin, vowed.

I didn't waste the psychic breath to respond, keeping my mental shields up as strong as I could make them, hoping that this gambit worked, silently apologizing to Kell in case I badly miscalculated.

Keeping a tight grip on the tapestry, with the djinn's hand still clamped on my shoulder, I brought the walking stick up between us.

I pushed the tip against the djinn's ribs and willed the fire into the creature's body, hoping I didn't incinerate myself along with it.

The djinn screamed.

I fought hard, struggling to keep the monster from possessing me. With magic fire consuming it from within, the creature had one escape —fleeing into the tapestry.

I felt his passage like fire in my blood and blisters on my skin as the djinn tore loose and hurled its essence into the nearest vessel that could contain it.

Teag, Donnelly, and Rowan suddenly gathered around me as they chanted and worked the spells necessary to bind the djinn to its new prison.

No longer essential to the capture, I sank to the ground. I felt utterly drained, my psychic senses scraped raw, skin heated from the too-close flame.

Strong arms caught me before I hit the ground. "What the hell were you thinking, Cassidy?" Sorren's tone was harsh, but worry warred with fear in his gray eyes.

"He was going to kill you," I whispered, finding even that to require monumental effort. "Couldn't let that happen."

"Archibald!" Sorren shouted.

I felt like I was floating, unencumbered by my body, no longer afraid. No threat loomed, and I couldn't quite remember why that seemed strange.

Donnelly's face suddenly filled my vision, bushy brows like thunderclouds. "I've got you," he rumbled, and the same familiar power that had led me from the nightmare vision once again enveloped something deep inside, anchoring me and bringing me back to myself.

I clung to his presence like a lifeline, and it enfolded me. It felt like being wrapped in a warm cloak and walked to safety in the darkness. Then I was alone in my own skin, all traces of an intruder gone, overwhelmed and exhausted as my eyes fluttered shut.

"Is she—" Teag's voice sounded far away.

"She'll be fine," Donnelly said, but I knew he wasn't talking to me. "She channeled a huge amount of power, and it's going to leave her soul burned for a few days, but Rowan and I can ease that and speed the healing."

"She was protecting me."

Even half-asleep, I heard the guilt in Sorren's voice.

"Of course she was," Donnelly said. "What did you expect?"

They might have continued to quibble, but I sank into a deep, dreamless sleep.

I WOKE ON MY COUCH—AGAIN. This was becoming a habit.

"I'm not a damsel in distress," I grumbled, although I couldn't quite remember why I felt like I'd just run a marathon while drunk. Baxter was lying next to me, and he wagged and snuggled once he saw me wake up.

"Of course you're not," Teag assured me. "You're a badass hero who makes questionable choices about attacking one immortal creature to save another."

"It sounds bad when you say it like that," I sulked.

"You were magnificent," Sorren added, "even if you terrified all of us. Thank you."

Bits and pieces came back to me. The fight at the salvage yard. Ghosts, zombies, and the djinn. Sorren, bleeding and in danger. Teag's tapestry, and the feeling like I was burning alive from inside.

"Drink this." Teag helped me sit and pushed a mug of tea into my hands. "Rowan made it before she left. Says it will help 'realign your energy streams,' whatever that means."

"How do you feel?" Donnelly shouldered past Teag to get a closer look. He put a hand on my forehead, but I somehow knew he was sensing my life energy, not just checking for a fever.

"Wobbly," I confessed. "Scorched." I looked down at my hands and arms, but the skin was unblistered.

"When you feel better, we're going to talk about how you did that." Donnelly drew back with a look that judged me satisfactory.

"Did what?" Parts of what happened still seemed a bit hazy. The tea soothed my throat and felt like a balm.

"You were able to use the emotional resonance from the walking stick not just for self-defense as usual, but you channeled the fire so tightly you burned the djinn from inside. How did you do that?"

"Beats me." I retreated to my tea once more as I struggled to recall. I saw fragments of the fight, of Sorren being hurt and the djinn advancing with the rebar, terror as his ugly gray face loomed close to mine—and then fire.

"Rowan says there's no lasting physical damage, and I detect no psychic or soul harm," Donnelly went on. "You'll feel drained for a while, probably have headaches, but all things considered, not bad compared to what could have been."

"I called Kell and gave him a short version—he's on his way," Teag said.

I vaguely remembered that Kell was out of town, but not where he was. "Was I out long?"

"Nearly the whole day," Teag replied.

"Thank you." I looked up to see Sorren, who was remarkably

undamaged. Vampires healed fast. "It was a reckless, dangerous thing to do—and it worked. I wouldn't have forgiven myself if it hadn't."

"You're welcome." Sorren's put himself on the line for us more times than I could count. Returning the favor didn't seem that extreme. "The djinn?"

"You trapped him in the tapestry," Teag said. "Donnelly and Rowan sealed him inside, and we locked it in an iron containment box."

"The Briggs Society has yet another new piece of 'artwork,'" Donnelly remarked. "Pity we can't display any of the new acquisitions," he added in a dry tone.

"So it's over?" Tired as I felt, I couldn't help a flare of optimism that we could close this case once and for all.

"Shaw is dead, and the djinn is captured," Sorren replied. "Teag's going to follow up on any other tapestries sold by the rogue gallery, and Moradi will keep an ear to the ground, but there won't be a witch or a djinn feeding off those items or sending them energy. They'll go dormant, and we can collect them as they come to light."

I looked up at Teag. "No bruises for the wedding?"

He gave me a tired smile and shook his head. "I'm tired from the magic, but it's nothing some sleep and food won't cure."

"Good," I mumbled. "Didn't want to explain that."

"Go back to sleep, Cassidy." Teag laughed. "I'll stay with you until Kell gets here."

I drifted off, hearing the voices of my friends in the background, Baxter next to me, and the djinn gone. For the first time in weeks, I slept without dreaming.

CHAPTER ELEVEN

"Any day that has afternoon tea is a very good day," Teag proclaimed as we took our seats.

Today was "Give Teag An Amazing Bachelor Party Day," and we had an agenda. The party kicked off with an early afternoon tea at one of the city's swankier hotels. Teag has a sweet tooth, and he fell in love with the whole British concept of high tea when he and Anthony took a trip to England.

"How can those little sandwiches fill you up?" He stared at the tiered serving plate in wonder. "But they do! I swear it's magic."

"I like the ham salad ones." I plucked another from the middle dish.

"Save the pimento cheese ones for me." Maggie helped herself to one of the little crustless triangles.

"I'm partial to the ham and brie," Kell confessed.

"That means more of the egg salad for me!" Teag crowed.

We washed down the tea sandwiches with plenty of Earl Gray and a couple of Mimosas, then finished off with new tiers of scones, tarts, macarons, petit-fours, tiny cakes, and other confections.

The tea room was busy at midday, with a décor awash in colors and patterns—chintz curtains, starched white tablecloths, mismatched floral cups and saucers, and shiny silver settings. Commemorative plates in gold brackets contrasted with the "country garden" wallpaper, and the oil portraits of nineteenth-century aristocrats made it feel like we had stepped into *Downton Abbey*.

"I think you've watched too much BBC," Kell teased at Teag's spirited recap of a plotline in the show.

Teag drew in a breath as if scandalized. "There's no such thing!" he mock-protested.

We bantered about the tea cakes that contestants had made on the baking show through the years and compared notes on the other English series we had recently watched. Teag wasn't the only one who was a bit of an Anglophile. Since Kell and I had recently visited the same castle where Teag and Anthony had gone, we regaled Maggie with details and plotted how to get her across the pond for a visit of her own.

For a weekday afternoon, the tea room was surprisingly busy. Taking the time for such a charming indulgence is the sort of thing people talk themselves out of doing, so it seemed like a perfect way to begin Teag's special day. And to my relief, nothing in the tea room appeared to be haunted.

"What's next?" Teag asked as I settled the bill, and we tumbled out into the street.

"You'll have to wait and see," I joked with a wink to Maggie, my co-conspirator.

Kell shrugged. "Don't look at me—I'm just here for the food."

Keeping the group small made planning easier. I hired a limo to chauffeur us around so we could get a little tipsy. It was Kell, me, Maggie, and Teag since Anthony had gone on a harbor cruise with his brothers and work colleagues. They were planning scotch, cigars, and imported cheeses. Teag assured me he liked our itinerary better.

After eating our fill at the tea room, we had an all-day pass at the art cinema, which was running a marathon of classic movies from the 1930s and 1940s, one of Teag's guilty pleasures. We hit the concession booth like kids with Christmas money and loaded up on popcorn, drinks, and candy, then carried our haul into the small theater and got prime seats. Even though we couldn't stay for the whole marathon, we had time to watch a couple of movies before our next stop.

"I love the rom-coms from this period," Teag said after he swallowed a mouthful of popcorn. "Everyone's so elegantly dressed, and the dialogue's witty. You'd never know times were hard in real life. Hollywood served up glamor galore to make people forget their troubles."

We had the theater to ourselves, so we oohed over the fancy clothing and elaborate ballroom sequences, enjoying the feel-good vibe.

By then, it was time for drinks and dinner at Teag's favorite restaurant, a cozy little place that served up New Orleans cuisine right, all the way down to the beignets. A live jazz trio made the meal more festive.

"The food is awesome, the Sazaracs are authentic, and you know how much I love jazz," Teag gushed. While it seemed like we had been eating all day, we'd managed to save room for crab étouffée over dirty rice, gumbo, jambalaya, and hush puppies, served family style. And of course, a mound of perfectly puffed beignets generously dusted with powdered sugar along with chicory coffee.

Next was the concert. The local music venue was perfect for the indie band Teag had loved for a long time, from before they cut their first album. The band was a regional favorite even though they hadn't broken out to national fame, which made them feel like a best-kept secret.

I'd called in a favor to get our gang front-row seats and a backstage pass to meet the band. Teag's pass dangled from a VIP lanyard, and the giddy smile and star-struck look in his eyes made all the effort worth it.

"Best bachelor party ever!" Teag proclaimed as we left the concert. He was decked out in a band T-shirt with a swag bag my co-conspirators had put together for him that included lots of merch as well as his favorite candy and some airline bottles of flavored vodka, just because.

"I can't believe we got to meet them." Teag adorably fanboyed over his favorites. "I met them a long time ago when they were just starting out, playing little clubs, but they're a lot better known now."

"I'm glad it worked out." I still felt a little high on endorphins from good music and a crowd that made up in enthusiasm what they might have lacked in not being stadium-sized.

After the concert was officially over, the warm-up band returned and the crowd moved to the lobby for a few hours of dancing along with a cash bar. We should have been sleepy from good food and stiff drinks, but we managed to storm the dance floor, partying like I hadn't since my college days.

All night we snapped photos, taking advantage of every selfie wall to document the evening.

"Okay, now one of you and Kell." Teag gestured for us to stand in front of a mural on one side of the lobby. "Now one with Maggie." He snapped the photo. "Let's get all of us this time!" I envied his ability to hold the phone and take the picture with long fingers.

"Do you have any room left on your phone?" I laughed as we moved away to let another group take our place.

"Pictures or it didn't happen!" he replied with a wide grin.

Teag and Anthony were texting each other throughout their parties, like it was a competition to see who could have the most fun.

Exhaustion and a hangover were worth the pure joy on Teag's face as we danced, making a big circle like a bunch of teenagers at prom. When the bar announced last call, and the band played its encore, we tumbled out to the street with the other guests, happy and a little tipsy.

The limo took us back to my house, which was already set up for an epic sleepover. Baxter yipped and wiggled to be the center of attention, greeting us at the door.

"Hi, Bax!" I picked him up and lifted him to eye level. "Don't worry—we brought the party to you, and there will be snacks!" Bax ran to the others in turn, demanding his greeting.

"Let's get comfy, and then there is even *more* food and a pitcher of Hurricanes because too much is not enough," I announced.

After we changed out of our party clothes into pajamas, we crashed in the living room on pillows and blankets to binge the baking show and munch out on chips, dip, homemade pimento cheese spread, and crackers.

Bax hopped from lap to lap, begging treats. We had all seen this season of the show more than once, so we called out tips to the partici-pants like they could hear our warnings.

"It's under-baked," Maggie cautioned one of the bakers.

"And that mirror glaze isn't smooth enough," Teag added. "You're not going to get a handshake."

We crashed on the couch, chairs, and floor like teenagers, and when I woke, it was morning, and the screen was frozen on the "Are you still watching?" prompt. Bax licked my nose to let me know he wanted to be fed.

Kell and I got up early to start cooking, and Maggie claimed the first shower.

"Last night I'd have said I would never be hungry again, but is that bacon I smell?" Teag wandered into the kitchen looking adorably rumpled. Bax was underfoot, hoping we would drop food.

"Bacon, link sausage, Belgian waffles, peach compote, fresh coffee, and Mimosas—if you dare," I told him. Kell and I loved to make indulgent breakfasts on weekends, so this was just scaling up a routine we had perfected.

"This has all been amazing," Teag said. "Thank you all so much. It's absolutely perfect."

I grinned because Teag and I have been through a lot together, and he deserves the best. "Hey, it's a once-in-a-lifetime occasion. Gotta do it right."

Maggie finished her shower and was the last to shuffle into the kitchen and join us, hair damp and still bleary-eyed. We drained the first pot of coffee, and Kell made another. I asked Teag about honey-moon plans.

"We're going back to the castle, the one where Anthony and I took my birthday trip to visit," Teag said enthusiastically around a mouthful of waffle. "The town is adorable, and everything we ate there, from the castle dining room to the pub in the town, was fantastic. I'm hoping that we don't solve any mysteries this time, and we can just relax."

"Good luck with that." I laughed. "Kell and I had a great time when we visited and nearly got carried off by the Fae. I hope your trip stays a lot quieter."

His phone chirped, and Teag looked at his messages. "That's Anthony. He says they had a great evening, got in really late, and he won five hundred bucks at poker. He says he's also going to stop at his parents' house for a shower and fresh clothes so I don't have to smell cigar on him."

"Don't forget the mouthwash," he said aloud as he returned the text. "I don't kiss ashtrays."

"Oh, harsh," I teased.

"It's the truth," Teag replied. "Start as you mean to go on, my grandmother always said. I don't mind him enjoying his smokes once in a while, but the smell makes me want to puke, which is decidedly *un*sexy."

Once we polished off the waffles and the second pot of coffee, Teag excused himself to get a shower, and Maggie helped tidy the kitchen. Bax got a few nibbles, which made him happy.

"Thanks again for everything," Teag returned with towel-damp hair and fresh clothes. "That was the most perfect party I could have ever imagined."

"We had fun dreaming up what to do." I shared a conspiratorial wink with Maggie.

"I didn't do the planning—I was just along as the wingman," Kell mock-protested.

Teag gave us all sleepy, hungover hugs. "Doesn't matter. It was still an amazing night. You're the best."

He took a rideshare home, and Maggie followed shortly after, leaving Kell, Bax, and me on our own.

I glanced around at the completely trashed living room and sighed. "I guess the bigger the mess, the better the party, right?"

Kell laughed. "Sounds right to me. And that was a pretty fantastic bachelor party. Much better than the few I've been to."

"Even though no one jumped out of a cake?" I teased.

He wrinkled his nose. "Ew. I don't think anyone's done that in fifty years except in movies. But it definitely beat going to a strip club or spending a weekend in Vegas that no one remembers."

I was extremely pleased that Teag was happy with the surprises

Maggie and I cooked up. We'd been taking notes for a while on things he said he enjoyed doing or wanted to do and then put our heads together to see how many of them we could check off in a single day. I didn't doubt that Anthony had a nice time with his brothers and friends, but I was convinced we threw the better party.

We showered and crashed on the couch with Baxter, happily exhausted. Kell's big video project had finally wrapped up well, and he had declared it worth the over-the-top effort. I was still trying to convince myself that we had seen the end of the djinn and that his century of terrorizing Charleston was at an end.

When my phone rang and I saw Sorren's number, I felt my heart in my throat. "Is everything okay?"

Sorren chuckled. "Only good news, I promise." Since it was light outside, I figured he was calling from the safety of his day crypt.

"Donnelly went back to confirm that the djinn is neutralized—at least for now, and probably for a long while. Donnelly put the djinn's remains in a lead and silver sarcophagus lined with salt, so it's going to have difficulty tapping into anyone's emotions."

"Good." I breathed a little easier knowing the creature wouldn't be coming back to track us down anytime soon.

"How's everyone doing? I have a few hangover remedy recipes from my time as a man-about-town back in Antwerp," Sorren teased.

I wasn't sure I even wanted to know about medieval cures.

"We actually did pretty well at having a great time without over-doing it." I was rather proud that none of us had to break out dark glasses or any hair of the dog. "Thank you again for what you did fighting the djinn. The outcome would have been very different without your help."

"You're most welcome. That's why I'm here."

"Are you ready for the wedding?" I was done talking about the djinn now that the danger was past.

"Looking forward to it," Sorren replied. "I'll see you then, if not before."

"Problems?" Kell asked after I hung up since he had only heard half of the conversation.

I shook my head. "No. Just Sorren calling with a wrap-up. I'm crossing my fingers and toes that everything remains totally boring between now and the wedding."

"I think we're overdue for a little bit of 'boring.'" Kell pulled me close.

∾

To my relief, the next week was as uneventful as we ever get. We cleansed four haunted items from an estate sale, un-hexed a locket brought in for appraisal, and tied up as many loose ends as possible for Teag to take a couple of weeks off.

When the time came for the ceremony at the St. Expeditus compound—which Teag kept calling the "pre-wedding wedding"—I secretly shared his jitters, although I was trying to be calm for his sake.

"You've got this," I assured him as I straightened his bow tie. "The only thing that matters is that you and Anthony will be officially married, blessed, and protected. It's all good."

"I know," Teag said, but I could tell he was still nervous. "I just want everything to go right."

"It will. And even if there's a glitch, no one will notice. Just make googly eyes at your boy and tie the knot."

He leaned in and gave me a kiss on the cheek. "Thanks, Cassidy."

I hugged him tight. "Go get hitched."

The chapel at the compound was smaller than a regular church since it was intended to serve the holy order's members and not the public. Its soaring hammerbeam ceiling and beautiful woodwork suggested transcendence without the need for ornate decoration. I found it calming and contemplative.

The compound and the chapel were warded against evil. At Teag's request, no salt or ghost protections had been made so my spectral ancestor Dante could attend. Sorren looked impeccable in a dark suit. Donnelly's choice of tails reinforced the impression he had just wandered away from a Victorian fete.

"Everyone cleans up well," Beckford Pendlewood murmured, standing beside me, holding hands with his partner, Logan.

"I could say the same about you two. How are things?"

Beck had given up his magic and inheritance as the head of one of the Caribbean witch dynasties to help save the world. That had earned him powerful enemies, which is why he and Logan remained in what amounted to supernatural WITSEC.

Beck shrugged, then flashed a smile at Logan and raised their joined hands. "Pretty good, considering. They take good care of us, and we're getting better at translating old documents and helping with the archive. It's…peaceful."

"I'm glad it worked out."

Kell continued talking to Beck and Logan while I looked around as guests filled the small sanctuary. Rowan sat with our medium friend, Alicia Peters. Lucinda Walker, a powerful Voudon mambo, chatted with root workers Mrs. Teller and her daughter, Niella.

Most of the same people would attend the "mundane" wedding a few days from now or at least join us for the reception. But tonight, our friends with supernatural abilities gathered to convey protection and blessings on Teag and Anthony by calling on a variety of traditions that might raise eyebrows among those outside of our community.

At the other wedding, I would stand with Teag as his "best person," and Anthony would have one of his brothers. Tonight, they stood at the front alone, with only Father Anne on the small dais.

Candles flickered all around the small chapel, and outdoor lights made the stained glass glow despite it being nighttime. The images, if anyone looked closely, were of St. Expeditus hunting monsters. Incense hung heavy in the air. An *a cappella* quartet intoned blessings and wardings in a Latin Gregorian chant. I couldn't shake the feeling that I'd been transported hundreds of years into the past and figured Sorren and Donnelly felt right at home.

Father Anne was her usual ebullient self, with purple spiked hair and her Doc Marten boots peeking from beneath her cassock. The wedding at the Marina would be simple and modern. Here, the ceremony drew on some of the oldest traditions within the lore, many of which had been largely forgotten over time.

Father Anne walked widdershins around Teag and Anthony three times and then reversed course three more, swinging a censer to the quarters as she went. She sprinkled them with holy water and lit a pillar candle on a small plinth between them. Then the choir stopped, and Father Anne withdrew a cream-colored cloth sash shot through with silver threads that I knew Teag had woven especially for the handfasting.

"Teag Logan—please give me your hand." Teag reached out, and Father Anne used an ornate silver dagger to draw and release a drop of blood from Teag's index finger over the candle. She did the same for Anthony.

"Please join hands," Father Anne instructed.

Teag and Anthony raised their right hands and clasped them together.

"Heart to heart, mind to mind, soul to soul." Father Anne wound the sash around their joined hands. "By love and will and faith you are joined in the sight of these witnesses and the eternal powers. May you be each other's shelter from the storm, sustenance in trying times, refreshment when hope is parched, and constant faithful companions."

Father Anne laid a hand on both men's shoulders. "By the power vested in me by the state of South Carolina, you are wed. You may share a kiss."

Fingers laced together and hands bound with the sash, Teag and Anthony leaned forward to kiss as the choir sang. They walked back down the small center aisle smiling broadly. The rest of us filed out behind them as Father Anne unwound the wardings and snuffed the candles.

One of the St. Expeditus monks led us across a lawn to the compound's dining hall, where a cozy reception awaited. We all clustered around Teag and Anthony for hugs and handshakes, congratulating them as they beamed.

"Did you see Dante? He was in the back." I'd noticed the ghost made a quiet entrance and early exit.

"I did," Teag replied. "I'm glad he could make it."

The simple spread of coffee and cookies from the compound's bakery was the perfect chance for us to share a more intimate celebration among friends. We lingered, nibbling at the sweets and savoring the excellent brew—roasted at the monastery. It felt like a private family gathering, and that's exactly what it was, for our strange little found family bound by everything but blood.

"This means the ceremony at the marina should be a cakewalk," Maggie joked as Teag and Anthony shared cookies.

"We'll already be married, but we still have to put on a good show for the relatives," Anthony said. "And Teag and I have a surprise for the first dance."

I knew they'd worked something up, but even I hadn't seen what they were planning, and I couldn't wait to find out.

The party gradually wound down and the guests said their good-byes. I knew we would see most of them at the marina, so Kell and I took extra time with those who couldn't attend that ceremony, like Beck and Logan. Eventually, the dining hall emptied. Kell and I were among the last to leave as we strolled arm-in-arm back to our car.

"Nice ceremony." Kell pulled me tighter against him. "I've been to all kinds of weddings, from Wiccan handfastings to Catholic high mass, and that was the most 'transcendent' version I can recall."

I looked at him, questioning. "Most transcendent? I'm not sure I follow."

Kell seemed to search for the right words. "The whole point with ceremonies is to carve out a special moment in time. Sometimes, they also create the feeling that the veil between this realm and the next is thin, a place where anything can happen. The high ceilings, pretty artwork, and style of music also play on psychology to invoke grandeur, something bigger than ourselves. So…transcendent."

I thought about it for a moment and how what we had just witnessed compared to the average wedding I'd been to, whether or not it was held in a religious space.

"You're right. And I'm sure that was intentional. It felt safe and protected like old power was wrapping around us and them," I agreed.

"And while the marina wedding will be pretty in its way, this ceremony felt sacramental."

He nodded. "Good word. Exactly. I understand why the style wouldn't be for everyone and why our 'gang' would appreciate that more than maybe other folks might."

We got in the car and Kell drove toward home. "Did the presents arrive?"

I nodded. "I got the confirmations. Two Oyster transit passes, two National Museum passes, and two round-trip Eurostar tickets for London to Belgium."

Kell and I went together on the gift, looking ahead to their honeymoon trip to England. I decided that it was better to skip the surprise and make sure it was something Teag and Anthony really wanted. The passes would make it easy to get around and visit a wide variety of museums. I also knew that Teag had always been curious about Belgium since that was where Sorren had lived when he was mortal.

"Sorren still goes back to Belgium fairly often, doesn't he?" Kell asked as if he guessed my thoughts.

"He has other shops like Trifles and Folly in a lot of cities, including one in Antwerp. So I'm sure he could give Teag plenty of tips on what to see."

"Do you know what else people are giving?"

"I've heard from a few folks who didn't want to duplicate. Sorren is giving them a framed piece of antique Belgian lace, which will definitely appeal to Teag as a weaver. Chuck and Robert Pettis are giving a non-haunted antique mantle clock. Travis and Brent picked out some holiday serving pieces from a place near Pittsburgh that specialized in hammered metal art. Mrs. Teller and Niella are giving sweetgrass baskets. Maggie saw Teag eying an antique samovar in the shop and bought it for them. Donnelly has a vintage Art Deco vase—knowing Archibald, it's probably Lalique." I rattled off the gifts I knew about.

"That's just from some of the folks on our side of the aisle. Given who the Bentons are, I imagine their guests will be generous, if not quite as…inventive."

"Did the wedding planner go along with the attendee gift idea?" Kell sounded amused.

"Kim thought it was lovely. She'll have one at every place setting." Teag had suggested 'sachet' bags that were actually a mix of protective flowers, herbs, and gem chips that would both look nice and protect the attendees and the venue.

"Do you think she suspects what they really are?"

I shook my head. "Doubtful. It's a little 'New Age-y' for the circles the Bentons run in. Sometimes it's just simpler to let people take things at face value."

My cousin Simon has a friend who is a bruja and owns a botanica in Myrtle Beach. She had been happy when Teag placed the order to create the 'favors' and knew us well enough to make sure the bags provided pleasant—but potent—protection with a touch of magic.

"I'm sure it will be beautiful," Kell said.

Neither of us drew any connections between their wedding plans and our relationship. Kell and I were still fairly new as a couple, even though we'd been dating for a while now, and Kell had mostly moved in with me, keeping his apartment as an office.

Occasionally we joked "someday, when" about weddings, more so lately with all the talk about Teag and Anthony's plans. Neither of us took the conversation to the next level, even though everything felt comfortable and awesome between us. My intuition told me that we weren't quite ready yet, and there was no need to rush.

What mattered was that I felt safe and loved with Kell, and he always had my back. We were best friends as well as lovers, and being together just seemed right. That was good enough for now.

CHAPTER TWELVE

"I never even knew this place existed." Maggie took a sip of champagne.

"Neither did I. It's amazing." I did a slow turn, taking in the big space where the wedding and reception would take place in a few hours.

The Marina Club provided a study in understated elegance. Floor-to-ceiling windows looked out on Charleston Harbor, with blue water dotted by white sailboats. Swagged strands of twinkle lights served as curtains. Come nightfall, the lights would be released to hang down over the dark glass.

"Do you think the cake tastes as good as it looks?" she asked.

"I sure hope so."

Real flowers adorned the four-tiered white cake that sat in a place of honor. The tables were covered in navy blue with arrangements of greens in clear vases—bells of Ireland, ferns, and eucalyptus—illuminated by white faerie lights amid golden glass stones. Gold ribbons in bows tied the look together and kept with the blue/green/gold theme Teag and Anthony had chosen.

In one corner, a jazz trio was setting up to play for the reception.

Across the room, the DJ was ready with a playlist for the pre-event time and ceremony. Bartenders prepared for the crowd at several stations. A table for gifts in the back of the room had an attendant to make sure all parcels were checked in and the givers duly noted.

Now and then I caught a whiff of the dried flowers and spices in the protective hex bags at each place setting, dark green tulle tied with gold thread next to gilt-edged white china place settings and crystal goblets.

Kell tapped my shoulder. "They want to go over the ceremony, and they need you up front."

I excused myself and headed toward where Teag, Anthony, and Anthony's brother Landon stood with Father Anne.

For this occasion, Father Anne tamed her spiked hair into a pink-streaked pompadour and traded her Doc Martens for black flats. Teag and Anthony looked amazing in their tuxedos, as did Landon. I wore a midnight-hued satin pantsuit with tuxedo lapels and matching heels that weren't too high to enjoy dancing afterward. Teag's blue bow tie matched my ribbon choker necklace. Anthony's tie was green to match the pocket square of his best man.

Father Anne called the four of us into an alcove for Teag and Anthony to sign the marriage license while Landon and I witnessed.

"Congrats! You're married! The rest is just for show," she told us. "Try to relax and enjoy the party. I'll go get in place, and when the music starts, that's your cue."

The DJ played "Marry Me" by Train. The four of us walked at a dignified pace from behind the curtained preparation area to the front of the ballroom. In the time we had been behind the curtain, the room had filled. Twinkle lights glowed in every direction. I spotted both a photographer and a videographer. Maybe I looked nervous; Kell flashed an encouraging smile, and I gave him one in return.

I was honored to be Teag's "best person." Even though we had seen Teag and Anthony make their vows in a very different kind of ceremony just a few days ago, it didn't detract from the emotion watching those two repeat their promises and exchange rings. I was so happy that I probably grinned like a loon.

"I now pronounce you wed. Congratulations!" Father Anne concluded the simple, contemporary ceremony.

Teag and Anthony exchanged a chaste kiss, then sashayed down from the dais for their wedding dance as the DJ switched to the Glenn Miller standard, "In the Mood."

No one expected the two of them to burst into an energetic jitterbug, perfectly choreographed and joyously executed. An audience I expected to be quiet as a golf tournament erupted into clapping and cheers at the flawless moves. When the song ended, Teag and Anthony took a bow and got a standing ovation.

"We'll be back with more music after dinner," the DJ said as we took our seats. The jazz trio began to play, keeping the music low beneath the hum of conversation.

Teag and Anthony sat, flushed and breathless but with broad grins.

"You were amazing," I told them, and Kell added his praise.

"Quite the show, little bro." Landon shook his head. "Didn't know you had it in you."

Kell and I had the sea bass with fingerling potatoes and asparagus. Teag, Anthony, and Landon chose the Wagu beef with wasabi mashed potatoes and baby carrots. Perhaps not the original plan, but it was delicious all the same. Everyone raised a champagne toast to the happy couple, and servers kept our glasses filled. I was glad we had hired a driver for the night.

In between courses, we mingled. My cousin Simon Kincaide and his husband, Vic D'Amato, had driven down from Myrtle Beach and greeted Kell and me with big hugs.

"It's so much more fun to be a guest at one of these shindigs than in the spotlight," Vic observed. It had only been a few months since he and Simon exchanged vows. Simon just rolled his eyes and shook his head.

Teag's skill as a researcher and hacker has helped many hunters in the supernatural community with lore, spells, and hard-to-find data. Our crew often lent a hand when Simon and Vic were chasing a paranormal predator. Gifts and well-wishes from others in our secretive circle of colleagues appeared throughout the week. I strongly suspected that their presents either had a connection to lore or protective energy —or both.

Teag and Anthony made sure to circulate among the tables, greeting everyone and snapping photos with guests. Wedding planner Kim was a constant, comforting presence, making sure everything went smoothly and keeping Mama Benton from stroking out. Even Teag's mom seemed to relax and enjoy herself. Our gang had their own table and were having a great time. I saw Alistair McKinnon and Mrs. Morrissey deep in conversation. Mrs. Teller, Niella, Lucinda, Rowan, and Alicia looked like they were enjoying themselves. Even the more staid guests—people I figured were either Anthony's law friends or business associates of his parents—laughed and chatted with their tablemates.

As waiters began to clear away the dinner dishes, the DJ returned and kicked off a playlist of updated swing-era songs full of Robbie Williams, Michael Bublé, Natalie Cole, and Frank Sinatra. The tunes were danceable even for those of us who hadn't spent the past six months practicing steps. Guests of all ages spilled out onto the floor to try their luck.

At some point I kicked off my shoes and danced barefoot, enjoying a chance to catch my breath on the slow songs and loving the energy when the tempo picked up. By the time the DJ took a break for the newlyweds to cut the cake, I was ready to sit down for a while.

"Having fun?" Kell looked just as breathless as I felt and equally happy.

I nodded vigorously. "The playlist is genius. There's something for everyone."

The cake tasted as good as it looked, and even the flower decorations were edible. After that, the trio played a short set until it was time to wave goodbye to Teag and Anthony as the party wound down.

"I think you guys should end every case with a shindig," Kell joked as we collected Maggie and made our way to our waiting limo.

"I agree," Maggie put in. "We deserve it."

I was happily tired and a little buzzed for the drive home, nestled against Kell's shoulder.

We had saved the world—again. Defeated a djinn and his wicked witch. And still managed a kickass bachelor party and not one, but two weddings.

Even for our crew, that was some kind of record.

GREEN MAN BLUES

BONUS NOVELLA

INTRODUCTION

Green Man Blues first appeared in *Midsummer Mischief at Caynham Castle*, a multi-author, shared world series that takes place in a fictional castle and town in England near the Welsh border. Cassidy and Kell take a vacation to the castle their friends have told them about and end up with more excitement than they bargained for! You can find the other four novellas from the previous seasonal Caynham Castle books in the *Castle Magic* collection, featuring a trip by Teag and Anthony as well as three stories with main characters from my Morgan Brice books.

CHAPTER ONE

"It's just as awesome as I thought it would be." Cassidy Kincaide raised her camera to get a photo of the ancient British castle. Then she turned, pulling her boyfriend Kell Winston with her, and snapped a selfie of them with the towers in the background.

"We look good together," Cassidy said with a smile. Kell was tall and lean, with light brown hair and blue eyes, a contrast to Cassidy's strawberry-blond hair and pale skin. "And we've got a great backdrop!"

"All our friends who've been here have raved about the place—give or take some of the supernatural 'side quests' that happened," Kell replied.

"Would you expect anything else?" Cassidy laughed.

Cassidy owned Trifles and Folly, an antique and curio store in Charleston, South Carolina, that specialized in getting cursed and haunted objects out of the wrong hands. Occasionally, they helped save the world from supernatural threats. Her psychometric ability to read the history of objects by touching them came in handy.

"I left the recording equipment back in the States, so if the ghosts put on a show for us, I'm out of luck," Kell said. He ran SPOOK—the Southern Paranormal Observation and Outreach Klub—that documented hauntings in the Charleston area. He and his "ghostbuster" friends didn't have psychic abilities, but they shared a fascination with all things supernatural.

"Assuming any of your apps work here, you can probably do a lot from your phone if we run into anything." Cassidy craned her neck to look up at the tall castle walls, excited for the long-overdue vacation.

"I wasn't planning on ghost hunting, although I guess since the castle is supposed to actually be haunted, you can never say never," Kell replied.

Caynham Castle and the town that surrounded it, Caynham-on-Ledwyche, nestled into the hills near the Welsh border. Owned by the same family for centuries and now run as a hotel by its current earl, the castle had been preserved, restored, and in the case of the guest areas, remodeled.

"It's fun being here for the Midsummer Fayre." Kell took Cassidy's hand as they strolled the grounds. He yelped in surprise as she pulled him in for a sudden kiss.

"Gargoyle." She pointed upward. "There's a legend that if you kiss in front of the original gargoyle, your love will last forever. We're not sure which one that is, so we just have to work our way through all of them! I've got a cheat sheet of the locations."

Kell kissed her again and laughed. "I'm not going to complain. Sounds like a fun quest to me."

The inner and outer bailey areas of Caynham Castle would soon be transformed into a Renaissance festival with colorful banners, strolling performers, and musicians in old-fashioned garb. Special events were planned in locations scattered across the castle grounds and throughout the town.

"There's plenty going on," Cassidy told him. "A play, a joust, an archery competition, a kids' costume contest, a medieval banquet in the main dining hall—and more. We've already got tickets for the dinner!"

"It looked like the town was getting in on the action when we drove through," Kell replied.

Cassidy nodded. "They're going to have artisan booths, food

trucks, and other cool stuff. Although the town is interesting enough on its own—I can't wait to eat at the pub everyone raved about."

"How bad's your jet lag?" Kell asked as they walked into the castle's tea shop.

White tablecloths and the castle's official china graced each table. Portraits of the earl's ancestors hung on the walls. Up front, a glass case held an array of desserts that all looked fabulous.

"Not too bad," Cassidy replied. "Although I'm looking forward to some caffeine and sugar for a boost to get me through the afternoon."

They followed a server to one of the tables and poured over the menu, looking at the choices of tea sandwiches and small cakes as well as the extensive list of teas.

"Everything looks amazing," Kell said. "We could try something new each day and probably not get through all the choices."

"I'm totally up for that," Cassidy agreed. "Teag and Anthony raved about the food, and so did everyone else who's been here." Teag Logan, her best friend and assistant store manager, had visited with his fiancé Anthony Benton not long ago and passed on a whole list of "can't miss" things to do.

"Welcome to Lady Neville's Tea Shop." Their server, a woman in her twenties with brown hair and green eyes, greeted them. "I'm Amy. Is this your first time here?"

Cassidy nodded. "Yes—but we're already planning to be regulars while we're staying at the castle."

Amy shared a conspiratorial smile. "That happens a lot. Keep trying new things no matter how much you like what you've just had. Everything's good, and there are so many flavors of tea you might have to plan a second trip!"

"How long has the castle had a Renaissance festival?" Kell asked. "Does it date back to the actual period?"

Amy laughed. "No, it's actually a new thing. If it goes well, I'm sure they'll expand. The town's gotten into the spirit. Did you download the event schedule on the castle app? You won't want to miss any of the fun."

Cassidy held up her phone. "Yep. Got it right here. Figured it would come in handy. Have you made the rounds to see everything yourself? Got any favorites?"

"I like seeing the performers dressed up and listening to the music," Amy said. "And I'm hoping I get to see the joust. I read about those when I was a kid and always wanted to watch the knights in shining armor."

"It sounds like fun," Cassidy replied. "Even better being in a real castle."

Caynham Castle looked like what Cassidy thought a proper castle should. Its tall outer walls guarded an inner walled area, and inside was the keep and tower. Unlike many fortifications, Caynham had survived centuries and battles largely intact. During the 1920s, the family decided to convert some of the space to guest rooms, offering a unique experience with excellent food, seasonal events, and beautiful grounds.

"I love visiting here, but I can't imagine living like this." Kell looked around them at the tea shop. "It's wild that the guy who owns this is a real earl."

"I guess we're thoroughly American," Cassidy said. "Although I'd rather drink tea than throw it overboard. I want to see the rooms that Teag and Anthony mentioned that were preserved like back in the 1920s. There's supposed to be a real dungeon too."

"I also heard about a 'Midsummer Memories' display with items that have a connection to the solstice and the spring holidays," Kell added as Amy brought their tea and a tiered plate of small, triangular sandwiches.

"Cucumber, chicken salad, and watercress." Amy pointed out which was which. "When you're done, I'll bring the desserts. Enjoy!"

Although the sandwiches were small, they hit the spot. "These are delicious," Cassidy said, polishing off her third. "I agree—this is addictive!"

"Back to the display," Kell picked up where he had left off. "It sounded like your kind of thing. Antiques, family heirlooms, and you can just enjoy them being pretty and not have to worry about them."

"I hope there's nothing to worry about." Cassidy nibbled another sandwich. "Everyone else we know ended up tangling with a ghost or a creature of some sort."

"Maybe because nearly everyone we know is involved in the monster hunting/ghostbusting business," Kell supplied. "I bet hundreds of normal people come here every year and don't end up saving the world."

"Are you saying we're not 'normal'?" Cassidy teased.

Kell raised an eyebrow, and she had to laugh.

"You're right; we're not. And I like it that way. But for once, I'm okay with not having any extra excitement. I want to enjoy the food and the scenery, curl up in a comfy chair, read some books, and be completely pampered."

Kell reached over and took her hand. "I think that can be arranged."

The second course included a variety of tea cakes and petit fours, all of which were scrumptious. Happy and full, she and Kell walked hand in hand into the sunlight.

"It's cooler here than back home," Kell noted.

"You mean we're not broiling in the heat and sweltering in the humidity?"

"Exactly."

Much as Cassidy loved her hometown of Charleston, summer temperatures and humidity weren't her favorite. "On the other hand, I bet our winters are nicer," she added loyally.

Brightly colored bunting and banners bedecked the inner and outer bailey walls in red, white, green, and blue. Flags jutted on poles from the stone, fluttering in the breeze. Although the festival hadn't started yet, it didn't take much imagination for Cassidy to envision costumed musicians and performers roaming the grounds and interacting with guests.

"I hope the festival is popular," Kell noted. "They're doing a nice job. Plenty of opportunity to expand for next year."

"I imagine it's like with the historic sites where we live—they're always looking for a reason to bring new people in and get prior guests to return."

They headed toward the Great Hall, which held the dining room and some of the historic displays in the adjacent solar.

"I want to stick my head in and see the dining room," Cassidy told Kell. "Simon raved about the architecture."

"And Vic couldn't stop talking about the food," Kell added. Simon Kincaide, Cassidy's cousin, had visited at Halloween with his fiancé.

"That sounds right." They strolled toward the Great Room, and Cassidy's eyes widened when they stepped inside. "Oh my. It's even grander than I expected."

A hammerbeam ceiling vaulted overhead, with English Gothic open timber roof trusses. Hand-cut beams arched downward at intervals, embellished at the corners with intricate woodcuts. The huge, ox-roaster fireplace at one end of the room had a carved firebox and ornate mantle and was large enough for a grown man to stand upright inside.

"Now I want to come back when it's cold because those couches look like a perfect place to nest with a good book," Kell said, taking in the seating area in front of the now-dark fireplace.

Cassidy nodded in agreement. "The regular dining area is over to one side, although I think they'll use the whole space for the medieval dinner. That should be fun! I went to a medieval event in Myrtle Beach once with Simon, and they made us eat everything with our hands—no utensils."

Kell chuckled. "I've been to shows like that. Although I doubt they'll have a joust right here in the middle of the dining room."

Original oil paintings graced the walls everywhere Cassidy looked. The furnishings in the public areas were reproductions, but Cassidy's experience with antiques meant she couldn't help admiring the pieces.

"There's one of the display areas." Kell tugged on Cassidy's hand and pulled her into the solar. While Kell's interests lay more with film-making and vintage movies, he knew how much she liked history.

"Just imagine having all sorts of priceless items in storage, too many to display all at once," she murmured as they took in the glass cases. "And staff to catalog them."

"I don't know—it's just a larger version of Trifles and Folly," Kell teased. "The shop has a pretty amazing inventory, even if most of the stuff isn't this old."

Cassidy didn't doubt that the art pieces displayed in the cases were genuine. Each had a note about its significance to the family and who had acquired it.

"I guess it's keeping with the midsummer theme, but it's interesting that everything in this display has to do with the fae," she mused.

"Aren't you supposed to call them the 'Fair Folk' to keep from getting on their bad side?" Kell asked.

Faeries weren't among the creatures Cassidy usually worried about back in Charleston, although she and her friends had a few run-ins. She knew the ethereal creatures were real and not to be trifled with.

"You're right. I should use the proper terms." She glanced at the items on display. "No offense intended," she whispered, in case anyone was listening.

"I like the ones with the…Fair Folk…riding corgis." Kell pointed to a display with that theme. Painted porcelain plates, figurines, and oil paintings showed tiny, beautiful, pointed-eared creatures in diaphanous clothing riding corgis like battle steeds. One painting showed a mushroom circle beneath the trees and faeries, depicted like dandelion puffs, flitting among them.

The only other person in sight, a middle-aged man in a blue windbreaker jacket, stood in front of the next case, staring at the contents as if mesmerized. When he realized they were moving closer, he hurried off, giving them room.

"That's pretty cool." Kell's comment drew Cassidy's attention to where he stood admiring an elaborate bronze mask of a man's face wreathed by oak leaves.

"It's the Green Man," she replied. "He's sort of a forest god. People worshipped him for harvests and believed he honored the life cycle. Some of the stories say he guards the threshold between realms."

"The living and the dead?" Kell examined the mask more closely.

"Or the mortals and the Fair Folk," Cassidy supplied. "One world and another."

"That's not spooky at all," Kell said sarcastically. "I know I've seen versions of this before. This one looks very old." He checked the tag beneath it. "This was made by a local artist four hundred years ago."

"I suspect it has protective qualities." Cassidy reached out with her psychometric ability, although she was careful not to touch anything. "It's not just art. It's been touched by magic—not a type I'm familiar with."

"Fae?" Kell asked in a whisper.

"Actually, I'd say that's likely. They say the old families have long-standing 'agreements' with supernatural creatures. I don't doubt that. These were once wild and dangerous places. Humans needed all the advantages they could get, and clever, ambitious people would have found every angle."

"Do you think this is some sort of warding for the castle?"

Cassidy nodded. "I'm certain it is. Maybe a treaty of sorts as well. I'm glad it's in a glass case. It would be valuable as a decoration, but if I'm right about what else it is, that mask is priceless."

They meandered around the castle grounds, holding hands and pointing out items of note. "I'm glad we came in early," Kell said as they walked to the garden folly with its statue of lovers. "It's nice to figure out where everything is when it's not crowded. More relaxing."

"I appreciate getting our bearings before the crowds get here," Cassidy agreed. "Although for the earl's sake, I hope this is successful enough that they decide to make it an annual event."

"I checked the app—even though the festival doesn't start until Friday, there's still a lot going on. Plenty of fun things every night and lots to explore," Kell said. "Including ghost tours!"

Cassidy grinned. "I don't know if it's true about all the tours, but the one Simon went on, he said the ghosts kept whispering to him how the tour guide had embellished their stories!" Her cousin Simon—a spirit medium—had come with his fiancé Vic for New Year's.

"The stories are interesting whether or not they're true." Kell shrugged. "And I'd love to capture some footage to show the rest of the team."

Even though they were on vacation, Cassidy never traveled without some supernatural precautions. She packed the old wooden spoon that had been her grandmother's, which she used as her wand because of its strong emotional resonance. The onyx spindle whorl in her pocket once belonged to a Norse demigoddess and helped her focus and amplify her magic. And the faded dog collar that had belonged to Bo, her late golden retriever, summoned his ghost as her spirit protector.

A quick stop, once they left the airport, supplied them with salt and iron nails, two basic protections against paranormal threats. While they hadn't been able to bring weapons with them, they weren't completely defenseless.

Back at the castle, they meandered through the gift shop. "What do you think Baxter would like?" Cassidy headed straight to the dog section.

"I imagine Bax would like his own title and serving staff," Kell replied. "But beyond that? Maybe a sweater with the earl's family crest."

Cassidy bought the sweater for Baxter and added a Christmas ornament of the castle as well as tea towels. "I know we'll be shopping in all the booths for the festival, but I wanted to make sure we had something from the castle before they sold out of everything."

"Baxter is going to be so spoiled staying with Maggie," Kell said as they took their purchases back to the room. "He's got her wrapped around his paw."

"She's besotted, so they're suited for each other." Cassidy grinned. Maggie worked at Trifles and Folly and had become a good friend.

Their room was comfortable and luxuriously retro. Cassidy eyed the bed and felt a rush of jet lag.

"How about a nap, and then we can head into town and take a look around? We can have dinner at the pub and maybe even catch a nightcap at the bar in the Keep Tower." Cassidy kicked off her shoes.

"I was thinking the same thing, but I didn't think you'd want to slow down," Kell replied.

"We have all week, and being dead tired is no fun. I want to be awake for sightseeing."

Cassidy stretched out on the comforter, sinking into the feather duvet. Between the air conditioning and the stone walls' natural insulation, their room was slightly chilly despite the warm temperatures outside.

Kell joined her, and they kissed for a few minutes before they snuggled back-to-front with Kell as the "big spoon." Despite being a long way from home in a strange place, Cassidy let herself relax into the feeling of safety and security she felt with Kell near. He wrapped his arm around her with his hand splayed on her belly, and she covered his hand with her own as she fell asleep.

In her dream, Cassidy saw herself walking toward a set of standing stones at dawn.

She carried a bottle of milk and a shallow silver dish, and just outside the circle, she set the dish on the ground and poured the milk into it.

"Fair Folk...accept this tribute for your protection, and in gratitude for your watchfulness. As I will it, so mote it be."

The peaceful morning scene shifted. The wind picked up, raking through the tall grass and blowing Cassidy's hair into her eyes. The temperature dropped, and her breath misted in the air. The sky grew dark, and fog roiled in the open space at the center of the stone circle.

A figure emerged from the mist, gaunt, haggard, and empty-eyed. Cassidy stared at the doppelganger in horror, wondering where it had come from and what it meant.

"There's no way home," her dark twin said in a chilling, toneless voice.

"Cassidy—wake up!" Kell shook her gently, sounding worried. The dream slipped away, and Cassidy came back to herself, shivering in Kell's arms.

"Are you okay? What happened?" He held her close, letting her shake off the last tendrils of sleep.

"Bad dream," she replied, although Cassidy wasn't so sure that was all.

"Need to talk?" Kell's voice steadied her, low and quiet next to her ear. She leaned back into him, welcoming his warmth and the strength of his arms around her.

"I might just be overtired," she said.

"When has it ever been that simple?"

She sighed. "Okay. You're right. It's probably not. I don't usually get visions without touching an object. But maybe the castle counts." Cassidy described what she had seen, and Kell listened silently with a look of concern.

"Let me check something." He got up and went to his shaving kit, where he had packed his EMF meter to check for ghostly activity. Kell switched the device on and walked around the room, but it remained silent and dark.

"Nothing." He slipped the meter back into his kit. "No ghosts or unusual frequencies. That doesn't rule out your psychometry or other entities, but if there's something else going on, it doesn't show up on the meter."

He brought Cassidy a glass of water, which she accepted gratefully. "Do you need tea? Something sugary?"

Cassidy knew that Kell had been present enough times when she had read a difficult object to know how to take care of her afterward. A strong, negative resonance could knock her out, and waking up afterward usually wasn't pleasant.

"I think I'm okay, but thank you. I don't know what to make of it." Cassidy took several deep breaths to ground herself and went back over what she had seen.

"I think it's a warning," she said finally. "Definitely not something that already happened, but something that *might* occur. But why?"

"I'm a little freaked out that you saw a ghost of yourself," Kell admitted.

Cassidy frowned, replaying the scene in her mind. "I don't think it was a ghost. More like a dark double. But where such a thing would come from, I don't know."

Kell gave her an appraising look, making sure she was recovered. "Let's go out, get some fresh air, and walk into town. It'll help you get your mind off the dream."

Cassidy resolved not to let the dream spoil their first day at Caynham Castle, but she knew it wouldn't be far from her thoughts until she had figured out its meaning. Still, she made an effort to put it out of her mind as they crossed the bridge and headed toward town.

"It's beautiful here," Kell said.

Cassidy took in the view. Caynham-on-Ledwyche had "character." Most of the buildings on the main street were old enough to be historic, although they had been updated and repaired over the years to suit modern uses. A few buildings even had thatched roofs.

"I feel like I've walked into a movie," Cassidy confessed. "It's hard to believe that real people live here."

"I imagine tourists think the same thing about Charleston," Kell replied. "But when you live there, it's just home."

They passed the area where many of the vendor tables would be set up later in the week and kept going toward the heart of the town. Small shops lined the main street, and Cassidy couldn't wait to explore the bookstore, curio emporium, and a second tea shop. The Boar and Knight pub was a favorite of all their friends who had visited.

"Let's eat there tonight," she said. "I've heard their signature beer is pretty amazing, and Simon raved about the food."

"Isn't that where your art-expert friend found a real Knight Templar helmet?" Kell asked.

Cassidy nodded. "Yep—up on a shelf where no one noticed it for a long time. Turned out there was a whole secret story involved and an old legend."

"Maybe you shouldn't touch anything," Kell suggested.

"Probably a good idea," she agreed. "Although it's a very old pub. I imagine even the furniture has more resonance than usual."

"You're used to that in Charleston. Things are just a little older here."

Despite what her jet-lagged inner clock tried to tell her, it was already mid-afternoon. The shops were open and decorated with colorful bunting, signs, and banners.

"I want to spend some time in the bookstore and the curio shop," she told Kell.

"Remember that anything you buy has to fit in our luggage to get home," Kell warned.

"I'll be careful," Cassidy promised. They strolled past the decorated windows, commenting on the displays.

"Everyone seems to have put a lot of effort into making the festival a big deal," Cassidy said. "I definitely need to pick up some yarn for Maggie, and some tea, to thank her for watching Baxter."

"By the time we pick out gifts for all our friends, we'll need a whole separate plane to get it all home," Kell teased.

"Maybe. That's what happens on vacation," Cassidy joked. The next shop was Curiouser and Curiouser. "I can't wait to see the antiques they have here—the UK is so much older than the States. The castle has furniture older than our country."

"True. But Charleston is one of the oldest cities, so it's not quite as much of a difference as if we lived in a newer place."

Cassidy peered through the glass, past the gilt lettering of the shop's name. Beyond the display, she could see tables full of treasures and glass cases filled with old, rare items. Her attention returned to the display in the window, and she caught her breath.

Cassidy pointed to the weathered, leather-and-iron-bound box in the front. The lid was open, revealing the contents. Jars of salt, iron filings, and dried plants that she recognized as St. John's Wort, red verbena, daisies, and four-leaf clover, nestled in the silk-covered interior, all known as useful to repel the fae.

"What is it?" Kell asked. "It looks a little like an old-fashioned vampire hunter kit, but the supplies are wrong."

Cassidy tried to reconcile the Midsummer festival's faerie-friendly focus with the relic in front of her. "It's a fae hunting box. I don't know what to make of it," she murmured. "Is it a warning? To whom? I can't believe the proprietor wouldn't know what it is. Why display it now?"

"Let's go ask."

Before Cassidy could object, Kell stepped through the door, obligating her to follow.

Maybe we can pretend to be clueless tourists. Unless the store owner has strong magic, he's not going to pick up on my abilities.

"Welcome," a man greeted them from behind the counter. "I'm Mr.

Porter, and I'll be happy to help you find what you're looking for. We have a little of everything."

Cassidy tried to focus her gift without triggering a full-on vision. Strong resonance could cause a reaction from the floor through the soles of her shoes, and she froze, then relaxed marginally when nothing happened.

Trifles and Folly carried a large inventory of antiques and unique items, but by comparison, Curiouser and Curiouser was a jam-packed treasure trove. It reminded her of paintings of a dragon's hoard, and she wondered whether the proprietor or owner—or both—had paranormal abilities.

"I'm interested in the box in the window," Kell said. "It reminds me of something I saw in a movie."

"That's not for sale," Mr. Porter replied. "It's over two hundred years old, one of a kind. It makes a striking display, but it's got sentimental value for the owner. We couldn't let it go."

"What's it for?" Kell played the "clueless American" perfectly, wide-eyed and non-threatening. "Is it a doctor's bag?"

Mr. Porter's smile never wavered, but Cassidy sensed a wariness that told her he didn't completely buy Kell's act.

"Not a doctor. A faerie hunter."

Kell's eyes widened. "Faeries are real? Why would you want to hunt them?"

Mr. Porter looked from Kell to Cassidy, and she had the uncomfortable feeling that he saw more than she wanted him to.

"The real ones aren't like in the movies," Mr. Porter told him. "They can be generous—but there's nearly always a cost. The dark fae can be ruthless and tricky. Of course, we want a good relationship with the Fair Folk, but it's wise to be prepared."

I wonder if the earl knows about this? If the Mortimer family has had a truce with the fae for centuries, was it forged diplomatically or in some kind of permanent stand-off?

"Was it ever used?" Cassidy spoke up. "It looks old and kind of battered."

Mr. Porter gave them a smile that didn't reach his eyes. "There are stories, of course. Every good antique has them. And its provenance is interesting—an old English family long rumored to have magical abilities."

"How did it end up here?" Cassidy asked. Something about the story didn't add up.

"The same way most things come to us. Old families fall on hard times and need money, so they sell everything that's been taking up space in the attic. Or the line dies out, there's no heir, and everything is sold off. Sad, but it's the way of things."

It didn't escape Cassidy that Mr. Porter hadn't answered her question. "Do you believe in the Fair Folk?" she asked and saw Mr. Porter try to hide a flinch.

"Don't we all, down deep? Collective cultural memory and all," he answered. "All those children's stories sink into our minds."

Another non-answer, Cassidy noticed.

"Have a look around," Mr. Porter invited. "Everything else in the store is for sale, and I can ship to the States—or just about anywhere."

Cassidy decided to take a risk. "You have a beautiful store. I'll admit that this is a bit of what my grandmother would have called a 'busman's holiday.' I run an antique store in Charleston. We've been around for over three hundred years—old by our standards, not so much by yours. My shop is Trifles and Folly."

For a second, Mr. Porter froze at the name. "I think I've heard of it. What brings you to Caynham-on-Ledwyche?"

He knows more than he's letting on. Wonder if he's ever crossed paths with Sorren?

Sorren was Cassidy's business partner, a nearly six-hundred-year-old vampire who had founded Trifles and Folly with one of Cassidy's ancestors when Charleston was newly settled.

"We're here for the festival," Cassidy said as Kell began to roam the aisles. She figured he would surreptitiously use the EMF reader and braced herself for its squeal if it revealed a resident ghost.

"Business or pleasure?" Mr. Porter met her gaze, and Cassidy felt a tingle of magic.

"Pleasure—unless something comes up," Cassidy replied. All her friends had come to the castle expecting to leave their roles as supernatural protectors behind, only to be pulled into Caynham's hidden mysteries.

"I hope you enjoy yourselves," Mr. Porter said as Kell returned to Cassidy's side. "People will have a lot of fun with the legends for the festival. But if you know history, you realize that there's usually a truth under the stories that might not be shiny and bright. Those who believe in the Fair Folk treat them with respect and never let down their guard."

Cassidy fought a shiver despite Mr. Porter's congenial tone. She took the warning seriously, as one paranormal professional to another.

"Thank you. I'm sure we'll be back," she told him and headed for the door.

Outside, it seemed to Cassidy that she could breathe easier, as if a weight was lifted. They waited to talk until they had walked a block, leaving the curio shop behind.

"What did you make of all that?" She needed to see if Kell's impressions matched her own. Cassidy had grown to value his opinion and knew he was an excellent observer.

"He's hiding something. I think he picked up that you might have abilities, and when you mentioned Trifles and Folly, I'm positive he recognized the name. He knows more than he's letting on."

"Agreed. And while he's giving lip service to it all being legend and lore, I think he believes in the Fair Folk…and knows what they're really like."

Kell took her hand as they headed into the Boar and Knight. "Let's just hope we don't need to borrow his kit."

CHAPTER TWO

"THIS IS EXACTLY WHAT I'D PICTURED WHEN I HEARD ABOUT THE BOAR and Knight," Cassidy said as they found a table inside the old pub. The small building had dark wooden beams, well-worn tables, a soot-blackened fireplace, and a sign on the wall tracing the tavernkeepers back in an unbroken line to the 1400s.

All sorts of antiques from various periods ringed the room on a high shelf. Cassidy couldn't avoid eyeing them with professional curiosity. If they were authentic, some were ancient and valuable. She got the feeling that the Boar and Knight wasn't likely to decorate with substitutes.

Cassidy ordered the chicken tikka masala, while Kell got the Sunday roast, along with pints of one of the pub's signature beers. Even though the fireplace was empty and cold for the summer, Cassidy thought she could catch a whiff of woodsmoke. It didn't take a wild imagination to picture customers swapping tales while puffing on long-stemmed pipes like in the movies.

"Everything smells good—and I'm hungry." Cassidy glanced around to see what the meals on nearby tables looked like. The buzz of conversation punctuated by occasional laughter made Cassidy feel at home.

As she waited for her meal, Cassidy took in the atmosphere and the decorations. She frowned as she spotted a horseshoe nailed to a beam above the bar and a small set of bells hanging by the window.

"What's wrong?" Kell asked.

"I'm back to wondering about the town's history with the Fair Folk." Cassidy kept her voice low to avoid being overheard. "For all the banners and bunting, someone nailed an iron horseshoe and put bells by the window. Those are protections against fae magic."

"Maybe folks are okay with the fake sort of faerie, but aren't too comfortable with the real deal," Kell suggested. "Like the people who love horror movies but faint dead away if there's an actual ghost anywhere near."

"Hmm. Maybe," Cassidy allowed, not entirely sure what to make of the contradictory behavior.

Their plates arrived, and they dug in with gusto. The snippets of conversation Cassidy overheard focused on the upcoming festival.

"…a lot of nonsense and bother, but it's for a good cause."

"…I imagine it'll be good for the shops and such, even though it's going to be a bloody nuisance to go anywhere."

"…exactly what we need. Shot in the arm and all. There's nothing to bring people here between the big holidays. Sounds like fun."

Cassidy was glad that the festival seemed to be supported by the townspeople because she knew from experience in Charleston how much tourist traffic could snarl getting around.

"…just hope the Fair Folk take it all in good spirits," an older man groused to his companions. "They leave us alone, we leave them alone. We don't need that kind of trouble."

Interesting. At least some of the townspeople believe that the fae are real. And they're not so sure about them being friendly.

The conversations shifted to the weather, the big soccer game, and the price of eggs. Cassidy finished her meal, and found Kell eyeing the menu for dessert.

"I'm stuffed, but I can't pass up the chance for real sticky toffee pudding," Kell groaned.

"That sounds fantastic. How about splitting it? I don't think I could eat a whole one myself after that big meal," Cassidy said. The serving ended up plenty large enough to share, the perfect end to the meal.

After dinner, they strolled around town. "Look there." Cassidy pointed to small saucers of cream left by the doorways to several shops.

"I guess they like cats?"

She shook her head. "Those are offerings to the fae to curry good favor." Cassidy grabbed Kell's hand. "Let's go in."

The yarn shop had a large variety of brightly-colored skeins made from locally-sourced wool, and Cassidy bought several for Maggie. A tea shop in the back of the store supplied both Cassidy and Kell with hot cups of strong Earl Gray to wake them back up after a heavy dinner.

"Take a look on your left," Cassidy said quietly to Kell. He followed her gaze to a set of bells hanging by the window and another horseshoe on the wall.

Cassidy and Kell worked their way up the street, noting how many of the merchants left an offering for the Fair Folk, only to have protective items inside as a safeguard.

"I get the feeling that the folks here have mixed feeling about faeries," Kell said quietly.

"Yeah, so do I," Cassidy agreed. "Maybe it comes from actually believing in them, as opposed to thinking they're just an interesting legend. After all, they're immortal and very powerful. Regular people can't really hold their own against them unless they're very clever."

"I don't remember Simon and the others mentioning the fae gifts or protections. Do you think it has to do with the festival?" Kell asked.

Cassidy considered that for a moment. "Could be. Maybe people are worried that the fae won't be pleased by the event for some reason. I'd love to find out more, but I don't think people are likely to talk to us."

"If we can find a book on the subject, maybe they don't have to," Kell suggested.

They ducked into Cadwell's Book Shop, and Cassidy took a deep breath, inhaling the heady scent of old paper and bindings.

"Welcome. Can I help you?" The man behind the counter, a short, bald fellow in a plaid shirt, sweater vest, and corduroy pants, greeted them cheerily.

Cassidy gave him her most disarming smile. "I hope you can. We're here for the festival. I saw the mask of the Green Man up at the castle and wondered if you had any books about that legend."

As with the other shops, Cadwell's had a saucer of cream outside and a horseshoe on the wall behind the register.

"Well, there are quite a lot of stories about the Green Man. I'm Ptolemy Cadwell, the owner. As I'm sure you can guess from looking around, I try to have books on every topic."

Floor-to-ceiling shelves were packed with books of all types. The new volumes and bestsellers were gathered in the front. As Cassidy and Kell followed Cadwell down the narrow aisles, the selections shifted to older, used titles on a wide variety of subjects.

"Folklore is a popular topic." He paused to look at the books on the shelf before selecting one. "Stories about the Fair Folk go back to antiquity in these parts. I know people elsewhere think they're made up for movies and children's tales, but when you live here, you sense that there's more than meets the eye.

"The Green Man is a nature spirit, generally a positive entity." Cadwell flipped through the book until he came to the right chapter. "Many of the Fair Folk are…ambiguous. Sometimes they help, sometimes they harm. And then you've got creatures like Herne the Hunter, a phantom who haunts wooded places and leads the Wild Hunt. He's not someone you want to meet up with—unless you care to ride off with his hunting party and never be seen again."

"Do the shopkeepers here usually leave offerings for the fae?" Cassidy watched Cadwell closely for his answer. He hesitated as if unsure how to reply, and then seemed to come to a decision.

"We're all very excited about the new Midsummer Fayre." He seemed to choose his words carefully. "It's going to be fun, and it gives folks like you a reason to visit. But there's also a lot of disturbance getting things ready, right at the Solstice when the fae world and ours are closest. I guess you could say we're hedging our bets."

"That bronze mask of the Green Man up at the castle." Cassidy felt like they had found a friendly source. "Is there a legend about him and the earl's family?"

Cadwell handed her the book and found two more before answering. "If you go back far enough, no one knows these things for sure," he prefaced his answer. "When the Mortimer family built the castle, this was still a wild area. Vast forests covered large stretches of land. They weren't like the woods are now. These were old-growth, huge trees, with forests so deep that people who wandered in without knowing what they were doing didn't come back out."

He absently stroked the cover of one of the books he held, with a cover drawing of a man with large antlers standing next to the Green Man.

"There were wolves back then and other wild animals. Life was… precarious. It wouldn't have been hard for people to believe that all kinds of supernatural creatures lived in the forests. And maybe they did," Cadwell added with a faint smile.

"There's a story that says the land was secured by making a treaty with the fae of the forest and received the blessing of the Green Man himself. The castle wouldn't harm the Fair Folk, and in return, the fae would offer protection."

"I heard that there's at least one household faerie in the castle," Cassidy prompted. Some of her friends had a run-in with the creature.

"I wouldn't be surprised. That's said of nearly all of the great houses," Cadwell replied. "The agreement the earls came to with the Green Man seems to have extended to Herne, a promise to not bring the Wild Hunt to these forests. I don't know how the deal was brokered—and honestly, I don't want to know. That's old magic. But the castle has prospered, and although the forests are thinner than they used to be, I've never heard of the Hunt near here."

"I'll take the books," Cassidy said. "One more question. I couldn't help noticing the strange old box in the window at Curiouser and Curiouser. Mr. Porter confirmed that it was a faerie hunter kit. If the Mortimers have always had a good relationship with the fae, why would someone have a kit like that?"

From the expression that flitted across Cadwell's face, Cassidy got the impression that he wasn't a fan of the display.

"Even a very safe town has a constable in case something bad happens," he replied. "From what I understand, Caynham-on-Ledwyche also had a supernatural constable through the years who had the training and knowledge to step in if a problem arose. It was a hereditary position passed down through the generations. But the last constable died without an heir. I think that's how Porter came to have the kit." His expression suggested that he thought it was poor form to put it on display.

"Will there be a new constable appointed?" Kell asked. "Seems like an important position to stay vacant."

Cadwell shrugged. "I don't know. I would think so, but that would be a matter for the earl. He's a very modern fellow, but he does respect tradition. Perhaps he just hasn't had the chance to appoint a new one."

They paid for the books, thanked him again, then headed out. Cassidy took Kell's hand, and they walked back across the bridge toward the castle.

"Looks like they've brought in materials to start setting up for the festival," Kell noted. "I think that's a stage they're building over the dry moat."

Cassidy nodded. "Maybe tomorrow would be a good day to take a hike in the woods. I've heard there are standing stones nearby. That way the workmen can pound away and it won't bother us."

"Sounds good. I saw something about being able to borrow walking sticks for hiking from the castle gift shop," Kell replied. "Might be nice to have while we're here."

"We can stop on the way back," Cassidy said. "I don't think we're going to have trouble finding things to do. The town website has a big list of evening programs going on this week—probably for the tourists like us who came in early. We could do the ghost tour, and then there's a concert series at the church downtown—classical, string quartet, choral, something different each night."

They walked the rest of the way in comfortable silence, enjoying the lovely evening. At the gift shop, the clerk on duty guided them to a selection of sturdy, beautifully hand-worked wooden walking sticks.

"A good walking stick makes for a great hike, but they're too big to take home on a plane," the clerk said with a laugh. "So we let our guests check them out from our 'library' and return them when they leave. Of course, if you really want one of your own, our craftsman takes commissions and ships internationally."

Cassidy and Kell admired the careful finishing on the walking sticks, making each one unique. None of the pieces gave off bad vibes. Instead, Cassidy picked up a sense of peace and contentment, and she wondered if that came from being handled by visitors happy with their outings.

"What kind of wood is this?" Cassidy asked.

"They're all made of rowan," the clerk replied. "It's a tradition around here. Sturdy."

Kell chose a long walking stick that suited his height, and Cassidy picked one that attracted her to it as if the stick was choosing her.

"Enjoy your hikes," the clerk told them after registering the loaned equipment to their room. "Just bring them back when you're done, or leave them in your room when you check out."

When they got back to their room, Kell pulled Cassidy in for a kiss. "I love traveling with you. You always manage to find the most interesting things."

Cassidy kissed him back. "I'm not sure whether that talent is a blessing or a curse."

"Most of the time, it's a very good thing." Kell ran a hand through Cassidy's hair, and pressed kisses down her neck.

"How about we celebrate our first day of vacation? I have some ideas." His husky tone got to Cassidy.

"Hmm…I was thinking the same thing." She tugged him toward the bed. "Let's see if we're on the same wavelength."

THE NEXT DAY was perfect for a hike. They set out on well-marked trails and soon found themselves near the Saxon's Hundred Wood standing stones. Their borrowed walking sticks helped where footing was uneven, and Cassidy felt a calm, protective resonance from hers.

The trail was surprisingly quiet. Only one person passed them, heading back toward town in the opposite direction of the stones.

Something about the man caught Cassidy's attention, and she realized he was the same person she had seen in the Great Hall staring entranced at the Green Man mask.

The thought lingered, even as she tried to put it out of her mind. Soon, they stood before the three large upright rocks that sat in the center of a clearing.

"It's not as big as Stonehenge, but there's definitely a similar vibe," Cassidy said. "I wonder if this had anything to do with the treaty between the earl's family and the Fair Folk."

"I know people are still debating what the stones are for, but I don't have your special abilities, and I still feel something…unusual…at a place like this," Kell confessed. "It's peaceful, but there's also an energy."

Cassidy nodded. "I suspect it's partly the resonance that's built over centuries—maybe millennia—of people holding rituals here. I wouldn't be surprised if the location was chosen because of good magnetic fields or a positive genius loci. People were more intuitive about picking their special places in the old days. They did ceremonies at locations with good energy and avoided the spots with bad vibes."

A flash of white in the green grass caught Cassidy's eye, and she walked toward it. Mushrooms grew in a nearly perfect circle not far beyond the standing stones. She heard Kell heading toward her and held up a hand in warning.

"Don't step into the circle. It's a Fair Folk thing." Now that she was paying attention, she saw several other mushroom circles dotted the clearing.

"Do you really think we'd disappear if we stepped inside?" Kell asked.

"Probably not—but why take a chance? Especially in a place like this, with the energy of the stones. It feels special here. Holy. Mystical. Whatever you want to call it. The fancy term is 'liminal space,'" Cassidy replied. "Somewhere the line between our realm and beyond is thinner than usual."

"It supports what Mr. Cadwell told us last night about there being Fair Folk in the area," Kell said.

"I don't doubt that they're here." Cassidy dropped her voice as she walked back toward the stones. "And I think the local Wiccans have paid a visit recently as well." She pointed to a fresh wreath of lavender, rosemary, thyme, and lady's bedstraw that had been left along with several smaller bouquets at the foot of the tallest plinth.

"It's the Solstice. I guess it's not surprising they would celebrate here," Kell said. "I wonder if they acknowledge the Fair Folk—and whether they're welcoming or wary."

They'd brought a picnic lunch with them that they bought at the castle tea room and set out a blanket beyond the stone circle, well away from the mushrooms. The sun shone through the leaves, sending dappled shadows across the grass. As they ate, Cassidy became aware of an odd silence and felt a frisson of strange energy.

"It's too quiet," she whispered.

"I was just thinking that. And I wasn't sure if I should mention it, but I feel like we're being watched."

Cassidy looked around and saw no one. She didn't have a talent for seeing ghosts unless they made themselves visible, but she suspected that spirits weren't responsible for the odd feeling. Out of the corner of her eye she thought she saw dandelion tufts floating on the breeze, but they were gone when she turned her head.

They finished their lunch quickly and rose, careful not to leave behind any trash. Cassidy saved a few cookies, knowing the fae's reputation for liking sweet things, and set them near one of the mushroom circles.

"We mean no disrespect," Cassidy said, just in case they had an audience. "Thank you for letting us enjoy the beauty of this place."

By unspoken agreement, they walked back to the castle a bit more quickly than they came.

After they left the woods behind, Cassidy glanced at Kell. "What did you make of all that?"

He frowned. "Not sure. I thought the standing stones were interesting, and the trail was gorgeous. But I agree that it felt odd. Not sure that means anything, but I was getting that feeling even before you said anything."

They put the incident in the forest out of mind for the moment, stopping for a snack at the pub and trying a flight of house-brewed ale. They split an order of the fish and chips, and Kell vowed to try the meat pasty on their next visit.

The Boar and Knight was busier than Cassidy had expected. Then she spotted the yellow stickers many of the patrons had on their shirts —"Cross-country Bus Tours."

"Looks like you've got your hands full," Cassidy said to Melanie, their server.

"Oh, the tour? They're here for the festival. Came in a little early and made arrangements with places in town for special demonstrations and the like. I heard the presentations are open to everyone else for a small fee," Melanie said. "Just look for the tour logo next to the event in the listings."

As they waited for their food, Cassidy checked the town website. "There are a lot of things planned even before the festival starts." She angled her phone so he could see.

"We don't have an agenda, and we're not saving the world today," he replied. "We can do whatever you want."

"We have dinner reservations for the Lamb and Bee later tonight and tickets for the ghost tour after that," Cassidy replied. "Everything after that is open if there's something we want to do."

They wandered through the yarn shop, which was hosting a demonstration. Cassidy watched the weaver work, enthralled.

"Teag uses a loom like that, doesn't he?" Kell asked.

Cassidy nodded. "Sometimes. He has looms of all sizes and sorts. I love to watch him. From the items we've picked up in the store, I think that at least one person creating the shop's merchandise has a bit of textile magic like Teag."

The demonstrations lasted half an hour, designed to be quick. Many of the bus tour people who stopped to listen also bought woven goods or went to the tea shop in the back for a snack, so Cassidy figured the events were good for business.

The florist shop had just started their wreath-making presentation when Cassidy and Kell ducked inside. The owner kept up a spirited discussion about flower lore, the Victorians' secret language using flowers, and other interesting tidbits as she wove a beautiful wreath. When the crowd moved on at the end to shop the items for sale, Cassidy stepped forward.

"Thank you for the presentation. It was very interesting. Can I ask you a few questions?"

The owner glanced over her shoulder and saw the staff handling the rush of customers, so she nodded. "Sure. What do you want to know?"

Cassidy thought of the wreath she had seen at the standing stones. "I'm curious about faeries and flowers. What do the fae like—and which ones keep them away?"

The shop owner's polite smile never wavered, but Cassidy saw a flash of caution in her eyes. "The Fair Folk love nature and pretty things, which means they're drawn to most flowers. In a lot of the tales, they're even named after them. Pansies, petunias, bee balm, and foxglove are some of the main ones people plant in a 'faerie garden.'"

"How about the ones that they don't like?" Kell asked. Cassidy thought the shop owner's expression grew wary.

"They say St. John's Wort, daisies, and red verbena are plants the Fair Folk aren't fond of," she said with less enthusiasm than she had shared the first information. "If you believe that sort of thing."

"I saw a lovely wreath out at the standing stones that was made from lavender, rosemary, thyme, and lady's bedstraw," Cassidy added. "Might they have bought that here?"

"I'd have to see it to know," the woman said. "Those plants look nice together. They're also said to enhance magic."

"We have to fly back to the States, or I'd love to buy one of your arrangements to take home with me," Cassidy told her sincerely. "They're all beautiful."

Once they were outside the shop, Kell took her hand. "I got the feeling the flower lady wasn't happy answering questions about the Fair Folk."

"Yeah, I picked up on that. I spotted another horseshoe tucked into the corner of the store, despite the bowl of cream by the door," Cassidy replied. "I think people here believe in the old stories more than they want to admit."

Dinner at the Lamb and Bee, Caynham-on-Ledwyche's newest restaurant, was even better than Cassidy hoped. The "upscale casual" atmosphere hit between the grand luxury of the castle's Great Hall and the no-frills comfort of the Boar and Knight. Cassidy ordered the steak and kidney pie, while Kell got Beef Wellington. Generous portions of swoon-worthy dishes kept conversation to a minimum. Afterward, Cassidy ordered a serving of trifle while Kell took a chance on the Eton Mess.

"I'm glad you were brave enough to try it because it's a lot better than I expected from the name," Cassidy told him when they ventured back outside.

"I'm happy the ghost tour will keep us on our feet and moving," Kell replied. "Otherwise, I feel a food coma coming on."

The tour guide spun fascinating stories about the town's resident ghosts. Cassidy didn't really care whether the tales were true, since the guide's performance kept the crowd's interest. By the time they wandered back to the church for a candlelight Vivaldi concert, the sun was setting.

"We packed a lot into one day," Kell said as they wandered back to the castle arm in arm.

Cassidy leaned up to kiss him. "Too much?"

He kissed her back. "No. Everything was great, and we came all this way, might as well see what we can."

THE NEXT TWO days passed in a blur. Changes happened hour by hour on the castle grounds and in town as the final stretch of preparations occurred for the festival. Booths went up in the village green and near the bridge for vendors—both for shops from Caynham-on-Ledwyche and other small businesses. Food trucks rolled in and staked out their corners. Even more bunting and flags celebrating the event appeared at every turn.

Within the castle walls it was easy to spot where the games of chance would be, fundraisers for local charities. The areas for the play, joust, and archery competition were already set up. A canopy offered shade for the musicians.

"Looks like they're getting ready for a barbecue." Kell nodded toward a section near the Great Hall. "I didn't know they cooked that here."

"It's a hog roast. I read it on the app," Cassidy replied. "Starts on Saturday. I've got to admit, I'm curious."

They spent Wednesday at a slower pace, starting with exploring the drawing room and the men's parlor. Those two rooms in the Bride's Tower had been furnished and decorated as they would have appeared in the 1920s when the castle first became a hotel.

After that, Cassidy pulled out the cheat sheet of gargoyle locations she had gotten from Simon, so they kissed their way around the castle grounds, something Kell didn't seem to mind.

"I'm already pretty sure our love is going to last forever, but I don't mind a little extra gargoyle luck," he told her as she captured a photo of them at one of the locations.

In town, the library had a presentation about the standing stones. Cassidy and Kell found seats in the back, and she frowned as she recognized someone a few rows up.

"Doesn't that look like the guy we saw coming back from the stones that day in the forest?" she whispered to Kell.

"Pretty sure it's the same man. He's probably in town for the festival, same as we are."

Cassidy didn't know why the man caught her attention, but she had learned long ago not to ignore her intuition. Still, he wasn't doing anything unusual, just sitting quietly in the audience as the librarian gave a half-hour presentation on stone circles around the UK and the small grouping in Saxon's Hundred Wood.

"I didn't realize there were so many," Kell said when the program finished. "I had only ever heard of Stonehenge. Apparently, they're everywhere!" He started to rise, but Cassidy tugged on his wrist, wanting to wait until the man left his seat.

Kell gave Cassidy an inquisitive look but didn't argue. She tried not to stare while at the same time, committing the man's features to heart as if she expected to make a police report.

He didn't seem to notice them, which made her relax. They followed him out of the library and onto the sidewalk. Almost immediately, he stepped off to the side and lit up a cigarette.

Cassidy thought the man looked careworn, with an expression suggesting his thoughts were elsewhere. She wondered about his story and what had drawn him to Caynham-on-Ledwyche.

They continued on and stopped back in the yarn shop. Today a woman demonstrated using a spinning wheel and a drop spindle, both age-old techniques to turn fiber into yarn or thread.

"Every time I watch how things were in olden days, I'm grateful to be alive now," Kell said. "Even getting yarn and thread for clothing was a major process."

Cassidy nodded. "That's something Sorren mentions when I can get him to talk about the past. He appreciates modern conveniences."

Her hand went to the pocket of her jeans, brushing over the smooth agate of the ancient spindle whorl, a stone with a hole in it to weight a spindle and make it turn faster. This one held the magical resonance of a powerful entity, something Cassidy could draw on when necessary to give her own magic a boost.

After a chicken satay lunch at a food truck, Cassidy and Kell meandered to the village green to watch the booths go up. They ate ice cream sitting on the library steps and then bought tickets and hopped aboard a shuttle set up for the bus tour group that took them out to the earl's distillery. A couple of flights of whiskey left them pleasantly buzzed despite the ample charcuterie board.

Cassidy dozed in the shuttle until they arrived at the castle. Kell jostled her to wake up.

"We're home," he murmured, leaning in to kiss her temple.

They had a little time before their dinner reservation in the Great Hall. "Kell, do you mind having another look at the mask? There's just something about it that I can't get out of my mind."

Now that they had spent time in the castle and town, the artifacts in the exhibit meant more to Cassidy as they admired them. "I'm looking forward to seeing what will be in the larger display in the outer bailey once the festival starts."

"At least I know now why there's a corgi parade tomorrow." Kell pointed at the plates and paintings with the stubby-legged dogs being ridden by faeries.

"Not just a parade," Cassidy replied enthusiastically, "they're going to put them through an agility demonstration and have them herd sheep. Don't tell Baxter, but I've always thought corgis were cute."

Her little Maltese was small, but he had a personality much larger than his size. Cassidy felt sure that if it ever came down to it, Baxter could give a corgi real competition. "I bet Baxter would never let a faerie ride him."

"Now that would be something to see," Kell agreed with a laugh.

They rounded the corner toward the case with the mask, and Cassidy caught just a glimpse of someone leaving. She recognized the blue windbreaker and knew it was the man they kept crossing paths with. *Maybe he's just a fan of the legends. It might not mean anything.*

Deep inside, Cassidy's intuition disagreed.

"The mask really is a work of art." Kell moved from one side to the other to admire it better. "I don't have any doubt that it's powerful— and I don't have a smidge of magic or psychic power."

"I would want a lot of protections set up before I touched it." Cassidy was aware of the mask's resonance even from a distance. "I don't think it's harmful—but there's strong energy that's very old. I could believe it was touched by the fae."

"I've always thought that out of all the legends, the Green Man and Herne the Hunter were the most unsettling." Kell still stared at the beautifully wrought mask. "They seemed to be rooted in something ancient, and I always felt like there might be a grain of truth to them. I certainly never want to run into either of those two."

❧

DINNER at the Great Hall was even better than Cassidy's high hopes. She had mutton with leeks, braised potatoes, and mint jelly. Kell had the cod crusted with walnuts, root vegetables, and sweet potatoes. They shared an apple crumble for dessert and lingered over glasses of port.

The sound of a string quartet filled the dining room. Cassidy and Kell took their drinks to the large, comfortable couches near the fireplace and settled in with the e-readers they had in Kell's messenger bag.

"Seems like a perfect end to a great day," Kell said as they sat close, enjoying the music as they read.

"Tomorrow will be even better," Cassidy said, sleepy from dinner and the wine. "After all, there's a corgi parade."

❧

"I CAN REALLY SEE the festival taking shape," Cassidy commented as they finished breakfast the next day. The preparations around the castle grounds were complete; just waiting for the events to begin.

"It's been fun even before the festival. For a small town, there's a lot here," Kell said. He gave Cassidy a sidelong look. "You're still thinking about the mask."

She shrugged, wishing she could put the artifact out of her mind. "Yes. I don't know why. Once the festival starts, I'm sure I'll have much more to take it off my mind."

His hand was warm in hers, and he leaned in for a kiss. "Or maybe not. If your intuition is telling you it's important, maybe you should listen."

After a morning spent relaxing, they took a tour of the castle's newly uncovered dungeon. Then they headed into town after enjoying lunch at the castle tea room. "I want to get a good spot to watch the corgi parade," Cassidy told Kell as they found a place along the sidewalk.

"The queen was crazy about those dogs," Kell commented. "They're feisty."

Dozens of proud corgi owners and their dogs strutted down the town's main street. According to the website, the parade included several nearby corgi clubs as well as Caynham-on-Ledwyche residents.

"I didn't realize they came in so many shades of brown. Those fluffy buns are adorable," she said, clapping as the last of the parade passed by.

"You think my buns are adorable," Kell murmured close to her ear.

She grinned. "No, I said they were 'hot.' That's completely different."

Cassidy had never seen dogs herd sheep except on television. Watching in person was amazing as the canines moved the sheep around, easily running circles around the herd despite their short legs.

"I'm glad Baxter isn't watching this," she told Kell. "He'd decide it was his new mission."

"There aren't many sheep in Charleston."

"He'd find some," Cassidy said. "Or maybe he'd round up the cats and squirrels."

After the agility demonstration, they hurried to the old Mortimer crypt beneath the church.

On the way, they passed Curiouser and Curiouser. Cassidy tugged at Kell's arm. "Look." She drew him to the side so he could see into the shop through the front window but not be easily seen by those inside.

The man in the blue jacket appeared to be arguing with Mr. Porter. Cassidy couldn't hear them through the glass, but the disagreement looked heated. The stranger kept pointing toward the window.

Or maybe, he's not pointing at the window. He's pointing at the faerie killing box. Is he a faerie hunter?

When the argument appeared to end without the resolution the stranger wanted, he stomped toward the exit. Cassidy and Kell hid in the darkened doorway of a nearby closed store until the man headed off in the opposite direction.

"There's something going on," Cassidy said quietly. Chancing a look inside the curio shop, Mr. Porter paced, clearly agitated.

"I doubt Porter will tell us if we ask."

"No. At least, not now. Maybe if the circumstances change—"

"Change, how?" Kell asked.

"In the usual world-ending way," Cassidy said with a sigh. "If the stakes are high enough, people start telling the truth."

"Do you think the man's here to hunt the fae? That can't end well."

"Not unless there's something else going on. Something big. I've heard about there being political squabbles among the great families of the fae that sometimes spill over into our world. Taking sides would be dangerous."

"Maybe he's just a guy with a grudge," Kell suggested. "Or he's read too much epic fantasy."

"That's a possibility, but I don't think it'll turn out to be that simple. If he's a misguided fan-boy, I imagine the fae will just play tricks on him, swat him on the ass, and send him on his way. Or suck him into their realm, and he'll never be seen again."

"Is it our problem?" Kell's question was sincere.

Cassidy knew that her mixed feelings showed on her face. "I'm not sure. And we're not going to figure it out tonight. I think we just need to keep our eyes open and stay alert for trouble."

"And make it up as we go?" He gave her a bright smile that made her love him even more.

"Just like always," Cassidy confirmed, leaning in to kiss him.

"Let's stick to our plans for tonight." Kell returned the kiss with a hint of tongue, which Cassidy read as a promise of things to come. "We'll keep an eye out for the guy, but I suspect he's given up on whatever he was doing for the evening."

"You're probably right." Cassidy glanced in the direction the man had gone, though he was already out of sight.

"Come on." Kell tugged at her hand. "You've been looking forward to the crypt tour all day, and it would be silly to miss it."

Cassidy did her best to put thoughts of the stranger out of her mind as they wandered toward the church. *I'm not going to let this ruin our vacation. We're here to relax, not solve a mystery.*

"I'm excited that the Mortimers are allowing a tour," she told Kell after they finally reached St. Paul's. "This is where Ben and Erik found the secret Knights Templar code that led to the lost treasure. I'm hoping some of those pieces might be in the larger display at the castle. I'd love to see them."

The priest told the story of the secret cipher worked into the carvings around the ceiling of the old family crypt and how they led two guests to find the long-hidden, legendary treasure.

Afterward, he took the group around St. Paul's and explained the history behind the stained glass and the art, followed by a piano concert of Beethoven's Pastoral Symphony.

"I've heard Erik tell the story, but it was fun to hear it from the priest's side," Cassidy said as they walked from the church.

"It's different when you see it all for yourself," Kell agreed. "I wish they could open the cave where the relics were found to the public, but from what Erik and Ben said, it was unstable."

"I don't think the cave was ever meant to be a public place," Cassidy agreed. "But even without the legend, the old crypt was interesting all on its own."

She did her best to put everything else out of her thoughts, intent on enjoying the evening.

If there's really something we need to worry about, we'll handle it.

The last stop of the day was the school, where a large screen had been set up on the lawn facing the front steps.

"The movie is perfect for the festival," Cassidy said as they found a spot on the steps, which doubled as amphitheater-style seating. "*Brigadoon*. It's all about faeries and getting pulled into their realm."

They watched the free movie under the stars, snuggled together. Cassidy couldn't imagine a better end to the day.

CHAPTER THREE

"They've really outdone themselves—it's hard to believe this is their first Midsummer Fayre," Cassidy said when they took in the transformation to the castle and town.

White tents and canopies with red, blue, or green stripes dotted the landscape. Matching banners and bunting adorned walls and windows. The faraway strains of a flute carried on the breeze.

"It's a pretty impressive display," Kell agreed. They'd enjoyed a leisurely morning and afternoon, waiting for the festivities to begin at five o'clock on Friday. The heraldic blare of trumpets accompanied the earl cutting the ribbon at the entrance gate to welcome the visitors who streamed inside.

Cassidy saw a flute player and someone with a lute, then she spotted a juggler and a man doing card tricks. She paused to watch the juggler. He pretended to "accidentally" drop the colorful balls until he started his real performance and showed off his skill.

"Let's go into town and stop at the booths on the village green and work our way back to the castle," Cassidy suggested. "That way, we'll end up in the right place for the Medieval Dinner in the Great Hall."

"And we have the next two days to explore, so we don't have to do everything tonight," Kell reminded her.

"Or we can do things we like over and over," she joked.

"Hey, look over there." Kell gently elbowed Cassidy to steer her attention. "Those costumes look familiar."

"The Green Man and Herne the Hunter."

One of the performers must have been on stilts, although his costume of brown cloth woven with vines hid them. He looked like the drawings in the books Cassidy had been reading the night before, with a thin, strong form covered with green body paint, silk leaves, and a mask eerily similar to the bronze artifact on display in the solar.

His companion was more muscular and broad-shouldered, wearing a green cloak and cowl. Although his face was hidden by the hood, there was no mistaking the large deer antlers that protruded from either side of his head.

"They're a little…overly authentic." Kell kept a wary eye on the pair.

"I was going to say 'creepy,'" Cassidy supplied.

They watched for a few minutes as the duo interacted with guests, but everything seemed normal, and Cassidy didn't pick up anything dangerous or otherworldly about the two performers.

"They're an interesting addition, and the guy on stilts is impressive," Kell said. "They're going to be in lots of selfies, which is good publicity for the fayre." A line had formed for eager guests to take photos with the two costumed actors.

Cassidy and Kell strolled over the bridge toward town, enjoying the summer day as they walked hand-in-hand. Cassidy resolutely refused to do more than glance at the rows of tables that stretched from the end of the bridge along the bank of the dry moat, promising herself they would stop for a closer look on the way back.

They bought strawberry ice cream at one of the food trucks, not worried about spoiling their dinner since they had plenty of walking to do. Caynham-on-Ledwyche had added even more striped swags and decorations, making it clear that the town was a full participant in the area's newest event.

Cassidy glanced at the front window of Curiouser and Curiouser, checking to make sure that the faerie hunting kit remained on display.

"Whatever that guy was arguing about with Mr. Porter, it didn't make anyone move the box," Kell observed.

"I'd still love to know what that was all about." Cassidy scanned the crowd and didn't see the stranger.

A juggler dressed in motley and a roving lute player entertained the crowds that had filled the streets. Busy foot traffic boded well for even more attendees on Saturday and Sunday. Cassidy silently cheered for the castle and town to do well with their inaugural event.

Striped awnings rippled in the breeze on the booths across the village green. Many of these tables were extensions of the stores in town, carrying special merchandise for the event and offering coupons to encourage shoppers to explore the shops as well.

"I could fill a cargo crate with cool stuff if I wasn't careful," Cassidy said as they checked out the merchandise. Cadwell's had a large display of books, including plenty of fiction and children's picture books about faeries. The curio store offered a spread of vintage costume jewelry, hair accessories, inexpensive pocket watches, and other fascinating trinkets.

"Anything with mojo?" Kell whispered as Cassidy paused to look over the items.

She shook her head. "No—thank goodness. Everything's nice and mundane." Still, she thought about the man in the blue jacket.

Cassidy closed her eyes for a moment, enjoying the sun and letting the breeze ruffle her hair. *Maybe I imagined anything being weird about that stranger. It would be nice to have a very quiet, unmagical vacation.*

They didn't try to see everything in town, leaving more to explore during the remaining days. A magician in Renaissance garb had replaced the juggler by the time they headed back toward the castle, and he kept children and adults amused with his sleight of hand. Nearby, a man playing a recorder had taken over for the musician with the lute. Cassidy enjoyed the uncommon instruments and loved getting caught up in the excitement of the street fair.

"We've got time before dinner," Kell pointed out, checking the time. "Let's make a quick pass through the vendor tables on the way back, and we can start there tomorrow."

Unlike the tables in the village green, which were mostly from town or very nearby, these booths hailed from all over the Welsh Marches. Most had a decidedly mystical bent, in keeping with Midsummer. One sold tarot cards and offered tarot and palm readings. Another had protective amulets. Cassidy could tell from the materials and the resonance that the maker understood light magic.

"Candles, bath products, incense—I'd love to take some home with us, but everyone on the plane would be able to smell our luggage," Cassidy confided to Kell.

She promised herself she would take a longer look the next day at the hand-thrown pottery and the beautiful skirts and shawls. Another booth with handmade clay figures of dogs, cats, and dragons overcame her resolution to hold off buying when she spotted a Maltese among the mix.

"I had to," she joked with Kell. "It was too cute—it would be gone by tomorrow."

Kell pulled her close and kissed the top of her head. "Baxter will approve."

They didn't linger, making a quick reconnaissance before they were due for dinner. Cassidy made a mental note of which booths might be perfect for gifts for friends and planned to come back.

She paused at a table where a young woman in a fanciful costume of silk and gossamer offered an array of handmade candles and sachet bags. One side of the table had a calligraphy sign that said, "Attract Luck," while the other had one that read, "Repel Evil."

"I'm curious," Cassidy asked. "What do you put in the bags?"

The woman smiled. "I can't reveal all my secrets, but I can tell you that the 'attract' bags include yew, holly, honeysuckle, and foxglove," she confided. "The 'repel' bags include St. John's Wort, red verbena, daisies, and four-leaf clovers."

"I'll take two of the 'repel' bags." Cassidy hadn't missed how the sachet ingredients just 'happened' to line up with what faeries liked or didn't like. She thanked the woman and tucked the bags into her pocket.

Toward the end of one of the rows, raised voices caught their attention. Cassidy looked down the line of tables to find the stranger in the blue jacket arguing with a vendor whose booth appeared to be strewn with odds and ends.

The stranger didn't seem happy with the outcome. He threw his hands up in the air in frustration and stormed away. As he left, the sleeve of his jacket caught on the edge of the table, and Cassidy saw a glint of metal as something fell to the ground.

The merchant, a young, stocky man with a thick beard and shaggy black hair, watched him warily until he was out of view. Cassidy and Kell gave the vendor a few minutes to recover before coming to the table. "Looks like you've had a busy day." She hoped her smile eased the man's mood.

Kell surreptitiously walked a few steps and then bent to pick something up and put it in his pocket before returning to stand beside Cassidy.

"Some folks are just like that." He stared after the stranger before he reoriented his focus on the customers in front of him. "How can I help you?"

It only took seconds being close to the odd mix of items on the table, for Cassidy to realize that some had negative resonance. A few gave her a strong sense of grief, others carried an edge of old anger, and one in particular felt drenched in despair.

She exchanged a glance with Kell. *Some of these pieces shouldn't be for sale.*

"You've got quite a collection." She kept her tone light. "How do you find such interesting pieces?"

The vendor preened at the attention. "Estate sales, mostly. I find some unique stuff that way. Jumble sales, too," he added, and Cassidy knew that was British for "thrift store."

That sounded plausible, but Cassidy suspected that some of the pieces had less legitimate provenance, perhaps scavenged from caves or deserted ruins. While her psychometry could confirm such origins, she didn't want to risk it in public.

"We couldn't help overhearing. That man didn't seem to find what he was looking for," Kell said in his mildest tone.

The merchant snorted. "That fellow was an arse, pardon my language. He kept going on about 'faerie crosses' and 'hag stones.' I know what they are, but I don't carry them."

Cassidy had seen the odd natural rocks before. Some were crystals that formed a natural "X," while others were rocks with swirls or a hole in the center. While the stones had geologic explanations, they had been the subject of folklore for years, and many considered them to be good for luck or protection.

"He seemed upset. Did he say why he wanted the charms?" Cassidy offered her most persuasive smile.

"Nothing that made sense," the vendor replied. "Just said he needed to 'walk the path' and wanted extra help. When I didn't have what he expected, he went off in a huff."

"That's too bad. You have some very unusual pieces," Cassidy replied. Kell stuck close, bumping shoulders, probably worried she might touch something and trigger a reaction.

"Do you know anything about the pieces' history?" She pointed to the ones that had awakened her gift.

"Got that bunch from an estate sale. Old lady died and didn't have anyone to leave her stuff to, so it got sold at auction," he replied. *That covered the "grief" pieces.* Cassidy wondered if they had been wedding gifts from a partner who had been the first of the pair to die.

"I picked those up from a lady selling stuff that belonged to her ex out of the boot of her car," he added.

That explains the angry vibes.

"As for that last one, I don't know much. Picked it up out of a ditch by the side of the road when I was on a walk." He indicated a man's signet ring, the piece that gave Cassidy a sense of despair. "No one posted a lost-and-found, so I brought it along."

The vendor seemed immune to the resonance of the pieces. None of them were actively dangerous, although Cassidy didn't think the bad vibes would do any purchaser good. She thought about saying something and then doubted he would believe her.

Cassidy bought a cluster of small bells that had bright energy and made a pleasing sound. She also purchased two old iron hinges carved with protective runes. "Thank you for sharing the stories," she told him. "We might be back tomorrow."

Neither she nor Kell spoke until they had moved out of hearing range, heading back to the castle.

"What did you make of all that?" he asked.

"I think the vendor's just got a side hustle selling interesting old stuff," Cassidy replied. "It didn't sound like he was doing anything illegal. I got bad vibes from some of the things, but nothing dangerous, just uncomfortable. There's no law against selling something that's a downer."

"How about the strange guy we keep running into?"

Cassidy slipped an arm around his waist as they walked. "I don't know what to think. He's fascinated with the Green Man, and he got pretty hot under the collar over the faerie killing kit. Now he's looking for charms to protect him or maybe lead him to the fae. I've got a feeling that he's bad news, but I haven't figured out why."

Kell gave a knowing smile. "I found a button in the grass where the man had been. When you're up for it, maybe you can read the vibes, and we can find out why the guy keeps showing up."

Cassidy reached toward Kell's pocket, and he twisted away. "Later. In case it knocks you for a loop. Let's have a nice evening and a good dinner. We can check the button once we're back in the room."

"You're right. Even though it's probably nothing, I don't want to spoil our plans. That way if I end up flat on my ass, you don't have far to get me into bed." Cassidy gave Kell's pocket a curious stare.

Costumed performers and musicians still circulated within the walls of the inner and outer bailey. Kell and Cassidy tried several games of chance, tossing rings or attempting to knock over bottles. Since all the money raised went to charity, Cassidy didn't mind losing.

"The history exhibit is still open," Kell said when they had finished with the games. "You wanted to go through it, didn't you?"

"Do you mind? We could make a quick pass since it's still too early for our dinner reservation." Cassidy was always happy for a chance to explore a museum.

"Seeing old stuff goes along with being here." Kell grinned. "I knew what I was in for when we planned the vacation."

The exhibit included some fascinating old pieces but nothing from the Templar treasure.

"I'm a little sad that the Templar treasure is in London being studied," Cassidy said when they finished. "But maybe I'll get to see it if we come back again."

"There's plenty of interesting stuff even without it," Kell replied. "I like the way the castle shares history without making it stuffy."

The bells from the chapel rang. "That must be the ringing demonstration." She paused to listen. "It's being done several times over the weekend. The bells are beautiful—and loud."

"Maybe we can watch tomorrow. I've heard that the ringers nearly get pulled off their feet by the big bells," Kell replied.

"They drop the ropes through holes in a ceiling so that the ringers don't get pulled up into the rafters," Cassidy added. "I can see why they wouldn't want that to happen!"

Dinner in the Great Hall was a Medieval Feast made with recipes updated from real dishes favored in the castles of long ago. A series of small courses served stuffed chicken, veal with pomegranate sauce, and meat pie. Wine accompanied the meal, and afterward, a plate of cheese with honey and walnuts was a prelude to fruit-filled pastries, along with fine port.

A harpist played during the meal, providing simple, elegant background music. On each table, a large notecard shared facts about the foods medieval royalty and commoners ate.

"Now I know why the kings always look so plump in their portraits if they feasted like this at every meal." Kell put a hand over his stomach.

"And here I thought the queens just had too much fabric in their big dresses." Cassidy felt stuffed but happy.

They took a second glass of port to the large couches by the fireplace to unwind before heading back to their room.

"I'd love to see the fires lit—when it's colder outside," she told Kell.

"It must be impressive—that fireplace is big enough for me to stand inside. I bet it really warms the place when it gets going."

They lingered for a while, sipping their drinks and remarking on what they had seen.

A nearby commotion broke the quiet. Cassidy and Kell exchanged a glance and headed to investigate.

The solar was crowded with castle security guards, local police, and a man Cassidy guessed to be the earl.

"What's going on?" Cassidy asked one of the nearby officers, who gestured for them to stay back.

"Please give us space. There's been a theft," the man said.

Cassidy had a good idea what might have been stolen. She couldn't see the glass case from where a barricade cut off access, but she felt certain the Green Man mask was gone.

By the time they wandered outside just after midnight, the fayre had ended. After a busy day, their excellent dinner, and some wine Cassidy should have been nodding off. Instead, questions about the theft kept buzzing in her mind.

"Think the culprit is the guy we've seen?" Kell asked.

Cassidy raised an eyebrow. "Don't you?"

"Seems to be the most likely suspect. Although I don't think we could convince the cops."

She sighed. "He hasn't done anything to report him about. Sure, he argued with Mr. Porter and that vendor, but he didn't break any laws. There's nothing to tie him to the missing mask except that we saw him staring at it."

Kell took her hand. "Maybe it's a good time to have a closer look at that button."

Once they were back in the room, Kell poured a glass of water and set out a package of honey candy they had bought in the castle gift shop. Cassidy sat on the floor with her back against the bed, figuring it was safer than falling out of a chair if the images from her vision were intense.

Kell pulled out a small tissue-wrapped bundle from his pocket. "Are you ready?"

Cassidy nodded. "Yeah. Apologies in advance if you have to scrape me off the floor."

Kell winced. "Let's hope it doesn't come to that." He sat beside Cassidy and handed her the bunched tissue, watching as she pushed back the paper to reveal a worn decorative button.

She took a deep breath and let the button fall from the paper into her palm.

Cassidy saw flashes of images. A young girl laughing as she played on the beach. A brightly colored beach ball floating on the waves. Tragedy, as the child chased the ball into deep water. An overwhelming surge of grief took her breath away, and desperation bordering on madness flooded her thoughts. Her body went cold and numb, and her heart felt as if it would break.

Daughter. It was his daughter. She drowned. And now he'll do anything to get her back.

"Cassidy? Wake up. Come back to me. Let it go."

Cassidy felt Kell's hands on her shoulders, and she woke from the vision to find herself nearly in his lap. Her head spun, and she still felt the heartbreak of the stranger's loss.

"Drink this." Kell pressed the glass of water into her hand. When she finished, he gave her the honey candy. "Take your time. You can tell me what you saw after you recover."

Cassidy ate the sweets and leaned against Kell, drawing strength from his presence. He stroked her hair, and she listened to the sound of his heartbeat as the sugar revived her.

"His daughter died," Cassidy said when she felt better. "She drowned. He couldn't prevent it, and so he blames himself. He's let guilt drive him mad with grief. I felt overwhelming sorrow—and desperation. He's obsessed with finding a way to bring her back."

Kell frowned. "Bring her back from the dead? That's not possible."

Cassidy set the glass aside, and Kell helped her stand. She pulled the book she had been reading from the nightstand, one of the titles she'd bought at Cadwell's.

"It's possible for the fae," she replied. "But not the way the stranger thinks."

Cassidy sat on the edge of the bed and drew Kell to sit next to her. She opened the book to the page she had read and passed it to him.

"'The Green Man mask opens the threshold between living and dead…or it could be translated between the faerie world and our own.' That doesn't sound good, either way," Kell said.

"It's not. The old tales are clear. Trying to bring someone back from the dead never goes well. The person doesn't come back the same. Whatever comes across that threshold isn't the human who died. It's a changeling—a type of dark faerie called a *draugr*. At first, it impersonates the person who has been welcomed back. But after a while, the *draugr* stops pretending and kills the dead person's family," Cassidy told him.

"Like in your dream?"

She nodded. "Except it doesn't stop there. It will keep on killing until someone destroys it," she added.

"The faerie box." Kell caught his breath in surprise. "Maybe the stranger intended to be prepared if the fae double-crossed him. That might be why he was looking for relics from the vendor too."

"I think you're right," Cassidy agreed. "The things we could see in the box were very old, but not uncommon. There might have been something else hidden inside, and some of the pieces could have taken on energy through generations of use, but the materials themselves weren't rare."

"What are you thinking?" Kell looked worried.

"We suspect that the stranger stole the Green Man mask so he could open the threshold and bring his daughter back from the grave," Cassidy said. "The police won't believe us—and if he's trying to use magic, they can't do anything about it. We can't prove anything. The earl can't help. The constables have died out. That means it's up to us to stop him."

CHAPTER FOUR

"YOU THINK THE STRANGER IS GOING TO TAKE THE MASK TO THE standing stones?" Kell asked when Cassidy roused him early for a quick breakfast.

Cassidy nodded. "He's not going to wait around and get caught. We're also close to the solstice, which adds a lot of power to rituals." She remembered the desperation she had picked up from the man's button.

"I think he's obsessed. He couldn't get into the forest by midnight last night, but if he knows anything about magic, he might work the ritual at noon today, the next best time when magic is strongest."

"Then I guess we're heading back to the stones," Kell agreed, and Cassidy gave him a grateful smile.

"Thank you for loving me enough to follow me into a faerie forest to stop something that could be a monster."

Kell leaned in for a quick kiss. "I love you enough to follow you to the gates of hell and bring you back," he told her. "Not to mention more haunted houses than I can count."

Cassidy rummaged through her things. She pulled out the salt and iron they'd picked up on the way from the airport. Cassidy added the bells she had bought from the vendor outside the castle and the two iron hinges, plus the "Repel Evil" hex bags.

She took the old wooden spoon that she used as a wand and tucked it up her sleeve. It had been her grandmother's, and the strong emotional resonance of her memories of their time cooking together gave the unassuming object a well of power for Cassidy to draw on.

"Bringing Bo along?" Kell asked as he added a compass and a first aid kit to the bag. He checked in the mirror to make certain he had all of the protective charms and amulets Cassidy had given him.

"Of course." She patted herself down to ensure that she had her amulets as well. Cassidy pulled a worn dog collar from her bag. The tags jangled with the movement, making her smile fondly as she wrapped the collar several times around her left wrist and buckled it. The ghostly shape of Bo, Cassidy's late golden retriever, appeared, sitting at her feet.

"Glad you're with us." Cassidy reached toward the apparition, moving her hand as if scratching Bo's floppy ears. She couldn't feel anything, but the ghost dog wagged his tail before blinking out.

"I wish we had more backup," Kell said.

"So do I. And I wish I could convince you to stay here and let me handle it." Cassidy had been fretting about Kell's involvement. Without magic, he was vulnerable despite the protection of his amulets.

"Not a chance." Kell set his jaw. "I'm not letting you do this by yourself. You go, I go."

"I don't want you to get hurt."

"How do you think I feel? Cassidy, you're going up against a fucking faerie, and I don't have any special powers." Kell's voice hardened. "I can watch your back in case the mask guy just turns out to be nuts. I can get you out of there if you collapse or call for help. I might not be able to do much to fight the faeries, but I'm going along."

"I love you." Cassidy threw her arms around Kell, grateful for his protection and support.

"I love you too." Kell pressed his lips against the top of her head, then pushed back just far enough for a proper kiss, full of longing. "So be careful."

Cassidy took another look at the two iron hinges and the sachet bags. "I think the love/hate relationship with the Fair Folk goes back a long way in these parts. Those old hinges have protective runes carved into them to keep away evil—and iron repels the fae. It's odd that all the walking sticks are made of rowan—a wood that faeries hate."

"That can't be a coincidence," Kell agreed. "The castle folk might have been protected by the Green Man mask, but it sounds like the people in the farms and villages took matters into their own hands."

Kell slipped two bottles of water and a couple of candy bars into the bag, and Cassidy appreciated him thinking ahead to revive her if the magic took a toll.

She padded to the fireplace and took one of the iron pokers. "It's a little clunky, but it's the best we're gonna get."

"I checked cell signal when we were at the standing stones the last time," Kell told her. "And I've set my GPS, so we should be able to find our way back even if we go off the trail."

Just in case, Cassidy scribbled a note and left it on the dresser. *Went for a walk to the standing stones. If we aren't back by afternoon, send help.*

"Not feeling optimistic?" Kell asked, and Cassidy saw the worry in his eyes.

"I think we're pretty well prepared, and I'd wager we know more about dealing with supernatural threats than the mask guy does," she replied. "But it's always smart to tell someone where you're going."

"I wish Sorren had someone nearby he could send to help," Kell said.

She had called Sorren before they went to bed, catching him before dawn in his time zone to discuss options. "He agreed with the logic that the man was likely to attempt the ritual at noon, and he said he didn't have anyone with more experience or better magic who could get here in time. While I'd love to have help, he didn't try to talk us out of going—and he would have if he thought we didn't have a chance."

Sorren had conferenced in several of their friends with knowledge of the fae and together they had fine-tuned a plan. While their input boosted Cassidy's confidence, it didn't reduce her fear. Anything involving the fae was extremely risky.

What she had picked up from the button's resonance made it clear the man's desperation wouldn't wait. Between his obsession over bringing back his lost daughter and the very real likelihood that the police would track him down for the theft, he had no reason to delay.

"Come on. I'd rather be a couple of hours too early than a few minutes too late." Cassidy grabbed the bag and the poker.

With the fayre ramping up for the day, no one paid them any heed as they walked out of the castle and headed toward the forest. Cassidy kept the poker down at her side, inconspicuous by her leg, but with all the costumed performers to look at, no one gave them a second glance.

Cassidy's gut tightened with nervousness. The plan was simple—go to the standing stones, wait to see if the mask thief showed up to attempt the ritual—and stop him.

As always, the devil was in the details.

No one passed them on the way, and the clearing around the stones was empty. Cassidy felt sure that if the thief had already attempted to work the magic, some trace of residual power would have been left behind.

"I don't think he's been here—so now we wait," Cassidy said.

"Where?" Kell looked for a good spot.

"Not inside the stone circle," she replied. "Maybe somewhere we can see the path, but anyone coming wouldn't spot us."

They found a suitable place and prepared to confront the stranger. Staying quiet made the time pass slowly, but they didn't want to be overheard. Kell took Cassidy's hand, and they shared a nervous smile.

During their previous foray here, Cassidy had felt uneasy because the woods were too silent. Once again, an unnatural hush had fallen over the clearing, and Cassidy took it as an omen.

Footsteps sounded too loud, and Cassidy elbowed Kell. They gathered what they needed and stayed out of sight as the mask man came into view.

He wore the same blue jacket as before, clutching a bundle wrapped in an old T-shirt. The stranger hurried toward the standing stones and paid no attention to his surroundings, likely too intent on finally achieving his goal.

As soon as the stones hid the man from view, Cassidy crept to follow. She had the iron poker, her rowan staff, and the bells and protective sachet bags in her pocket. The plan she and Sorren had devised was fairly loose, a series of contingencies and reactions more than a single course of action.

The man stood in the center of the stone circle and held up the unwrapped mask.

"Stop!" Cassidy's voice rang out.

The thief turned on her with a snarl. "Get out. This has nothing to do with you."

"It won't work. You can't bring your daughter back." Cassidy hoped that she could argue the man out of opening the portal.

"She will return. Leave me." He turned back toward the stones and lifted the mask, beginning to chant.

Cassidy let her staff fall and allowed the wand to drop from her sleeve into her hand, then pulled hard on its resonance, sending a blast of cold power that should have thrown the mask out of his hands.

Instead, the stream of power bounced back, repelled by an invisible barrier.

Cassidy tried again, this time aiming at the man and not the mask, drawing extra power from the spindle whorl in her pocket. The energy should have knocked the man off his feet and sent him tumbling. It rocked him, but he remained standing, and the power flowed around him.

Through it all, he hadn't stopped chanting. A black line appeared down the center of the largest stone, wider with every passing second.

It's the threshold. We're out of time.

Cassidy realized that Kell had come up behind her, backing her so she wouldn't fight alone. She jangled the dog collar, and Bo's ghost appeared at her side.

If I can't use regular magic, then maybe what fights the fae will stop him.

She slipped her wand back into her sleeve, then picked up the rowan staff and the iron poker and ran forward past the stranger toward the growing portal with Bo beside her. In the doorway of the standing stone, a figure took form, but as Cassidy had feared, it wasn't the thief's lost little girl.

The *draugr* looked like a reanimated corpse, with gray skin sunken against its ribs, bones visible in places, still clothed in its tattered shroud. Its eyes blazed with the brilliant blue of another world.

The rift hadn't opened completely, but the *draugr* was poised to step through. Cassidy's plan shifted as she ran, hoping to close the portal or shove the *draugr* back where it belonged. Bo barked furiously, and the bells jingled in Cassidy's pocket as she ran.

Behind her, the thief kept chanting. Out of the corner of her eye, Cassidy saw Kell sprinting toward the opponent to which he was best matched—the very human thief.

Kell swung his staff for the mask, and it connected not with the clank of wood on metal but with a clap like thunder. The impact tore the mask from the man's grasp, knocking him in one direction, Kell in another, while the mask flew in a third. Bo leaped toward the man, pinning him to the ground.

The air quivered with otherworldly power, shimmering and iridescent. For precious seconds, Cassidy felt sure they hung in a place "between" their world and the faerie realm.

Kell got to his feet and darted forward, picking up the fallen bronze mask and holding it high. "Remember your vow," he shouted, invoking the covenant between the Green Man and the Mortimer family.

In the distance, the bells of the castle's chapel tolled in another ringing demonstration.

Cassidy wielded the rowan staff like a lance, striking the *draugr* in the ribs. The wood blazed with green fire as its point crossed the threshold into another realm, and the creature howled at the touch of the staff, poison to his kind.

Her momentum carried her toward the rift, dangerously close to the *draugr*. At the last moment she swung the iron poker, slamming the length of it across the opening to bar the gate.

Green light flared, and a deafening clap of thunder shook the ground despite the clear blue sky. The *draugr* vanished into the darkness of the portal, and the threshold thinned once more to a line before disappearing as if it had never been.

Cassidy shook all over, gasping for breath. Her right arm ached from the impact of iron on stone. The staff wasn't charred by the green fire as she feared, but new silver lines traced around and up its length like a vine.

Kell stood holding the mask aloft, looking stunned.

Behind him, the thief sat where he had fallen, guarded by Bo's ghost. The man sobbed inconsolably. "She's gone. Gone forever. There's nothing for me now."

Cassidy turned and saw that a new figure had entered the stone circle, a tall man in a cowled cloak. The hood's shadows obscured his face, but nothing could hide the stag antlers protruding from his head.

If Cassidy had any question whether the man was one of the performers, the waves of ancient energy rolling off the cloaked creature settled any doubt.

"Ride with me," the cowled man said to the thief, extending his hand. "We will hunt together. You will have a purpose and never be alone again."

The thief took hold—and both of them disappeared.

Kell still held the mask, although he had lowered it to chest height. His eyes were wide, and he'd gone pale. "What...the fuck...just happened?"

The thunder had stopped, and the air no longer sparkled with iridescence, but Cassidy still felt an old, powerful presence. Just beyond the ring of stones, she saw the Green Man.

No one who witnessed the real thing could ever be confused by even the most elaborate costume. The vines and leaves that covered the being weren't painted or sewn onto cloth; they were clearly part of flesh and body.

"You were here," Cassidy accused, adrenaline from a near-death experience making her reckless. "You could have stopped them. Why didn't you?"

Her impudence seemed to amuse the Green Man. "If you had

failed, I would have stepped in," he replied in a voice like the rustle of dry leaves. "But I have found that humans need to be the agents of their own rescue, lest they become too reliant on the gods and grow weak."

"Did you come for the mask?" Kell's voice quavered, and he looked shell-shocked, but he moved to stand shoulder to shoulder with Cassidy. Bo's ghost hovered beside them, hackles up, growling a warning.

The Green Man shook his head. "That remains as a symbol of my promise to the castle. Please return it to its owner." His smile showed a glimpse of sharp teeth. "Thank them for the festival in our honor."

He took a step back into the shadows and vanished.

Kell and Cassidy stared at each other.

"That really all happened, didn't it?" he managed.

She nodded, dumbfounded. "Yeah. Although I don't know how we're going to explain returning the mask."

Kell's gaze roved around the circle of stones. "Maybe for once we tell the whole truth," he replied. "Several of our friends have helped the earl with a supernatural problem. After all that, he might be inclined to listen."

He bundled the mask and carried it to avoid Cassidy accidentally touching it. The walk back was uneventful, with the forest no longer silent. Bo's ghost accompanied them to the edge of the forest, then he gave a yip, wagged his tail, and disappeared. Cassidy sent a mental surge of thanks and knew he would hear her.

"Simon told me who to ask for to get a direct line to the earl." Cassidy headed for the castle's front desk.

"We need to see Priscilla," Cassidy told the woman behind the counter. "It's about the mask that was stolen last night."

The woman looked hesitant. "I can put you in touch with the police—"

"There are circumstances that I think are best handled without the police," Cassidy replied. "Please call Priscilla. Tell her that Simon Kincaide's cousin is here."

The woman's eyes widened as if she recognized the name and

made the call. A few minutes later, a vivacious woman, perhaps in her thirties, with dark brown hair pulled back in a ponytail, walked out to greet them.

"I'm Priscilla. And I remember Simon well. How can I help you?"

"Can we speak privately? It's about the mask—there's a little more that's involved than meets the eye," Cassidy replied.

Priscilla seemed to take her meaning. "Of course. This way."

Cassidy and Kell followed her to an office, where Priscilla motioned for them to have a seat.

"Like Simon, I have strong psychic abilities, only mine involve touch magic instead of being able to talk to ghosts," Cassidy said. "We spotted a man who seemed to turn up in all the wrong places before the mask went missing, but when the theft happened, we didn't have hard evidence for the police. I was able to get a reading on a button he dropped and realized he stole the mask to try to get the fae in the forest to bring his daughter back to life. We confronted him at the standing stones and got the mask back."

Kell took the mask from the bag and handed it over.

"Where is the man now?" Priscilla seemed surprisingly unrattled by Cassidy's story.

Cassidy and Kell exchanged a look. "He left with a man who offered to take him hunting," Cassidy replied, trying to make the story sound less fantastic. "I don't think we'll see him again."

Priscilla gave Cassidy a knowing look. "Hunting, huh? Interesting. We're grateful for the return of the mask. Thank you for going to such lengths to retrieve it. I'm certain the earl would like to hear your story. Please wait here."

She excused herself and left them alone. Cassidy looked to Kell. "Think we'll get arrested?"

"Doubtful. We went to the standing stones and found the mask. And we have witnesses who saw us at dinner last night when it was taken. Returning stolen goods isn't against the law," Kell reassured.

Before long, Priscilla returned with a sharp-featured man with blue eyes and black hair. Cassidy guessed the earl to be in his forties, and while his collared shirt and khaki pants were casual, he had an air of formality even when he smiled.

"Cassidy and Kell, I'd like you to meet the Earl of Caynham," Patricia introduced.

"Call me Ward." The man shook their hands and perched on the corner of Patricia's desk. "Now, I hear there's a tale to be told about recovering the mask—and that you are connected to our prior guests who have done us a good turn dealing with the paranormal."

His smile warmed his blue eyes and made him more approachable. "If there's anything you've left out of the story you told Priscilla—no matter how difficult you might think it would be to believe—please tell me. You might be surprised at what passes for 'normal' around here." His look to Priscilla spoke volumes.

Cassidy took a deep breath and told the tale again, but this time she didn't omit her vision from the button, the fight at the standing stones, or the appearance of Herne and the Green Man.

"The rowan staffs we borrowed came in handy, and I'm guessing the choice of wood wasn't by chance," she said as she wrapped up the story. "My staff was slightly damaged—or 'fae-touched' if you want to think of it that way." She handed over the walking stick with its new silvery marks.

"That's quite an adventure," the earl said. "But I've come to expect no less from your circle of friends. And I'm grateful for your help. Our local constabulary certainly wouldn't have anticipated a run-in with dark faeries. Thank you for returning the mask."

Cassidy smiled. "If you had any doubts about the legend of it being a covenant, I think we've confirmed that the deal is still in effect."

Ward shuddered. "I'm not sure I could be quite so blasé about having encountered either of those two rather storied creatures. I'm glad you're both safe and that the mask is back where it belongs. Thank you again."

He shook their hands once more and took his leave. Priscilla smiled at them, still unflappable.

"To show our gratitude for your help, I'm arranging some upgrades and credits so you can truly relax for the rest of your stay," Priscilla told them. "Please accept them with the earl's gratitude."

Kell and Cassidy left the mask and their staffs with Priscilla and headed back out to the festival, which was still in full swing.

"I don't know about you, but I'm hungry after all that," Cassidy said as her stomach growled. "Let's get lunch and go back through those vendor stalls. I need some retail therapy."

They stopped at a food truck that offered Indian street food, settling on the grass to eat chaat, kebabs, and tikka fries while they watched part of the production of *A Midsummer Night's Dream* and washed the meal down with spicy chai.

"Looks like their Midsummer Fayre is a success," Kell noted. The Saturday crowd was bigger than Friday's audience, with plenty of guests perusing the vendor booths, watching the play, and stopping to listen to the strolling performers.

"I'm glad. It's perfect for the castle—and the town," Cassidy agreed. "Let's check out those booths again in a little more detail. Then I'd like to make sure we see the joust and the archery exhibits before it's time to get ready for the dance tonight."

"Don't forget—we still have tomorrow. So we don't have to do it all today," Kell said.

Cassidy picked up a few more decidedly un-haunted handmade pieces from the booths for their friends back home, as well as a couple more Christmas ornaments and a stuffed corgi dog toy for Baxter.

As they walked over to the joust, they spotted two costumed performers on a bench in an alcove taking a break. One was dressed as the Green Man, and the other was the Herne the Hunter actor they had seen the day before. Both young men had removed their elaborate headgear to have a soda and a snack, which reassured Cassidy that they were very human.

After the joust, they returned to their room to shower and dress for dinner. Cassidy changed into a summery blue dress with a matching shrug, and Kell paired a sports jacket and collared shirt with khakis.

"You look beautiful." Kell pulled Cassidy into his arms for a kiss. "This is the best vacation—ever."

"Even with a battle with the Fair Folk?" Cassidy teased, returning the kiss.

"Wouldn't have missed it for the world. And after dinner, I'm going to show you just how much I love being with you."

"Mmm." Cassidy nibbled at his ear. "I like the sound of that."

Decorations for dinner and the dance to follow turned the Great Hall into an enchanted grove. Cassidy ordered the roast duck while Kell took a chance on the chicken, leek, and mushroom pie. Both were delicious. The earl sent out an expensive bottle of wine with their dinner, part of his gesture of thanks. For dessert, they shared a syllabub and a slice of Victoria Sponge.

"All the things we've ordered are new to me, but I'd love to have them again," Cassidy confessed.

"Same here. I've seen people eat some of these dishes in movies or on television, but it's an adventure trying them myself," Kell agreed.

"I liked the duck—but the desserts are definitely the keepers," Cassidy added with a laugh.

The string quartet that had accompanied dinner gave way to a DJ afterward for the dance. He had a good feel for the pulse of the audience, offering up a mix of slow and energetic songs that got people onto the dance floor and kept them there.

Cassidy tugged Kell out to dance when one of their favorite songs came up, and they stayed when the mood turned mellow. She snuggled against him as they slow danced, hands clasped against his chest over his heart, swaying to the music.

"Pretty good way to end the day, huh?" she murmured.

He smoothed a hand through her hair. "One of the best. But the night's not over yet." The low rumble of his voice sent a shiver through Cassidy.

When the dance was over, Cassidy and Kell strolled back to their room. The fayre was closed for the night, and the castle had gone quiet. With no large city nearby, the clear sky showcased a dazzling array of stars.

"What are you thinking?" she asked as they paused to stare up at the heavens.

"Just that people from the Middle Ages would probably think it was funny that we dress up and pretend to be them. If they were here, they'd probably all want to be watching television and eating pizza."

She could hear Kell's smile in his voice, and it warmed her heart. "It's fun to play pretend, but I'm glad we live nowadays. Sorren's stories make the old days sound much less glamorous than they look in the movies."

When they reached their room, they found a bottle of champagne, two crystal flutes, and a tray of cookies, with a note from the earl. Cassidy's gaze went to a bouquet of columbine, oak leaves, and foxglove on the bed.

"Odd that they didn't put the flowers in a vase," Kell commented.

On a hunch, Cassidy called the front desk. "We came back to our room to find a beautiful bouquet but it didn't have a note on it, or a vase. I want to thank the person who sent it. Can you please check?"

The woman put her on hold, and returned after a few moments, sounding confused. "We sent up champagne and biscuits courtesy of the earl, but there were no flowers in that order, and there's nothing in our records."

"Did someone else's bouquet come to us by mistake?" Cassidy had her suspicions, but she needed to check.

"No ma'am. There were no flower deliveries to any room tonight. I can notify security that someone accessed your room, and send up a vase if you care to keep them."

"I think the flowers are from a friend," Cassidy told her. "No need to involve security—but a vase would be great, thank you."

Kell was watching her when she turned back. "A friend? Maybe a *green* friend?"

"That's my best guess, wouldn't you agree?"

The vase arrived faster than expected, and Cassidy arranged the bouquet in the water. She felt a shimmer of residual magic on the plants that confirmed her suspicions.

They changed out of their clothes into fluffy robes that had appeared in their bathroom—another upgrade, courtesy of the earl. Kell poured them each a nightcap and they nibbled at the shortbread.

"It's definitely been a day to remember," she said.

"How about making it a night we'll never forget?" Kell asked in a sinful voice, drawing her toward the bed and loosening the knot on her robe's belt.

"It's like you read my mind," Cassidy replied, returning his kisses as she slipped his robe from his shoulders and followed him onto the bed. "Let's make some vacation memories."

AFTERWORD

I promise—this isn't the last we'll see of the Trifles and Folly crew! There are plenty more adventures ahead. It just seemed to be the right time for Teag and Anthony to move to the next level of their relationship, and it was a lot of fun planning their wedding without needing to foot the bill! Watch for more from Cassidy and the crew in the future.

The locations mentioned are generally a mash-up of real places and inspirations rather than actual settings. Even the marina exists just in my imagination. Some books lend themselves more to specific locations than others, and in this case, the "what happened" mattered more than the "where."

In case you wondered, Simon and Vic have their own Badlands series under my Morgan Brice name. Travis and Brent are in the Night Vigil series, written under Gail Z. Martin. Erik and Ben star in the Treasure Trail series, also by Morgan Brice. If you haven't already checked those out, take a look! All the Morgan Brice books and the modern-day Gail Z. Martin/Gail Z. Martin & Larry N. Martin books cross over!

Thanks for reading. Because you read, I write!

ACKNOWLEDGMENTS

Thank you so much to my editor, Jean Rabe, to my husband and writing partner Larry N. Martin for all his behind-the-scenes hard work, and to my wonderful cover artist, Lou Harper. Thanks also to the Shadow Alliance street team for their support and encouragement and to my fantastic beta readers and the ever-growing legion of beta and ARC readers who help spread the word! And of course, to my "convention gang" of fellow authors for making road trips fun.

ABOUT THE AUTHOR

Gail Z. Martin writes urban fantasy, epic fantasy, and steampunk for Orbit Books, Falstaff Books, SOL Publishing, and Darkwind Press. Urban fantasy series include *Deadly Curiosities* and the *Night Vigil*. Epic fantasy series include *Darkhurst, The Chronicles of The Necromancer, The Fallen Kings Cycle, The Ascendant Kingdoms Saga, and The Assassins of Landria*. Under her urban fantasy MM paranormal romance pen name of Morgan Brice, she has six series (*Witchbane, Badlands, Kings of the Mountain, Fox Hollow, Treasure Trail,* and *Sharps and Springfield*) with more books and series to come.

Co-authored with Larry N. Martin are the Jake Desmet Adventures and the *Storm and Fury* collection; and the *Spells, Salt, & Steel*: New Templars series (Mark Wojcik, monster hunter) as well as the *Wasteland Marshals* series and *The Joe Mack Adventures*.

Gail's work has appeared in more than fifty US/UK anthologies. Newest anthologies include: *The Weird Wild West, Gaslight and Grimm, Baker Street Irregulars, Across the Universe, Release the Virgins, Witches, Warriors, & Wise Women, The Four ???? of the Apocalypse, Nevermore, Three Time Travelers, and Solar Flare.*

Join the Shadow Alliance street team so you never miss a new release! Get the scoop first + giveaways + fun stuff! Also where Gail and Larry get their beta readers and Launch Team! http://www.facebook.com/groups/MartinShadowAlliance

Join the newsletter and get free excerpts at http://eepurl.com/dd5XLj Gail is also a con-runner for ConTinual, the online, ongoing multi-genre convention that never ends. www.Facebook.com/Groups/ConTinual

Support Indie Authors

When you support independent authors, you help influence what kind of books you'll see more of and what types of stories will be available because the authors themselves decide which books to write, not a big publishing conglomerate. Independent authors are local creators, supporting their families with the books they produce. Thank you for supporting independent authors and small press fiction!

ALSO BY GAIL Z. MARTIN

Darkhurst

Scourge

Vengeance

Reckoning

Ascendant Kingdoms

Ice Forged

Reign of Ash

War of Shadows

Shadow and Flame

Convicts and Exiles: Collection

Chronicles of the Necromancer / Fallen Kings Cycle

The Shadowed Path: Jonmarc Vahanian Collection

The Dark Road: Jonmarc Vahanian Collection

The Summoner

The Blood King

Dark Haven

Dark Lady's Chosen

The Sworn

The Dread

Watch for the new Legacy of the Necromancer series.

Deadly Curiosities

Deadly Curiosities

Vendetta

Tangled Web

Inheritance

Legacy

Tapestry

Trifles and Folly: Collection

Trifles and Folly 2: Collection

Trifles and Folly 3: Collection

Assassins of Landria

Assassin's Honor

Sellsword's Oath

Fugitive's Vow

Exile's Quest

Outlaw's Vengeance

Dead Man's Justice

Night Vigil

Sons of Darkness

C.H.A.R.O.N.

Other books by Gail Z. Martin and Larry N. Martin

Jake Desmet Adventures

Iron & Blood

Spark of Destiny

Storm & Fury: Collection

Spells, Salt, & Steel: New Templars

Spells, Salt, & Steel: Season One

Spells, Salt, & Steel: Season Two

Wasteland Marshals

Wasteland Marshals Volume One

Joe Mack: Shadow Council Archives

Forged: Joe Mack Adventures Volume One